Accursed

Red

In dedication to all my friends who asked me about this book without a clear answer given in return—and my parents who gave me the confidence and support to write this ever since fifth grade.

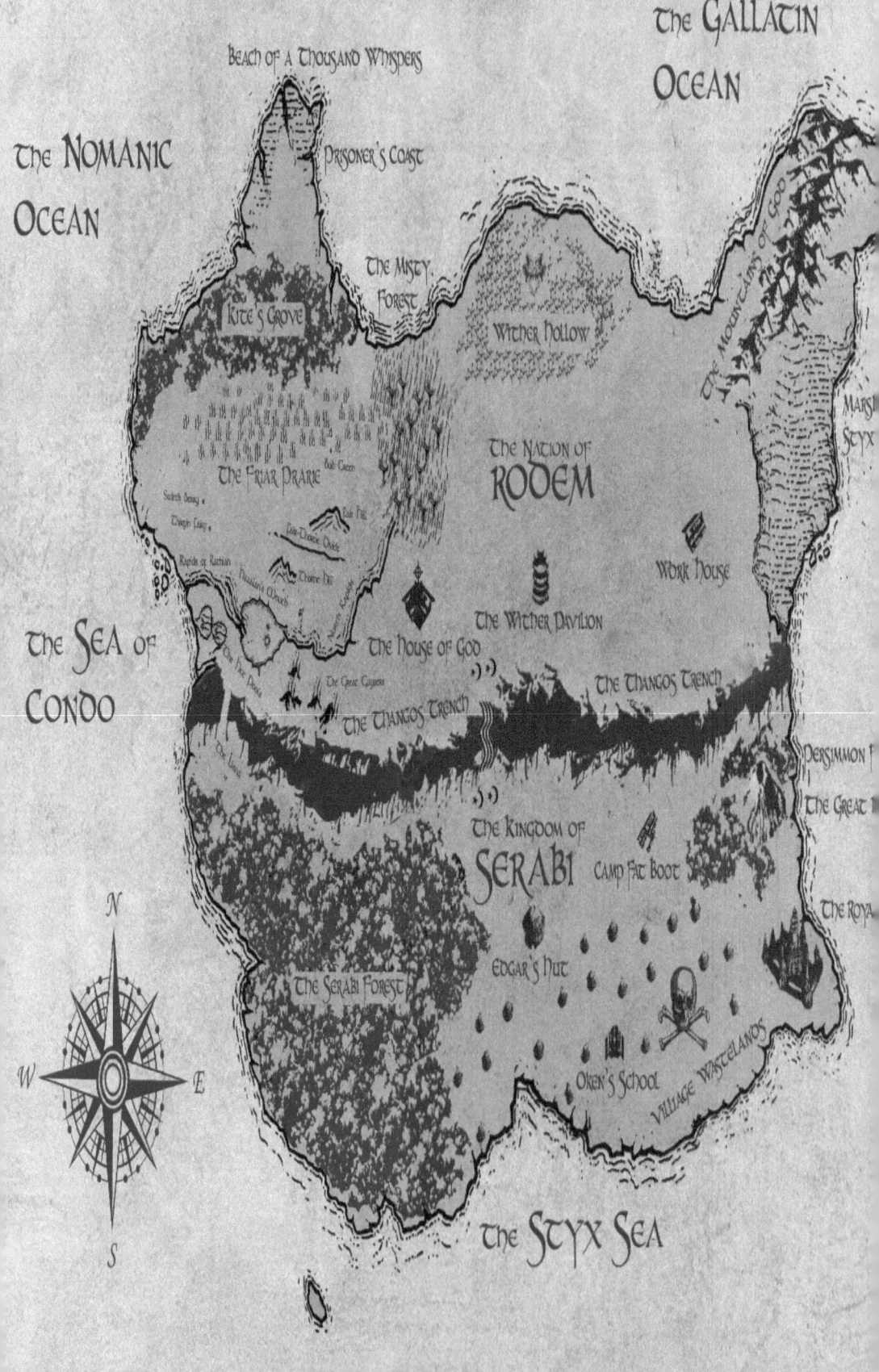

Born from the Darkness of a Sinner's Heart

The Curse is destined to split those who loved apart

Created to destroy the world, unleash darkness to eat it

Abolish light, and watch the world crumble to pieces

Let this day be known as The Day of the Shadow

The Curse, hair hellish—red, the one you must foreknow

This child, this Third Child of the Third King

Will be the end of all living things

The ones that are precious, filled without felons

Let this prophecy be known as the Foresight of the Four Demons

The world will indeed be killed, forever no longer aglow

Until the arrival of The Dark Hero

CHAPTER 1

FLIGHT – THE POINT OF NO RETURN

The air smelt profusely of fresh snow and morning dew as Ismus watched in the high treetops of the Serabi Forest, just beyond the kingdom. Frosted ice latched to the bottoms of Ismus's iced boots. She clung to the old, firm tree trunk, determined not to slip and plummet to the ground. Idiotic death was not an option for Ismus. Not yet. Ismus could not even yawn for she was so anxious that someone would find her and tell the Queen, Aloes. Ismus turned all of her attention to the castle grounds, watching for any sign of movement, any sign of her castle members—her *family*.

She cringed at the thought of that word.

Ismus was not someone who had people to depend on. She did not need people. She was lean and defined, compact and athletic. Her hip-kissed hair was the kind of red that struck fear into one's heart—the kind of red that brought out the paleness in her skin, the vivid purple in her eyes.

She had to go; she couldn't stand another second with those *members*.

Ismus took a long breath in, and her lungs filled with the rancid air of Serabi—one that smelled of death and grime. Just then, several thick, cold gusts of wind engulfed her, freezing her like an ice-cube.

Clutching her rabbit-skin pelt, she attempted to warm her cold hands, but the material was no match for the arctic day. She shivered, then turned away from the castle, reassured that no one was skulking out of the kingdom to follow her: no being would care enough to follow her.

Find me if you can, Aloes.

Ismus cursed as she grabbed hold of the rough branches. Her hands stung every time she touched it, drips of blood staying behind with every swing. Teeth chattering, watery lilac eyes straining, fog coating, she continued.

A second pack of wind hit her in the face, pain piercing her ears and cheeks. Her muscles pumped and swelled, and the wind stiffened her hands and arms. Then she came to an abrupt halt. She had made it to the end of the tree branch. Trembling, Ismus grasped more firmly to the branch with her left arm, fishing through her bag for her bow with the other. She pulled out her favored weapon and looked forward with anxious eyes.

And there she saw it.

When the branch ended, a long, green vine encased in thorns grew from the side of the tree and stretched over many miles of land, extending over the deep opening in the earth. As far as Ismus could see, the vine continued to wind its way down until it connected to another small, stubby tree boarding the creek's circular exterior.

That was where Rodem began.

Ismus rejected hesitation. She slipped her bow through its small opening and hung it tightly around the vine. She let go of the branch and held firmly to her bow.

Her breath quickened. She was hovering over the trench.

Blackness filled her eyes. It was frightening; the trench

stretched out farther than an ocean, until it disappeared on the other side of the border. Ismus could tell it was hundreds of miles deep, for she could not see the bottom of its endless dread. The Thangos Trench. Blood pounded in her left ear.

Regaining herself, she placed her legs on the back of the tree, and, with all her force, pushed off. Nothing happened. The winds died. Suspension above the trench with nothing but the bow to clutch made her legs tighten and cramp.

A sickness in her stomach churned, first with fear, then anger.

"*Pathetic!*" Ismus bellowed to the sky. "*PATHETIC!*"

She waited. Her breath hitched.

I'm pathetic.

"*ANSWER ME!*" Ismus was ready to puke up nothing but the one stale biscuit she had consumed that morning. It was over. One mistake, a second of lost grip, and she would be doomed to an endless fall. Forever in the vastness of the Thangos…

An electric shock snapped her to attention.

In the blink of an eye, she shot down, a bullet. She shrieked into the distance—out of fear, out of excitement. The gray world blurred into fuzzy nothingness. Tears formed from the winds and tossed her flaming red hair into her eyes. She raced across the open sky, losing control and consciousness of her body.

A thrilling sensation coursed through her veins. She grinned, madly, riotously. Ismus laughed, feeling free. *Free!* Freedom was uncontainable. That was a different feeling…*uncontainable.*

All her life, Ismus had been depressed. There was always a present and everlasting feeling of seclusion, of loneliness… until she felt nearly numb. She had always been contained, but for a reason she did not truly understand. As if they were afraid of her. Afraid of what she would do.

Yet now, she was experiencing a new, revolutionary feeling, one that no human being could take away from her. *The feeling of being uncontainable.*

Ismus sped down the vine, nearing the stout tree on the outskirts of the creek. She laughed in hysteria. Adrenaline burned throughout her entire body. She was more than halfway across. The wide ditch in the ground almost completely vanished from beneath her.

I'm so close.

Ismus thrashed to one side. Her laughter ceased. Her insides jostled. A surge of wind kicked her to the side.

She screamed for her life.

A jet stream sucked her into a windstorm, and her fingers froze. The winds howled as the bow began to slip from the vine.

CHAPTER 2
MEETINGS AND MEMORIES

Linnasoeta Choi woke, startled by the blazing toll of the iron bell. Lin sat up straight in her bed and surveyed her room with a sudden epidemic of surprise. "All workers rise!" A loud voice boomed over by the belfry, his voice seeming to have the potential power of waking the entirety of Rodem. The metallic vibration of the iron bell and the old man's cry hissed into the air and rang in the ears of any villager near or far. Lin sat alarmed in her cot-sized bed and itched at her face. Groaning, she shoved her pillow over her head before someone pulled the rope that started the warning bell again. The sound barely muffled under Linnasoeta's abrasive, cactus-like pillow.

The door screeched open. "Time to get up, girly," Nyoka snarled, his lethargic yellow eyes encircled with dark, prominent bags. "Don't want to upset Daddy again, now would you?"

Lin, after groaning by his presence, threw off her hairy, bearskin blanket, rising only to the dreadful thought of upsetting her father, and peeked out her window.

"Yeah, I'm coming," Lin said. She turned her attention from Nyoka quickly. It was best to avoid all unnecessary conversation with the thing.

The early chill of morning wind blew through the open, three-story high window of her bedroom, the Sun rising slowly. It cast shades of light pink across the land, accompanied by a soft red glow. Linnasoeta peered down the window to get a better glance at the world below her.

Loads of sleepy-eyed villagers lined along the rocky, unpaved paths, stumbling and grumbling, angered by the working call that had come much too early, especially on a week's end. The bell continued to ring on, the sheer scrape of metal caught in the villagers' ears.

"Lin!" Nyoka snapped, still standing by her bedroom door. She pivoted on one foot and blinked lazily at him.

"What…" a groggy protest escaped from her before she faked a deep yawn.

"Get away from the window and get dressed, now. Or Daddy will fire you, again!" Pointing to the old rusted blocktimer hung on her dirty-white wall, he barked, "In three minutes, you better be dressed!"

Slamming her door hard with a sharp, guttural screech, he hissed almost inaudibly outside her room door, "Don't keep us waiting again, Linnasoeta. For I will not wait. Not this time… nor ever again."

When Lin heard Nyoka's bare footsteps retreat down to the first floor of the Wither House, she threw herself onto her bed (following multiple swears, of course). **Maybe I can get a few more minutes of sleep**, she thought, **then I'll be ready.**

However, Linnasoeta, who lived somewhat near the iron bell, heard the sound as clearly as if she was standing right next to it. Her chances of more sleep were spent, and her father would not be keen on consecutive tardiness. Throwing off her cover again, an agitated, half-asleep Lin trudged to her bedroom closet and fetched her baby blue work clothes.

A draft of cool air formed goosebumps on Linnasoeta's arms. A fresh morning breeze had found its way through the open wicker windows of her room, and a faint fragrance of mid-winter drifted in. Lin dressed with fumbling fingers and tied a dark belt firmly around her waist. She untied her braids that hung by her face and pulled her thick brunette hair in a bun at the nape of her neck. Lin then slapped on some lotion and applied a bit of dark powder to her slightly discolored cheeks. She nearly poked her eyes as she rubbed on a bit of eyelasher.

As Linnasoeta started out her door, fully dressed in her baby blue uniform and hair in a messy bun, she noticed that the bell had not stopped ringing. Fear paralyzed her—from the top of her head down to her toes—as the bell clonked on. The bell seemed to ring inside her. **How many times did it ring?** She thought to herself. **10? 20? 30?** Linnasoeta saw the black smoke spew from the chimney of the Meeting Grounds through the stain-glassed building. That was an iconic sign. The smoke shrieked, *"Hurry Up!!!"*

Lin rushed out her door and down the stairs, running too fast for her brain to process. Nearing the last few steps of the dirty carpet, she tripped over her own feet, did a half flip, and landed hard on the solid wood floor.

Linnasoeta jumped up, despite the fact that her head felt near exploding. The bells raged on as Lin hurried to the Meeting Grounds. Surely she wasn't late. Not for the second time. Lin's breath grew heavy. Where was everyone? Had they left without her… again? Nyoka usually *was* true to his word, the bastard.

Many months ago, Lin had made the mistake of saying such a word in front of her father when speaking of Nyoka.

"Be wise enough to hold your tongue, Lin! You have no right to talk behind the backs of people who have done no harm to you, especially our good Nyoka. Do not swear either, do you understand? Now go, Lin, and leave me to the stack of work in which I must do!"

Yes, good Nyoka, Lin thought as she rushed down the main hall of the House. **The weasel of a man who *purposely* left his Master's daughter late in her bedroom to *purposely* prove a false point that she could not handle the responsibilities of Workclan Life. Yes, good Nyoka, indeed, Father!**

Once Lin was outside, the noise of the bell grew louder and more violent, while the man's call grew angrier and more disturbing.

"All workers rise!" he called for the one hundredth time. "All workers rise!"

Yet the slow development of morning seemed to be untouched and perfect. The winds were gentle. Dew-dropped grasses shimmered in the scintillating Sunlight. Cherry blossom trees formed a semi-circle about the lawn, their dark trunks looking, oddly, ever so delicate. Their pink fallen petals, crushed by the rain, brought out the sweetness from the fragrances of the roses and fruit.

Linnasoeta ran out barefoot onto the lawn in the back of the Wither House—the place she called her home—where the thick, earthy smell of rain and mulch greeted her nose. Moist dirt wiggled between her toes as she ran in the direction of the belfry.

Wedging through the opening between the cherry blossom trees, Lin saw a stampede of villagers bustling around on the streets, all of them in their blue work clothes. She could tell that they were angry; who wouldn't be on such an early morning, trying to get to the Grounds? Weary workers trudged across the unpaved roads with furious dispositions fixated on their bitterness, all the while holding onto the little ones that repeatedly tried to squirm away.

Lin dashed across the rocky streets where she greeted the villagers with a too loud "Good morning" as they half-heartedly grumbled the (rather meaningless) phrase back; she then cut across the North Pasture to save time. She was alone on the grassy trail. There were no roads, houses or huts, villages, or people back here.

Alone was rather nice, for a limited amount of time, to be honest. Linnasoeta heard the gentle crash of the North Rapids fall onto a bed of smooth stone. The trees hung firmly in the wind, towering over her like an earthy veil. She drew in a long, sweet breath and then exhaled, smiling a bit, getting a whiff of the flowers.

It was quiet and serene on the back pasture behind the streets; nature was at its greenest here, where velvety bushes and scratchy undergrowth snaked along the whole way of the pasture. Trees and rose bushes danced with grace in the wind. Little animals slept in their dark, cozy caves. Soon they would awaken.

Living in the Wither House was something very hard to do. It was passed down from generation to generation, a symbol of strength, an entity that represented the honor of the country.

But also a hellish place for a girl like Lin.

For one thing, the bedrooms were small, and the House was noisy. Secondly, about fifty people lived in that one building; some people even had to share three to a bed. (Perhaps that was why it was nice to be left alone.) Thirdly, Shen was Lin's father, and her father was the controller of the House and all the Workclan who lived in it. He led the people of Rodem, yet not in a... *tyrannical* manner. He was the head (accompanied by a fleet of consultants) and the man who received and delivered news first.

But with all his work, he had little time for his daughter.

The gentle crashes of rushing water by the riverside, the quiet chirp of the birds in the distant shrubbery, and the warming Sun that had risen up to the horizon line were the only things that made Linnasoeta continue forward to make it to the Meeting Grounds. Also the thought of disappointing her father, which she may have already done, made her run even faster.

All tension and worry began to fade upon her entrance into the Soreyth Woods, however. In fact, Linnasoeta's speedy jog slowed to an unhurried stroll, as if she had forgotten everything. As if she had forgotten that she was doomed to be late.

Something stirred in her brain.

A sudden memory came to Lin when she was promenading through these peaceful woods. It was random, how the memory just came and went as it pleased, and it was rather strange that she remembered such a great deal of it, from the last detail of her mother's distinctive face to the taste of the air from the salt river nearby. The memory came at unexpected times, times where Linnasoeta was alone, especially by the Banks of Soreyth (or the North Pasture, as those who couldn't remember the name called it).

The memory forced her to walk. In fact, it made her not walk at all, and Linnasoeta soon forgot where she was going, for she was so engrossed in the rolling film in her brain. Linnasoeta thought for a moment and pictured her mother, Kima Choi, with every description she could find possible. It was not hard to do.

The rapids crashed, and she was back at the age of seven.

Kima—the rebellious, confident woman—had held her hand and led her through this sundrenched passage eight years ago. She was indescribably unique; and she was indescribably beautiful. Kima's body was one of great strength: powerful back and arms, wide hips, and firm, sculpted legs. Her smooth, caramel skin shone with youth. Thick black tresses swept down to her mid-back. Though she had a strong connection to her brown-eyed lineage in Jainu, her eyes were a penetrating, iridescent blue. Intimidating? Most definitely, but that woman was too astounding. To Linnasoeta, she looked like an almighty goddess: strong, gorgeous, *radiant*.

Linnasoeta then tried to picture the day with her mother itself, the day after the glorious spring festival party, the day before the Demon Queen had… **Stop!** Linnasoeta shook her head at the thought and instead remembered the *good* day.

It was indeed a good day; light from the Sun cast a sleepy golden afterglow upon Lin's skin and shone on the slightly damp, deep green hills and grass; the shallow, cream-colored river bank was quietly humming in its flow; and her mother had packed a delicious picnic for them to share.

The picnic lunch consisted of many delicious items, all of them Lin's favorites; Mailberry Fool; vegetable-stuffed dumplings; chicken sautéed in a bed of spices and herbs and cheese crust; Hot Rolls drizzled with golden syrup and pecans; Creamer Bread, a vertically cooked dough with butter and sweet-berry honey; Sherry Wine – for Kima; and Strawberry Cider for Lin.

"Linnasoeta," her mother said when she had finished a small portion of the picnic lunch, "these moments I shall treasure forever with you, and I must not trouble your young mind with the Demon

15

Queen. However, I must ask you something. Your friend, Isthmus, is that her name?"

"Ismus," Lin nodded, wagging her tongue as she did. "I-S-M-U-S. Ismus."

"I see, *Ismus*. From what you have said of her, it sounds as though she is very sweet. Your loud exchanges across the border must be exciting."

"Yes, Ismus is my friend," Lin explained with a smile as she recalled their constant shouting. It was hard to hear when they were miles apart; usually they would shriek nonsense and laugh and wave stupidly.

"She is my friend because, um, we are nice to each other."

Her mother responded with a distressed nod. "Yes, but will Ismus *always* be your friend, Linnasoeta? She is a one-way system to that Demon Queen—Lin, stop screaming at that bird and listen—and I must not let you be directed into that path. Linnasoeta, do you hear me?" Lin stayed quiet in confusion, her mother's eyes full of anxiety.

One way system? She thought.

Silence hushed them. The only sounds heard were the bird's awkward chirp; the slow movement of the river; the crash of the waterfall; the loud smack of Lin's jaws as she chewed on her Creamer Bread. Sickness swelled in her stomach.

"*What do you mean, mother?!*" Lin cried out, "*What path do you speak of?!*"

"Lin!" Her mother said sternly as she reached for her little hand. "Lin… I know this is quite complex for you to understand, but—"

"No! It's quite complex for *you* to understand because you know nothing about Ismus! Nothing! She isn't taking me on any path! There is no path!" She snapped her neck back to drink her tepid cider and stuffed her mouth with antelope.

16

"You must—!"

"And I'm never gonna stop talking to her!" She growled with a mouth full of meat. "I love her!"

"*Lin.*" Her mother gave her an upset stare, the dark, penetrating force of her eyes choking Linnasoeta's throat at once.

"One border divides each of you… " her mother had rasped. Then, raising her voice to a terrifyingly loud tone that Linnasoeta recognized as the "Beast", she said, "Stay within the borders of your own kin, Linnasoeta, and there you shall stay out of trouble. Those people are much too different for our bearing… and safety. Not with that history of theirs. I think it is time for me to tell you this story… this pressing matter." Kima hesitated, as if she were thinking of what *not* to say.

"Listen to my words, child; one hundred and ninety-three years ago, there was a land which people were sent to. They were exiled people from a dimension unseen to our very eyes. Our people came from crossing into unknown lands, and settled in Jainu—do you know where that is, Lin? A century later they traveled across the Gallatin Ocean and came upon our current continent. They explored and called this land home, naming it Rodemina. We fished and ate and built homes and lived happy lives, and it stayed peaceful for two decades.

"But, as things go, nothing can stay peaceful forever; soon, the Chidaria Royals of Grudale came, and they fancied these lands just as much as our people. In fact, they loved it so much that they took it as their own. Since they had royal rulers, anything could come and go with a flicker of a royal's wrist, and we loathed them very much.

"Yet our people were strong, knowing that the enemy could not just take our beloved land on a whim, and they fought against them to keep it. But—alas!—the reign of the country in which the settlers had come were too powerful for our people to tolerate. We battled bravely in the Night War, but our numbers were too few, and our soldiers too ill-equipped."

Her mother laughed, but bitterly, and bore a face that would have rotted the Creamer Bread Lin was finishing.

"We were not ready for war, and the enemy wiped us out quickly, forcing populaces to flee for their lives. By daybreak, our population had suffered… and was decreased by ten thousand."

Lin gawked, her mouth wide open in horror. "T-ten thousand?" She asked weakly, almost about to vomit her now tasteless bread. Her mother had nodded. Her gaze hardened as she looked far into the distance, toward the castle. Her eyes grew red and her cheeks faltered, but she stayed strong in front of her young daughter. She continued on in a hollow voice.

"They took control of everything: the land, the homes, the people. And it stayed that way for years. For years, our people suffered even greater losses, and not just their families were taken away, mind you. Everything our people ever cared about was deprived from Sorthon's—Borthor's Grandfather—command: their homes, food, money, farms, rights… Everything, Linnasoeta. *EVERYTHING*. They took over entirely and dominated the people with total power— brutal tyrants they were. Power was their fuel, and death was something of theatre. They fed on our torture. As we slowly died from disease or starvation, they would merely watch, just watch us rot away… and they loved it. They *loved* seeing us die, Linnasoeta. They enslaved us.

"Few of us remained to see the effects of the Fire Revolutionary War. The militia under the command of Sorthon was defeated, after ten years of his brutality, forced into Émigré, and soon killed by the beasts of Wither Hollow. That was when the country, the country in which we live now, was split in two: Rodem and Serabi. And that was when the Border of Thangos was put into place. Just think of it Lin, dear: a deep trench splitting it all in half like Mailberry Fool."

Lin's mother laughed again, but this time it was more of a scoff.

She continued, "So the king of his time, Sorthon, signed the

18

First Armistice of "Cease-Fire", as those who did not serve in the war had called it, and soon split Rodem in half, all the way from the Sea of Condo to the Marsh Styx.

"Of course the Serabians did not split it evenly, for the border was no more than an immense line with jagged crossings. If they so much as saw the Rodem people cross the border, they would torture them to death. And that is when they found the vine... The Liana. I have told you of its magical properties many times before. They found it impossible to chop it down: it would always grow back, holding onto the bark tighter than the last time. Yet, as time went on, our people submitted completely to the orders of Serabi and stayed within their own borders.

"And so you see, Linnasoeta, the Royals of Serabi are dangerous people. There was never even a *sliver* of humanity that came from that rat's nest. And I must not let you fall into the Queen's grasp. 'An apple never dwindles too far from the tree' people say. And that is quite true for the Royals of Serabi."

Lin nodded. She was not sure what she was nodding to. Her mother fell under a spell of momentary silence.

"Now, with that said and done, I need you to promise me something."

Lin snapped back into the present; she had been dreaming of butterflies. Kima's deep iridescent eyes startled her since they were wide with seriousness.

"I never want to see you near that border ever again in your life." Her voice was low and raspy. "If you do, Embarion Above, I will not be there to save you. I know what the Queen can do—." Kima touched her back and inhaled sharply. Lin recoiled as her mother's dress revealed a sliver of her opened skin; long, red cuts were engraved into her flesh.

"She can *hurt* you Lin. Aloes can *kill* you." Kima was looking Linnasoeta right in the eye. "Ismus is foul. I normally would not put that kind of negativity on youths, but she is rotten. Your *friend* is a

19

curse to our people. She brings malice into the lands; she tips the scale of balance that... that's enough." She sighed and clutched her forehead.

A moment's silence filled the air. Tension sliced the atmosphere in two.

"Don't cross the border."

Her memory faded and she came back from the darkness. Linnasoeta's mind stopped abruptly, and she forgot for a minute where she was and what she needed to do. She then continued forward, still strolling (for she was quite bemused).

The roads started to come back again once Lin had finished the trail. Lin increased her pace and dashed for the Grounds, which was now in her sight. Horse-drawn carriages and carts littered the rocky streets she sprinted down.

Even while she was several feet away, Linnasoeta could tell something was wrong. Once she neared the roads, she saw the entire village had gathered in a circle on the dusty, earthen floor around the old House of Gods—the Meeting Grounds.

Sea Serpent and Snake Biter (the confounded twin brothers) were having a discussion among themselves. The two men argued, both heated and angry, with their voices loud and fists in the air. Whatever they were arguing about, it must have been for a while because people were starting to yawn and nod off.

But, as Lin came up close to the circle, breathing heavy and a little too loud, a thousand pairs of eyes turned toward her. She stopped in her tracks and there fell a dead, awkward silence. And it was a *dead* silence. Her eyes darted about the circle. The birds coughed.

A shameful glance was cast from her father near the center of the circle who, without question, was just as embarrassed as his daughter. Linnasoeta pursed her lips, and she cleared her throat.

"Heyyyy, guys," she laughed as she snapped her fingers and

winked. They responded with blinks and a few eye-rolls before reinstituting conversation about themselves. The Workclan had become well accustomed to Lin's brashness and thought nothing of it.

Linnasoeta sighed and made an attempt to walk as effortlessly as she could toward her father. She hoped her attempts at confidence were not mistaken with arrogance; she was nearly certain they were.

Dragging herself along the dusty, red dirt, she reluctantly trudged to her father. Lin nestled right in-between her father and the rotten weasel Nyoka. Her father's Workclan sat nearby him. Lin didn't see it, but Nyoka was staring at her, a satisfied smirk resting on his lips. He placed his hand on her neck to feel her heartbeat. Lin swatted it away and scowled at him.

If only Lin's mother were here now...

~

The tedious meeting lacked refinement. That was a fact for certain. It lagged on and on until the ends of the earth, and half of everything the men were talking of Linnasoeta ignored.

Not only was the meeting as bland as a watery bowl of the petrifying oatmeal the Workclan called food, but it was just as sordid as one.

While Alto Jack, for example, was giving one of his death-worthy lectures about a bunch of nonsense, Linnasoeta heard many disgusting noises: someone on the far side of the circle hacked up saliva; the loud, putrid, and the occasional sound of a burp every now and then; and, this may just have been Linnasoeta's imagination, but she thought she heard someone... it was someone close to her who did it. She could say that because a foul odor had crept in the crevice of her nose, strong and repugnant. She twisted her face as if she were sucking on a lemon.

Alto Jack babbled on. Linnasoeta tensed once more. Then

21

she slumped over, bored. She hummed. A scary, pudgy woman turned her way with a demented grimace. Linnasoeta faltered and stopped.

"And dats why we need so-mo sword work."

Alto Jack smiled proudly—giving his toothless grin—after he had finished his speech, impressed with himself. He surveyed the crowd before the entire circle broke out in hisses and plenty of "BOOS!" to go around.

"You lump of baloney! The 'ell do you think we do all the time! Grow some sense!" someone shouted.

"Shut your face, you idiot!" Sea Snake and Snake Biter cried in harmony.

"Sit your ass down, Jack. Waste of time," the obese woman seethed.

(Linnasoeta was relieved that people were yelling at Alto instead of her, and she found this part of the meeting quite entertaining. Normally they would discuss if the country was running smoothly, or if the Queen was planning another horror on Rodem. The yelling was a nice variation.)

"*You are men, are you not?*" Shen bellowed at them all. Lin jumped.

"The fate of our people rests in Serabi's hands, and here you are laughing—at our loyal Alto Jack! Disgusting, the lot of you are who chortle along with this! I am in no mood to handle idiotic complications when there are larger, more fatal matters to attend to. If you are not men, then leave this meeting. Only those who intend to mend our nation's problems without a lark on their lips shall stay."

All hushed.

"Now on with the importance of this meeting: what I came to address is concerning our Demon—Serabi's Queen. A week ago, Aloes saw a gathering of innocent villagers, right on the Banks of Soreyth. They were on their way to the Huntington Village, just crossing Olde Taylor Farm. Aloes saw this as an opportunity to kill more of our people. She crossed the border yet again—someway, somehow—and captured them. I learned of this only four days ago, since I was extremely busy dealing with—" He gave Linnasoeta a sideways glance. "—some issues."

Linnasoeta frowned. She didn't *mean* to light the cavern on fire. Shen should have never hired her. Worse, rehire her. She could feel Nyoka's smile press into her back once more. She whipped her head around before he could touch her neck again.

"Starting tomorrow we will have the creek guarded, starting at dawn until dinner. I believe if this happens again, however, we will be forced to call upon War's aid. And that aid is not a certain, ideal one."

One workman, a young woman, answered this. "War is not the answer, Shen Lein of the Wither House. Her soldiers' numbers dominate and multiply over ours. Jainu refuses to come to our aid. Swords must be forged, and the country has no money to be spent on a war.

"And if we did somehow defeat her army, what then? Will we take over Serabi and throttle the other poor villagers as Serabi did long before the country was split in two? What then, Shen?" The young woman glared.

Lin's father returned the look, only calmer and deeper. "It seems as though you know not of my plan." He pulled a tattered scroll out from his crimson kimono, unrolled it, and held it out for the clan to see. He talked in a voice rich with importance.

"This is ancient text that I found after, well... whenever it had been. It was... *blowing in the winds*," (some people laughed at this as it was such in Shen's nature to keep the details to himself) "so I took it and examined it. The text claims that there is a dark power built right under Serabi's castle that may just help us win this war... *quickly*. If this information is true, it will lead us straight to the Guardian of Fire.

"I have not spoken of this before because I had lost this one day eight years ago, and I only now have I found it once more."

Another woman—the town teacher and mother of eight sons—from the circle raised her hand. "And what exactly is the Guardian of Fire? And what use is it to us?"

Shen's voice lowered.

"It is the only the most destructive power below the earth. It is—"

Just then, the belfry, directly above the circle, was hit, and rang with a loud purpose.

Filling their ears with an unswerving metal clank, a different man from the tower cried, "The border signal has been triggered! The girl has entered!"

Shen threw a look behind his shoulder, eyes and neck positioned like an eagle's. Chatter among the circle grew into shouts and yells. Complete confusion and worry excited and startled everyone. Shen instructed them to make haste to their homes, for it was *her*.

The Queen's daughter.

"Linnasoeta," Shen grasped for his daughter as he emerged from the crowd, "See if it is she." His dark eyes were pleading, yet influential. "Keep her from us."

Without another word, Linnasoeta ran off south toward the border and weaved her way through the crowd. Like a cat, she climbed up a maple tree, clawing her chipped nails into the eroding bark, and perched herself up on the top branch. Linnasoeta looked out past the tree leaves, having no need to squint due to her astonishing eyesight. She gasped and felt time slow for a moment.

Ismus.

After twenty seconds of staring at her unconscious friend in the meadow, Linnasoeta jumped from the tree and dashed to the Creek of Hazalen, waiting to join her best friend. Before she stepped in, she looked behind her to see if her father was still there. Lin's face fell.

He too had left.

CHAPTER 3

THE PROMISE LAND

Everything around her swirled, hypnotically. Ismus felt her mind soar, visions of dragons and confetti streaming throughout her brain. Lion heads sang and danced. Acorns with beards smiled and laughed. Babies chuckled and soiled their diapers. Things went black, then in color. Kaleidoscope views and phantasmagorias made Ismus think she had passed out on a bed of mellifluous pineapples and had inhaled coconut. Then things darkened again, the imagined coconut breeze turning smoky, poisonous, and coarse.

Had she gone mad?

Black.

Color.

Black.

Color.

Black.

Vibrant colors morphed into objects till her nightmare settled still in a dark world… a shadowy realm.

Ismus was hung in the uppermost corner of the suffocating dungeon before she heard a door creak open then slam shut. Inhuman footsteps stomped with a vicious purpose, bolting down the narrow hall. The chains on Ismus's wrists wrung into her flesh, then her bone, burning her. The fire that roared in the dark-red fireplace on the other side of the confined space grew higher until it gained the size of a giant building.

Wherever she was, it was murky and cold—despite the fire—like deadly shadows were hiding behind the walls. Water dripped onto her head. When it cascaded down her nose in heaps of red and into her mouth, and when she tasted its iron bite, Ismus then knew it was not water.

Gargoyles frowned from above, perched on platforms. Hideous statues (or things she *hoped* were statues) stared at her from below. As she looked down, Ismus was startled to find the pale beast stare up at her. It was slender and almost faceless and nearly bald… and it was one of the ghastliest creations in existence.

Calloused fingers found their way ten feet up, where Ismus hung, and slapped her filthy cheeks.

"You try to run, purple imp," Aloes rasped.

Her voice was the scrape of a sword, of nails against a board.

"You try to hide from me."

The fire was growing wider now, filling up the entire dungeon. Ismus bent her head down as her immobile body heated from the fire's approach.

"Do you think this could be forgiven? This life of damnation because of you? Turning me ugly? Ruining my perfect life? Forcing me to slaughter the innocent and the weak?"

The fire was burning her now, charring her feet.

"But know this—if I have to kill you myself, even if that means killing my Ismus—

"Then I will ensure that you will return to your own Underworld."

A second after Aloes spoke these words, a wrathful ocean of flames grew into a horrendous size and engulfed Ismus in its evil. The girl did not even scream. There was little point; this was what she craved. As the pallor of her skin turned to red then black then ash,

Ismus felt herself retreat to the state of numbness she had always known. And she smiled.

Hidden by the fire's flames, Aloes ripped from her horrid green dress and morphed into a winged, skinless beast. She flew up to the burning girl and bared her sharp jaws. She growled, sucking Ismus into her mouth, exploding from the fire. The bricks of the dungeon started to fall off piece by piece, until the entire room was crumbling into havoc.

"I will ensure it now!"

Everything was happening so rapidly until—

At that moment, Ismus had been awakened from her nightmare and startled by a squawking figure.

"Ismus? Ismus?!" Linnasoeta shrieked as she clutched Ismus by her satchel straps and began to shake her violently.

"What? What?!" A startled Ismus panicked, her neck bobbing up and down from Linnasoeta's great arm strength. "Hi, Lin. Stop shaking me—please!"

Linnasoeta parted her lips and stuck out a hand.

"What the hell are you doing here?"

Ismus staggered to her feet, clutching her head, and brushed herself off, ignoring Linnasoeta's outstretched hand.

"To get harassed, apparently."

Lin squinted and cocked her head. "Is you ear still messed up?"

Ismus didn't respond. She was fading out, staring blankly at the ground. She touched the quiver on her back; the arrows were still somewhat intact. Her bow had probably fallen down the trench. She was starting to reach for her sheath before she began to stumble.

"Gods," Lin sighed exasperatedly as she caught Ismus. "I

really was hoping that had gone away—"

Ismus wrapped her arms around Lin's back and about her shoulders and pulled herself into her. She buried her weighing head into her neck, and Lin could feel her fluttering lashes against her skin. Lin locked her arms about her as she concealed her face within red hair. For a few moments, they stayed this way, letting their chests rise and fall with every slow breath. It was not until Lin felt tears down her neck that she realized why.

"It must be awful," Lin faltered.

Ismus drew in a breath. "The worst."

"I'm so sorry."

"Don't be. You're the only one that keeps me sane."

When Ismus pulled away, Lin felt as though a great burden had been released from her body. That alarmed her.

"So I'm guessing you're here to get away from all those…"

Ismus interjected swiftly, wiping under her eye. "I needed to leave Serabi. They won't care." She pursed her lips as the nightmare flashed through her mind. She ignored it and took Lin's hand.

"I need you to show me around the Creek. I need peace and freedom, Lin. I have been feeling so contained and aching these last couple days and…" Her knees buckled.

"I think I hit my head on the…" she weakly gestured to the tree enwrapped in vine.

Linnasoeta nodded. "That's the tree that signals when an outsider has crossed the border," Lin explained as she hoisted Ismus up onto her shoulders with one arm and walked toward the entrance.

"I'm just spit-ballin' here, but I think you used *the Liana*. It can cut the length of travel, pure magic. It would have been, if you walked through the gap in the trench, a couple of hours to get across.

But with that sharp vine, just a few minutes. I should know."

"Gap in the trench?" Ismus asked.

"Yeah, I must be nuts because when I tried to show it to my father he had told me all he saw was a normal ole trench."

Ismus bit down on her lower lip. "That's... odd."

"Maybe it just doesn't work on old people. It might be some sort of gift brought by the goddess of youth... even though I'm pretty sure that doesn't exist."

"I'll give it a shot. Otherwise, I have no other way in getting home."

Lin huffed, "Trust me, it should be there. I had to use it a long, *long* time ago, and I check up on it every now and then."

Lin shifted her feet and turned her head to stare at the girl on her shoulders.

"Remember the first time we met, like face-to-face, Ismus?"

Ismus tried shaking her head as best as she could while holding on to Lin's strong back. "I can't remember the good. Only dark things, only sad things."

Lin then switched the conversation, not exactly wanting to talk about the dark things they both had once seen. "Shen, my father, and all the other clansmen went back to the Wither House. I guess he thinks I can handle stuff on my own. Stuff like you. I can't tell if he cares about me or not. It seems like he gives me too many chances to prove my worth, and it's like he's expecting disappointment if I screw something up. I just don't get him sometimes..." She came to a stop. Lin breathed in.

"Well," Linnasoeta announced after laying Ismus down onto a bed of mulch, "I present to you the Creek of Hazalen." A grumbling Ismus took Linnasoeta's hand this time before gazing at the most glorious, overwhelming, and complex scene ever made. Ismus stood with her jaw hung, awestruck.

For a moment, she couldn't see. Blind to the brightness of the new land, she paused as if she were frozen in place. All this time she had been kept away from beauty and peace. Her sudden immobility was due to a mixture of emotions: cheer, anger, melancholy. But now Ismus was here, freed.

Linnasoeta peeked at her awestruck friend. "Beautiful, right?" She asked with trademark complacency.

"Yes," Ismus said in a voice barely above a whisper, "Yes, Gods, it's... it's Heaven." The Creek of Hazalen was forceful and elegant at the same time; it made one not want to speak, but rather stay quiet and watch, smell, and listen. And that is precisely what Ismus did.

A vast, dark-green forest encircled the pair of fifteen-year-old girls, working its way around all sides of the Creek Land, except for a huge opening—an entrance—where the two stood. There in front of them was a garden; bushes of honeysuckle, wild berries, and strawberries cultivated around the mulch fields. Inside the shrubbery was a green lawn eradicated of any weed or slight imperfection. Grass specks trapped the Sunlight from their silver shine. Linnasoeta slowly walked to the crops and Ismus trailed behind; orange carrots, red, succulent tomatoes, sweet corn, onions, and vibrant bell peppers were among the various vegetables that they saw, glistening in the sparkling Sun.

"This part right here is Hazalen's Garden. Best crops to find in our country." Linnasoeta tried to state quietly, which was wholly difficult for her. (If one stayed quiet, one could hear the creek's gentle movements and the rapids' far away crash.)

Going along both ends of the Creek Land were two trails of channeled, reddish-brown brick, winding along ample beds of wild flowers, all assembled precisely in the colors of the rainbow. Some bees, butterflies, and blue jays had ventured through the exuberant flowers, feasting through the florae. The bubbly burble of the blue jays and the buzzing of the busy animals were all so overwhelming in their serenity.

Ismus dillydallied through the field before looking aloft.

"Lin, look!" Ismus half shouted, half whispered.

She felt, in this garden, a lost sense of youth, the lovely parts of a childhood she could no longer remember. Maybe one that was never hers. Numbness was replaced with childish precociousness and she let out a delighted scream.

Exploding with this newfound joy, Ismus said again, "Lin, *look!*"

"I know! Fruit looks delicious, right?" Linnasoeta said. Curved trees planted deep into the soil detained ripe fruits and the rare Heartful Harvest Flower (a red, heart-shaped flower, half of it being honey and the other a rich chocolate.)

"Can I take it?" Ismus asked, thinking twice. "I didn't eat breakfast this morning, except for some shitty biscuit—"

Linnasoeta was already clawing her way up the fruit trees and pulling down bananas, citrus fruits, green apples, mangoes, plums, and, her personal favorite, The Heartful Harvest Flower. "You'll love this one!" Linnasoeta called from above. She pulled down a few coconuts and an unattended bee hive.

"Will you hurry up with that, *Linny dear?*" Ismus said in a stiff accent before the two started to break out in laughs. (In fairness, Ismus wasn't trying to be funny.) Linnasoeta toppled down the tree, snorting, and the whole feast of fruits tumbled down from her callused hands.

"Ow!" Linnasoeta screamed when she made contact with the ground. Ismus chortled, grabbing a piece of Heartful Harvest. She bit into it, and a mouthful of juice dribbled down her chin. They ate for a few minutes, stopping every so often to exchange gossip.

Then Ismus made a mistake.

"Hey, I was wondering, I know your country is… awesome and everything, but how do you have all these fruits *and* have them all be ripe at the same time? I mean, this is a *little better* than the castle garden back home and you come from a…" Ismus came to an abrupt stop and hoped Lin would not fill in that blank.

Why would I say something like that?

Linnasoeta grimaced and raised an eyebrow. "*Not* a castle?"

There was a pause before either had the audacity to speak.

"Sorry. I… forget sometimes." Ismus's voice couldn't have been less audible. The girls sat in a tense silence for less than a minute…

It felt longer than a minute.

Linnasoeta sighed and then scoffed. "Whatever. If that's how you see me." Lin gave her a sharp look and a sneer. "Don't blame this on your depression again, Miss Princess."

Ismus could not see one sign of hurt in Lin now. She watched as her friend took a huge bite out of her mango and stuck her hand in the hive before shoving a honeycomb down her mouth.

The girls ate in silence, not with anger, but with a deep hunger. Soon the food was gone.

~

"Lin, where are you going?" Ismus shouted while pursuing her running friend. Linnasoeta threw off her shirt and much too tiny skirt. She stripped off her socks and ripped her hair out of the bun, running free with just her undergarments. Without bothering to fold up her clothes, she abandoned them on a sharp rock, ran full speed, twirled, and landed face first into the Creek. Ismus scanned the water. It was abnormally clear and glimmered in the reflection of the Sun.

She wasn't there.

"Lin?" she whispered. "LIN?!" Ismus leaned in before losing her footing.

Before she knew it, she flipped and submerged into the cool water.

Linnasoeta chortled wildly, choking as she laughed. "I can't believe you—(*choking and spitting*)—fell for—(*violent coughing*)—that!"

Ismus blinked. "Gods, why, Lin?" They exchanged small smiles and wordlessly agreed they were back on good terms.

"Look," Linnasoeta pointed out way in the sky, "those are the Rapids of Rathian, and they cascade into the Creek, see? And its sweet water... you know? Clean water, I mean. So you can drink it, too."

Ismus stared at the sky as she peeled off her pelt. Three rapids were tumbling down a platform of stone buildup, high into the sky, one from the left, another from the right, and another in the center. They all cascaded into the head of the Creek, as Linnasoeta had said, and some excess dripped into a small waterway that led to the forest. On the leeward side of the rapids, the flowers and lawn stayed dry and slightly shaded, an ideal spot to sleep, or maybe hide.

"The Creek of Hazalen was made right in the center of the entire Creek Land, and because of its position, it gets the most Sunlight. See how it sparkles in the Sun? And if you look close, you can see these little, juicy trout guys and their cute little babies swimming along." Linnasoeta spoke like a tour guide.

"And those closed parts of the Creek, you know, that small body of water that's broken up by that strip of land? Well, that's a hot spring—the Hot Pool. It's heated underneath so you can get nice and warm. Over there in the far corner, where hot gas spews up, is a geyser. *Don't get too close to 'dem!*

"Also, we're in Hazalen's Mouth, just something you might want to know, and that's pretty much it!" Linnasoeta straightened, turning her attention toward Ismus like an overexcited dog.

"Thank you, Miss Linnasoeta. Indeed, the Creek sparkles and glitters like pearls in the radiant Sunlight, but please, Miss, you still haven't answered my question I asked earlier: How do you maintain all of those fruits when they have different growing seasons and have them all ripe at the same time while its winter?!"

Linnasoeta tapped her chin and grinned. "Magic."

Ismus cocked her hip to the side, as well as she could in the water, and swam over to the waterfalls. Linnasoeta, like a fish, swam beside her.

"But really though, my mother told me a long time ago that a Goddess named Silvergrass had created this place. She made it as a protector over the people that once lived here years ago," Lin said as she caught up to her. "She's the Goddess of the greenery and all animals. That's why the crops grow without tending to them."

"A Goddess named Silvergrass?"

Lin nodded, tossing her chestnut hair around her shoulder. "Yeah, and then there's one named Waterleaf, Goddess of all rushing water, Redtarnish, Goddess of growth, Embarion, Offspring of Infinion, God of the Sun, who's like the most important of them all. And then there's Embore and Winterbreath. Embore is the Goddess of the Moon, and Winterbreath controls snow and hail and freezing rain. There are a few others, but those are the main ones. Cool, huh?"

"Very," Ismus agreed. "How did your mom know about all these?"

Lost in a memory not perceptible by Ismus, Lin grew quiet and mumbled, "Just basic House of God stuff," and steered her gaze toward the falling shadow above them. Ismus left it alone.

The crash of the waterfalls filled their ears (only the left ear for Ismus) now, and the water was much cooler and deeper. Sea plants and smooth rocks coated the deep-down bottom of the Creek floor. And the navy-blue water didn't sparkle, since the rapids blocked the

Sun. Ismus rang the water out of her clothes, hastily folded up her outfit, unlike Linnasoeta, and laid it down before she submerged under the small, centered rapid.

"Ismus, stop! You might drown!" Linnasoeta screamed, swimming after her. Her pale friend was deaf to her cries.

Ismus smiled, looking unhurt in the deep waters of the creek. She removed the band that bunched the ends of her hair up. Instantly, her mane tumbled down into the darkness of the waters, a shimmery inferno of fire. Her long, pale legs drifted in the air and she laughed, doing backflips in the water.

Linnasoeta froze to stare at her. Ismus was so weak and troubled, and yet so strangely strong and illuminating all the same. She was a mystery to all, even to Lin. A smile crept on her lips, and she swam towards her.

Ismus stayed under the crashing cascade, smiling in her own partially silent world. It was quite funny, and odd, that the water was just shooting out from the sides of her head, little slides going off in all directions.

"ISMUS!" Linnasoeta screeched, waving her arms.

Unable to hear Lin's screaming, Ismus had to look at her flailing arms to detect a problem.

"What's wrong?" Ismus yelled back.

Lin, exasperated, gestured to the waterfall and the fact that Ismus was not drowning from its weight.

"I got a metal head, remember?" Ismus screamed over the loud falls. "I guess I never told you about it when I saw you by the Border a few months ago! Brutus had pushed me down to the cement and then –" Ismus stopped, her voice hurting, and dogpaddled over to Linnasoeta. She tugged on her arm and pulled Linnasoeta away from the high water. "Come over here. I'm freezing, and I can't keep screaming." The water level started to shrink immediately once they left the bottomless part and approached the shallow hot spring. The rapids quieted.

Both girls sighed in the hot water and relaxed. The Sun was slowly sinking from the darkening sky, but the pair still had some catching up to do.

"So anyway," Ismus continued, "my *idiot* brother, Brutus, thought it would be funny to see what it was like to put a sharp rock across the dent in my forehead—which was already metal thanks to him pushing me down to the floor— and he thought my scalp was a good place to slit the sharp part of the rock. So, he cut it, two inches deep, as Dr. Rol had said, and then I got a metal head." To prove it, Ismus took her fist and banged it hard on her scalp area. It made a robotic sound like, *Chink, Chink.*

Linnasoeta gasped in awe. "But your head looks so normal… How is that?"

Ismus frowned. "What?" She pointed to her right ear. Lin nodded in knowing and asked the question on the left side of her. Ismus tapped her chin and answered with a sarcastic, "Magic."

Linnasoeta rolled her eyes and sighed. She gazed out beyond. Silence.

Ismus tucked a strand of hair behind her ears before the wind pushed it back into her face. "What's the matter? You seem down all of a sudden."

"It's Nyoka."

"Oh yes, I remember you telling me about him."

"Right now he would be threatening me to go to bed. He's an utter *bastard*, Ismus. He always seems to turn my father against. This wouldn't have happened if she just…"

Linnasoeta was quiet for a minute, frozen. Ismus could see her face harden with distress. "Don't beat yourself up about your mother. At least she doesn't have to suffer… not anymore," Ismus tried. Lin did not respond.

"Rather be Nyoka than her," Ismus tried jokingly. "Like getting rid of him instead... at least you *have* a family, Lin! No matter if Nyoka is your slithering pet snake."

Lin closed her eyes and leaned against the land near the Creek. "Do you remember the first time we met?" She asked again weakly, her mouth dry from the heat. "I can. We were both five, having 'no business to be on the outskirts of our countries,' as my mother would have said. I saw you there, with your long, red hair flowing in the wind. You waved, and I waved back." Lin's voice was tired and quiet, remembering something that Ismus didn't even know existed. It boggled her mind and made her feel restless to not know what her best friend was talking about.

"Yes," Ismus lied. "I remember it too. You were wearing a sparkly dress with your hair in curls. You looked very beautiful."

"Stop it," Lin barked. Her eyes snapped open, and she shot an angry finger. "You know that's not how it went. Why can't you remember?"

Ismus shrugged and decided to swim around in the water a bit. An angry trout treaded beside her.

"I don't know. I can only remember when you actually came to Serabi. My memories are too clouded, just gone..."

"But I remember you saying something like: '*Oh, you look familiar. Wait! Are you that Lin girl?*' when I walked behind that terrible, ugly, nasty, rocky, smelly, putrid castle—"

"—Alright, alright! I get your point and I couldn't agree more! And yes, I did say that, but I don't remember our first encounter."

"... Well, if you remember when I came back behind the castle when we were seven, how do you not recall us talking two years before then?"

"Dunno. I think you're a little—" Ismus took her index finger and started making a little circle right by her ear, "KOO-

KOO."

Taking that as an excuse to attack, Linnasoeta splashed the hot water straight into her friend's eyes.

"You bitch!" Lin laughed as she fired more water at Ismus.

Ismus breathed in, happy to play along. "How *dare* you treat a princess this way?!" She spoke melodramatically, in as snobbish a tone she could muster. "I will kill you, you damned *peasant!*" Ismus dunked herself under the water. Linnasoeta followed after her. They wrestled and tried to hold their ground. Bubbles flew to the surface as they laughed.

Grabbing her by the ankles, Ismus emerged from the water and flipped Linnasoeta around. "Who's laughing now?" Ismus said between Linnasoeta's screams.

The girls went back and forth, battling with water for several, quickly-passing hours, until the Sun vanished like smoke into the starless night sky. The two girls finally felt safe and wanted.

Yet, as the warmth of the hot spring decreased, the Creek felt hollow and cold, like the insides of a haunted grave. The trees cracked and moaned. A pack of wolves howled viciously and sounded much too close.

Just as Ismus was about to hurl another spray of water onto Linnasoeta's face, her wrists were grasped. They were alone in a pool of deep darkness. And it was soundless. Ismus thought Lin could hear the beat of her heart. They both swam, trying not to move the water around, listening to the sounds.

"Damn it, my dad is gonna be pissed," Linnasoeta swore into a whisper. She swam over to the far side of the Creek and hoisted herself up to land. She disappeared into the dark to find her clothes. Ismus did the same and swam over to the deep end with the rapids. Linnasoeta came back running, fully dressed in under a minute (she hated the dark). Ismus pulled her friend into a tight hug, squeezing so hard that Ismus feared for a second that she might pop her. She kissed the top of Lin's head.

"I love you, Lin. I'll be back soon," Ismus promised, as she broke away and swung on her satchel. "Meet me here in a week, on Saturday, alright?" Ismus placed a hand on Lin's cheek, resting her thumb underneath her chin.

"Alright," Linnasoeta sighed as she grabbed the pale hand that rested on her face. "Saturday, then."

Without another word, Linnasoeta smiled toothily, then vanished again into the invisible realm of darkness, this time not coming back.

She would not see Lin again for a long time.

Ismus slowly turned away from the opening to face a pitch blackness that consumed all objects of any color.

How long did Lin say the journey through the gap was?

CHAPTER 4

A CONFUSING (AND UTTERLY QUICK) TRIP TO EDGAR'S

The sixty pound trout Ismus was dragging along the unpaved footway had its eye scrapped clean off before she had even reached Edgar's. Three hours of sprinting, jogging, then the inevitable sluggish walking had drained Ismus of any energy she had gained during her time with Lin.

Serabi's moonless night sky feigned an attempt to mimic the soft, ivory glow that was produced in Rodem. Yet, instead, it flickered evil, like the wicked flames of an untamed hearth. This, alas, was her country.

Not one single ambler passed by at that late hour, though a rare exception of a rat or two was still part of the company. Filthy, oxidizing trash cans toppled over with moldy, waned apple cores and decomposing litter, the cold wind blowing the overflowed trash into the rocky roads. Slick puddles of muck and urine snaked down the gutters, the smell of it wafting into the air and reluctantly into Ismus's nostrils. The aligned houses were cardboard tents with stakes to support them. Ismus could see the wind rattle the tents. One blew off into the distance.

Even though these poor people were close to the Queen's castle, just on the doorstep of Ismus's reluctant home, Aloes would never help them… maybe kill them for bothering her prowling time, at most. Ismus would have done anything to help them; but that was unlikely, what with her family lineage of treating the poor.

But then, a thought rolled onto Ismus's mind: where were all the people?

As a matter of fact, there was never a single ambler in sight at *any* time of day, week, month, or year. The streets were always empty and remote; maybe the trash had just been there for years and no one had bothered to pick it up. **Where are all the people?**

After walking along the poor, vacant community, a shabby shed quaked up ahead. Running, Ismus could see the small thing in the distance. As she ran farther, she was able to see the neon lights of Edgar's shop light up the block:

Edgar's Hut

Come inside for the best of the best quality in the trading market!

Ismus knocked upon the glass-shattered door (which was pointless since there was a huge, horse-sized tear in the fabric of the hut) and waited for a split second before Edgar opened the creaky entrance.

A yellow lamp held a bright, gold light—he had told Ismus he had "once come from a place of pure wealth, of mountains of gold and silver in the world" and that somehow he had made his way here with all his electronic trinkets and neon lights. A bamboo fan chugged overhead—though it only blew around the warm air.

Edgar gave Ismus one of his famous chicken smiles—the one where he had large chicken pieces stuck in-between his teeth—and beckoned her in with a ginormous grin. His mustache was shaved, looking sophisticated in spite of the huge hot wing stain on his tattered, sleeveless shirt. He stained the white top further when he wiped his orange fingers clean against the collar.

The hut had an intoxicating bouquet of warm pine straw and thick compost (both sold in his store). He tossed the chicken bones he had finished eating into an iron trashcan and studied the princess, a frequent customer of his.

Edgar's Hut held all odd necessities; animal heads laid on shelves; jars of substances and unmentionable chemicals were thrown into a wooden crate next to his signature collection of jams and jellies, honeys and apple butters, and caramels; bloomers and bras and animal skin-anything hung from solo shafts from the straw roof. Anything could be found: from pots and pans to rugs and sofas. Spoons, knives, forks, juicers, and other kitchen utensils suspended from loose shafts. And that was only to name a few things. But what Ismus needed was a bow: a finely handcrafted one.

There in the weapon section was an artistically crafted bow; it was milky white with smooth edges. It caught her off guard until she realized Edgar was talking to her.

"Ismus! The princess, of course!" Edgar chimed, "What's this?" He asked, snatching the eyeless fish from Ismus's sore hand. "Oh, my g— you got yourself a sixty pounder trout! None like that round here, though… and I should know… I used to fish with your fath—," Edgar stopped, midsentence. Ismus frowned at him.

Is there anything I *can* remember?!

Changing the subject, Edgar interrogated, "You've been sneakin' out of the border, haven't ya? Tsk, tsk, tsk," he scolded, waving his finger in Ismus's face. "Shouldn't be sneakin' out like that, love! It's dangerous! You're extremely lucky I like trout… I mean, do business with trout." He hobbled off to his counter to his desk and mumbled on.

Shut up and listen!

Ismus cleared her throat. Edgar looked up from his register, almost scared. "Yes, princess?"

"I need a bow."

"I-I… I thought I gave you one. I remember it was exactly two months—"

"I need another one."

Edgar looked down at Ismus. And even though Edgar was looking down and Ismus was looking up, it felt as if Ismus was standing on a mountain looking down on him: She was giving him the "evil look" with her eyes, as the servants had informed her.

Edgar immediately showed her the bows, looking alarmed again.

No one mess with the Queen's malicious daughter. Ismus thought, ashamed. **Can I at least have one friend in *this* country?**

"Here we have an exotic bow, completely crafted of lemonwood. Not the best quality here, but certainly the cheapest. Would cost, roughly, an eye or leg of a drake. I kid, about three salmon... maybe four... I love salmon—I mean; next we have our top of the line quality, The Ule Bow, named after the oldest, fiercest warrior of Serabi. Two of this trout—" he stopped to shake the trout in his hand "—would do nicely—"

"Edgar!" Ismus stopped him. Usually she would have been joking, laughing with Edgar, but today she was weary and cantankerous. She had been up all night and woke up early to venture out into the other world. By this point, she needed an attempt at a good night's rest ... and for Edgar to shut up.

"I want that bow—the Ule Bow—but I have only one trout. Is there an exception?"

Edgar looked down at the dirt floor and let out a loud thinking sigh. "You do come to my store quite a lot, don't ya?" He asked as he turned his back away from Ismus and assembled the jars of jams and slime. "I don't make much running this store. I mean, love—hardly anyone steps a foot into this place other than us two. But...I'll tell you what. Since this is about your tenth time comin' here, it's free."

He walked back behind the counter where the weapons were (probably to keep it safe so the violent children wouldn't try to take the daggers and knives) and pulled up a mini ladder. He stepped onto each step thoughtlessly, even though it cracked and bemoaned for help, and lifted the Ule Bow off the wall with his free hand.

Ismus stood like a statue, opening and closing her mouth like the trout before she had fished it from the Creek of Hazalen. Edgar jumped off his little ladder, smacked the trout down onto his desk, came around from the counter, and handed Ismus the bow and slimy fish.

"There you are, my princess." He smiled softly, his mangy black hair moving as he sighed with happiness. He placed a kiss on the crown of her head and laughed at her frozen attitude. "You run back to the castle now, my royalty. The Queen will smack a whip at you too, and we both know it!"

Without another word, Ismus stepped out of the odd, warm, and Winter-Festival-scented hut to be embraced by the cold, dark realm of Serabi.

"Night, love." Edgar smiled, and he closed the door to his shack.

Confused, Ismus looked at the bow, alone again. The winds whipped her hair into her eyes. **He did *what* with my father?** Shaking the thought off, Ismus marveled at her bow, trudging back to the wretched castle.

~

An isolated queen, a crazy father, a demonic brother, and a quiet sister, along with a couple hundred servants and soldiers, summed up the company of Ismus in a few words. Ismus didn't consider her own family "family". Castle members did enough justice for their names, for Ismus knew that there wasn't even a swallow of hope that her fellow members could become a true household comprised of loving individuals. Sometimes her fantasies were to have real parents that loved her, or just a real family that was together and supported one another. Her life was like an unbalanced weight, her "family" always seeming to go way below even the lowest standards.

But what she so desperately craved was a state of being free.

After a couple of minutes walking in the foul-smelling, murky, poverty-stricken village, Ismus had found the castle: *her* castle. She studied it with a growing trepidation, deep in the hollowness of her stomach. She pushed open the black gate, which opened with a horrid shriek of corroded iron.

The rocky walkway turned into a chipped marble sidewalk, red and silver granite throughout. The color was starting to fade, so it was looking more gray than silver in some parts. The castle itself was constructed of gray limestone and painted down with metallic silver. The paint was starting to peel off, and cracks were forming at the base of the castle. Everything looked washed-out and dirty.

In the back, rats lurked by the trash cans. She dropped the dead fish on the black, crispy grass, knowing that a hoard of ants would come soon and feast upon its flesh.

There was nothing unique about this castle, except for the fact that it had plain towers and one large pinnacle at the top. There wasn't a moat, or little streams, or rustic drawbridges, or beautiful, green scenery surrounding it, or unique openings and secret passageways (if there were she hadn't found any), just a pool of liquid oil dripping from the shed and a handful of dead rats in the back. Nor was there a patio or pavilion or anything else quite exciting about it. It was just... foreboding.

The towers all peeked at the top, four lackluster mini mountains touching the even grayer sky. It was a small castle, but in comparison to everything else, it looked ginormous.

Ismus had lied a little to Linnasoeta: the castle garden was nothing more than some rotten mulch filled with rotten produce no one cared to pick. There were a lot of worms and weird insects in the bed of weeds. It was really more a *cluster* of weeds than an abundance of ample flower beds and vegetation. The lawn was shriveled and gray, and the wilting hollow trees hung naked and unadorned. Ismus had lied.

A lot.

The castle of Serabi was cold and lifeless. One could have found more cheer at a funeral. There was something wrong with this castle, and Ismus was ready to explore it, the spirit of adventure taking over her.

If she *wanted* to get in, of course.

Ismus approached the granite stairs with a deep, terrifying dread. **What will they do?** Ismus mouthed to herself. **What will *she* do?** Ismus suddenly tasted the iron bite of metal in her mouth. The frostiness of the post-midnight chill felt like gusts of ice were blustering onto her skin and freezing their way through her insides.

One foot after another, Ismus was a step closer to the door: the creaky, coffee-colored door with the bristly, black lock. Yes, *that* door.

The girl showed no grace as she approached the ugly, muck-colored thing. The wilting trees shook in the wind, first lightly, then flailing all around. The shriveled roses moaned in her presence as she rang on the doorbell. Half a second after Ismus touched it, a ferocious *"BOOM!"* gonged throughout the castle. Half a second after that, a servant opened the door, nose up.

"Who—? Princess Ismus!" Dandelide gawked. "When—what are you doing out of the castle?"

Ismus smoothed back her fiery hair and tucked her chin down to her neck, glaring her eyes. "I'm assuming you just now noticed?"

She pushed back the over-dramatic servant and stepped into the castle. Then the familiar whiff of lime and dust bunnies greeted her nose. She was home. Sadly.

She stepped onto the green-carpeted steps that lead to her room, her stomach growing heavier with every step. And there were *a lot* of steps. Thirty-two tiny steps with the throw-up green carpet that felt like sandpaper, to be specific. Once she reached the thirty-second step and turned down the corridor, she bumped into a meaty figure.

Ismus froze.

It's him.

CHAPTER 5

BITTERSWEET DREAMS

Brutus smirked. Brutus, her nineteen-year-old brother, was extremely dense; his thick legs and arms were like tree trunks, and he had a very full face. His eyes were completely black, and his teeth were a light yellow. His thick, low-cut hair was dirty blond.

"Hey, Demon. Where you been to?"

Ismus didn't dare speak. For all she knew, Brutus would beat the bone out of her if she told him where she had been. "Didn't you hear, Demon? Need to fix your left ear, too? I said, *where you been to?!*"

He shoved her down to the ground, placed his fat, reeking foot on her chest, and bent down. "Wherever you went, you should have stayed there." He smashed his foot into her chest, hard, and Ismus groaned.

"Get off me, Brutus. *Now*," Ismus growled.

"You dumb bitch. You make it so easy to hate you. Don't know why you haven't killed yourself yet."

"GET. OFF." Gasping now, helplessly.

"Keep screaming, whore, I *like it*. Gods, I should have killed your sorry ass the minute you stepped into this place. If it wasn't for you, Mom wouldn't—," Brutus paused and decided to slap her across the face to stall. "Whatever, it's still your fault she's like that, demon!"

"YOU DON'T MAKE ANY SENSE!" Ismus tried to

breathe. "GET. OFF."

Brutus always told her these things. He always made her feel like a monster, but he was the real demon. He always tortured her dolls when she was younger, swirling them in public commodes in the villages, and then threw them in pig manure. Brutus told her such awful things and had ruined her face on several occasions. Over the course of her fifteen years, she had replaced her initial sadness with indifference and attempted to ignore him. He always called her demon. Brutus always did that to her.

And he *always* tackled her down to the ground and said that he wanted to kill her when she was a baby. Yet the smell of his feet definitely had the potential power of killing her right then.

"Then I'll make you understand," the boy rasped.

He wrapped one hand tightly around her neck, revved his other fist behind his right ear, and was about to smash down into Ismus's face until Gwenda shouted out, "*Brutus, stop! What are you doing?*"

She was coming from the castle library upstairs with a boatload of books in hand. She placed them lightly onto the steps, so she would not muss the covers, and rushed to Ismus's side. She removed Brutus's foot and gave him a fretful look before turning back to Ismus. Gwenda crawled over to Ismus's left ear.

"Oh, Ismus, where have you been? It's been almost an entire day! I woke up and went into your room to say good morning and to bring you a chocolate pastry, but you weren't there! I could barely *read* I was so worried!"

(Ismus rolled her eyes. *Sure,* she thought.)

Brutus stomped to his room and mumbled something under his hot breath, griping. The hallway shook as he slammed his door shut.

Ismus lifted herself up. "I was... at the market." She pulled the bow from her satchel. "See? I got a new bow."

Gwenda looked like she was going to ask a different question, but instead she pressed, "Well, what happened to the other one?"

Ismus wrecked her brain for something besides "*Brutus smashed it.*"

"It just sort of… disappeared." Indeed, that wasn't *entirely* a lie.

Gwenda nodded, not asking any more of the matter. She was never one to interrogate due to her shyness. Ismus admired her eighteen-year-old sister, when she wasn't annoying the life out of her. She had a petite figure, sporting a flat stomach, thin waist, and a pair of long, slim legs. Her blond beach-waves fell to her shoulders. Lips full and glossy, skin creamy and pale, eyes a tantalizing dark-green, a perfect white smile… she was nearly flawless.

"Alright then." She swooped up her books and glided to her room, all the way down the hall. She sang—inaudible to her half-deaf sister—the lyrics from her book, "'Lacy Maiden in gown, heading off for a night in town, everyone stops to stare, but the Lacy Maiden has no time to care.'"

The perfect princess. Ismus sighed, wishing to be elegant yet intelligent like her remarkable older sister. She walked to the door right in front of her, past the clock. She twisted the golden doorknob and opened it to her room, a burst of gold punching her in the face: it had been cleaned after she left.

Her room was painted gold with a white trim and decorated with beautifully drawn red roses on each of her walls. Everything about the room was orderly and tucked away in drawers, something Ismus never bothered to do once she realized the maids would just reorganize it all.

The pillow was made of the softest goose feathers, and her bed had silk, gold sheets that made her slip and slide at night. On the other side of the room was a hearth, and by it one big dresser with twelve huge cabinet drawers and a wooden desk, also painted gold, with a golden accent mirror above it. To the right of the mirror was a

51

target stuck with arrows.

On the far side of her room, over by her closet, were a cappuccino sofa and ottoman and silky, golden ottoman covers. On top of the ottoman was a large radio, which had once amplified the best sound of music before the signal towers were destroyed long ago. Under the sofa was a mat that blended in with the glittering gold carpet. (Yes, gold carpet.)

She opened her satchel and out spilled fifteen silver arrows. Ten less than what she had before her escape to Rodem. Ismus gripped her bow firmly and pulled the string back enough to touch her lips. She aimed and released; the arrow spun and missed and ripped into her curtain.

"Damn," she murmured as she walked over to her arrow. She ran a hand through her now ripped curtain.

The thinnest of gold silk, sewn by a maid with the boniest of fingers, were her curtains. It was a useless fabric that could wake anyone up right at the crack of dawn. They were placed on a black rack, half-covering her lustrous crystal window. The window sill held little antiques, like a cat chasing yarn, and of course they were all golden.

Yeah, more gold…

The room smelled fresh, an ocean breeze type smell.

I hate the ocean…

The view outside her window gave Ismus the entire view of the deserted, poor town outside the castle grounds.

What a *lovely* thing to see every damn day!

She plopped down onto her bed, exhausted. Where was the Queen? Was she out doing something terrible again? She sat up and slipped off the bed. She landed on the carpet with a loud "Oomph!"

"Oh the joys and great comforts of being home…" Ismus

frowned out loud, her hair tumbling below her waist like a shield from the world.

~

Ismus did not risk bathing; she merely wanted to slip into bed. The servants, however, thought differently. One by one the servants came into the room, tidying up things that were already clean, and completely forcing Ismus to freshen up.

"Princess, you had nearly a week of adventure! I can practically smell the filth on your body you gained each day! You must bathe!"

"I'll fetch the Cherry Blossom Rice Milk lotion and Coconut shampoo!"

"Or at least be decent enough to put on some perfume or deodorant, for our sake!"

"My Heavens, what happened to your curtain? Were you firing arrows again?"

"—Maybe some Mint Butter Cream would fancy you?"

"Sugar salt bath, Princess Ismus of Serabi?"

(Most of these demands went unheard by Ismus, whether it was because of her deaf right ear or her indisposition to listen.)

Each servant had their own opinion. Wendell, the eldest servant, pleaded her to bathe. Her old eyes looked hurt when Ismus declined.

In actuality, Ismus did not care. However, the servants had instructed her that indifference was a sign of weariness, and thereby she was surrendering herself to weakness.

And weakness is a loss of power.

So she spoke:

"Please, you all! I don't need to bathe. I'm perfectly clean. Here, sniff me!" Ismus lifted her armpits. All the servants backed away.

Jansha, daughter of Wendell, burst through the servant-crowded room.

"My dear Princess Ismus!" The servant groveled at Ismus's feet. "Oh lass, where were you?"

Ismus looked down to her sockless, ragged feet. She smiled at one of her favorite servants—something close to a mother.

"I left the castle. And got a new bow."

A different servant clicked her gums, like a horse eating hay. "We know *that*, Princess." Jade rolled her eyes, leaning against a wall. Her blocky, dark boots were scraping against Ismus's stupid gold paint. Though she hated the color, it still bothered her to see it stained with black. Ismus flashed Jansha a look of annoyance and she immediately stood.

Jade. The only servant I actually hate.

Ismus did understand Jade, though; she was the only one in the castle who visibly did not like being a servant. Others would pretend or hide what they felt on the inside, but Jade, no—she expressed and voiced her opinion like she was the Queen.

Oh, no.

The Queen.

All sound muted around Ismus. The nightmare resonated in her ears.

"NO," Ismus commanded as it overtook her brain. *"STOP!"*

The pale beast without a face, without a heart, the flames engulfing her. A knife, held in Ismus's own hands, slipping into her chest.

"LEAVE ME ALONE!" Ismus screamed into the darkness of the dungeon. Her skin was burnt throughout and she was now only a thing of bones. Did she really mean it?

Ismus opened her eyes to find the servants cowering. Some began to exit.

"I-Ismus?" Jansha fretted. "You're... fading again."

Her eyes fell to her floor. "Oh. I'm... I'm sorry," she tried weakly, throat caught.

Jansha, who had been carrying something the whole time, handed Ismus her pink silk gown and the Mint Butter Cream she had been summoned to get.

"Here you are, my princess." Jansha smoothed back the mane of Ismus. "You sleep tight, and in the morning I'll have the cooks make you a big feast. By that time, you will be feeling better." She kissed her on the forehead and turned to Jade.

"Leave her, Jade." Jansha looked her up and down. "And you're not in *uniform*," she growled before exiting.

Jade stayed.

"You know you don't deserve any sort of feast." Jade slithered from the wall. Her tight black pants and big, black boots made her look like some evil cat-woman. "Wherever you went, just know, the Queen will find out. And I'm going to be there when she does." Jade cackled, and with that, she left the room with a satisfied throw of her head. "Good night, *Princess*," she smiled outside the door.

~

Ismus was tucked away in bed, dressed in her silk nightgown, but she could not drift off. She never really could. An odd symptom it was of her state, not being able to sleep.

Ismus had always tried to put on an act for her servants, the ones she loved, but it grew more difficult with every slowly, indistinguishable day that passed. Words—words that she had to strain to hear—blended into white noise. She had to ignore it. She would stay silent. It was the only option.

There was a heaviness that had weighed her down. The lavish items that were presented to her had little importance. Small tasks, things she once enjoyed doing, were now a chore. There was always a spontaneous surge of excitement that overtook her some days—like this day—but it often quickly relapsed to a disinterested mindset.

Then the nightmare seized her. Her heart palpitated. She braided and unbraided and braided her hair over and over again. She scratched the Mint Butter Cream that soaked her body in itchy moistness.

She tried to ease her mind off it by imagining she was talking to Linnasoeta. In her imagination, her friend sat upon a tree stump, dressed in a flowy, white gown.

Would the Queen really do that? Ismus would ask while pacing up and down the black void of her mind.

Duh! If she can execute peaceful peasants she could set you on fire. Lin would respond evenly with raised brows. Their voices echoed in the empty space of Ismus's creation.

But why doesn't she love me?

Maybe because you hang around me...

She doesn't know about you. She just doesn't care about me. I think she really _hates_ me, Lin.

Yeah, well, if it makes you feel any better my dad hates me too.

Least you have a dad who's sane. And he can't hate you!

Dunno, I think Nyoka poisons his mind or something.

Lin would shrug and say in her unintentionally humoristic sort of way.

My 'Father' is a crazy maniac whose mind is already poisoned. And Aloes? She's just a monster…

You live in a castle! Don't you have… like power or something?

Not over the *Queen*, Lin, Ismus would say, rolling her eyes.

Oh… well, just try and stay away from her, I guess.

Lin! She lives in the same building as me. What am I supposed to do, stay outside, run away?

I ran away to be with you.

I know. But—

I gave up my life for you!

Lin—!

My mom died because of the killer Queen! Your killer Queen! My whole life is for you!

I'm sorry. I know what you mean…

Hey, Ismus?

Yeah?

Wake up. A terrible scream erupted from the back of Ismus's mind. *That was not Lin's voice.*

What?

Wake up.

Who are you—?

Wake up.

Ismus sat up faster than a missile. Her eyes darted around the pitch-black room. Glassy blue circles of light puddled the floors of her room. The digital clock on her dresser read:

3:19 am

What was going on? Was Ismus dreaming or just going insane?

Ismus caught her breath and lay back down on her tear-stained pillow. She had not noticed she was crying. The constant ache in her temples returned to her now conscious mind. Her head was always burning: except when she was with Lin.

Almost the entire day, she had been cured of her symptoms. The weakness, the indifference, the craving of silence. All had dissipated when spending time with the greatest gift the cold universe could give her. Her only friend.

Though they each had their differences, they brought the best out of each other. When Ismus was around, Lin could somewhat drop her bold façade and conform to the weakness within her; and Ismus could forget the weakness she had made friends with and feel a rarity—happiness.

They both had superior eye sight, climbed trees well, and loved adventure. Each could respect the other's faults, like how Ismus would fade out sometimes, or how Lin fell under oblivious and ignorant spells.

They both had dark pasts… and they both had scars with the Queen. Everyone had scars with the Queen. But most importantly, they needed each other. And Ismus needed Linnasoeta right then. She lay awake in bed, hoping for a miracle, something to look forward to.

Living the life of luxury and all its comforts did not soothe the growing pain in the princess's mind. She did not embrace the fulfillment of royalty and comfort, and she took hardly any pleasure in it. The Princess had a fate of disaster. Immorality and danger lay ahead for young Ismus of Serabi.

For quite some time now, Ismus knew that she indeed had more than just a stroke of misfortune. As she was sleeping, her mind was still rolling. Still thinking. She was dreaming up of something faintly like her schooling days.

School worked differently if one was Royal, but not so for Grade School, as one might call it. At the age of ten, young Royals seem to become more important, due to the fact that they had now reached double digits. However, ages five through nine still attended the "Normal-Foke" schools. Because of this, Ismus had befriended one "Normal-Foke."

Old Royals of Grudale would have found that rule absurd—ludicrous some would think, but Aloes did not find it silly; instead, she grew infuriated. Day by day, she would watch Ismus go through the castle gates, walking along some threadbare, repugnant peasant (her thoughts) and would fantasize over all the things she could do to him (in terms of brutality).

One day at her "Normal-Foke's" school went like this:

Samir Nichols, usually known as Sam or Sammy, sat quietly beside his friend on her left side, the two on the snowy porch steps of Oken's School. She was in one of her miserable moods again.

Her gloominess seemed to affect everything, or, rather, everything affected her gloominess. The Sun had no purpose in the grim, steely sky, like it always had their entire lives, and it seemed to do nothing about the thick layers of solid, concrete-like ice that encrusted the entire Oken's Playground. The other children in the play area, who were at least attempting to be merry, shivered and froze before they even thought of climbing up the stairs to the freezing slide or the top of the cold rock wall. It was a boring recess day, indeed, every child's spirit lacking interest or joy. Instead, they shivered… and the teachers were doing the same, though the teachers never seemed to do anything at all when recess came.

Samir sighed with monotony. "Ismus, whatever is wrong now?"

She stayed quiet, gazing sadly into the seven-inch mountain of snow. Samir waited for an answer before getting impatient.

"Ismus," Sam urged loudly. Then, lowering his voice, he said, "*Is it Aloes, Ismus? Aloes?*"

Ismus shot him a dirty grimace. Samir leaned back, away from Ismus, looking a bit alarmed. Talking about her mother was a touchy subject for Ismus, and of course Samir knew better to speak of it when she was already down and depressed. He scooted farther from Ismus, leaving his "warm" spot, and sat on a thick, solid block of ice. He shivered fervently from the cold. Ismus looked up at him.

"I'm sorry, Sam," a weak Ismus apologized quietly, "and yes, it is my mother I am thinking of. She has been horrid these past few months, and Brutus... he's been more violent than ever. Father is never around, or when he is, he scolds me for no reason, and Gwenda..."

Her gaze subsided and fell back to the snow, breathing harder. "I wish I had a better family." Ismus muttered these words very low and hollow, as if she were swallowing back tears. Samir scooted close to his best friend, brushing up against her, and stroked her soft, long, fire-red hair. It looked incredibly glowing and lustrous (sparkling like diamonds even, he would say) that it dared Sammy not to touch it. That was when he saw tears were forming in her eyes.

"Ismus," Sam said, beaming brightly, "I'm here for you, and no matter what the Queen or your brother or sister or father do to you, I'm always going to be right here—right here with you." Ismus looked up at him, smiling a small smile, heavy tears eloping down her cheeks from her blood-red eyes.

Ismus punched Sammy hard in the gut, forcing a laugh. "Don't get so syrupy with me, Sam. Yuck!" She giggled, and the boy watched her closely. He loved the rare moments when he could make her laugh.

The love-struck Samir grinned mischievously and continued to stroke her hair, mesmerized by it. "Wow! What conditioner do you use?"

"Get off it, Sammy Nichols!" Ismus shrieked, pushing him. She tackled him off the stairs, and they rolled into a heap of glittering white snow.

"I'm gonna get you now, girl!" They ran like wild beasts, screaming so loud that even the teachers turned their heads. The world seemed to have paused that day as Sammy Nichols and Ismus of Serabi chased each other around Oken's Playground.

The next day, after coloring in pictures with strawberry paint, the children were making their way outside. The fire was crackling loud in the hearth that day as Ismus and Sam stayed in the dark room. He wrapped his red scarf around his neck and pushed the blond curls out of his face. "Um, are you ready to go?" His round, intensely blue eyes gazed upon her. And to Ismus's disgust, they shone with pure innocence.

Ismus gave him an upset stare. "You sure were talking to that new girl quite a bit today."

Sam gave her a confused smile. "Arraw?" he asked. "Is that who you're talking about? Oh, I was just talking to her about the paint, that's all. Nothing much, I suppose." Sam seemed to be huffing a lot more, a big confused smile stuck on his face.

Ismus paled. "You like her, don't you?" Ismus twisted her face. *"Don't you?"*

Samir blushed and turned away. "Uh, no."

"Well, why didn't you ask *me* about that paint instead?"

"Er, you wouldn't know." Sam tried slowly. "And you sit at another table…"

"Yeah, I would! I found a bunch of paint stuff in Gwenda's bathroom! And you should have sat with me, then!"

"Ok, calm down. She said that her family used fruit paints

61

to—"

"Oh, exciting, aye, it is!"

Sam looked down at the brass floor. "Can we just go, please?"

Ismus crossed her arms. "I'm. Not. Leaving."

"Teacher will yell."

"I don't care!"

"I'm leaving."

"I don't need you to escort me… I already have people for that."

Sam sighed and buttoned up his coat, pushing his hair from his face again. "Ismus, I'm always going to be your best friend, but I hate that you're a princess. It…. It really sucks."

Ismus didn't know what to say.

So Sam left.

A couple of years went by, and the new girl had Samir wrapped around her finger like a snake slithering up a staff. The days turned even colder and lonelier for Ismus. She would trudge around the other side of the school and sit alone on the back steps, and dawdle with a stick in the snow. Ismus never seemed to appreciate her friendship with Sam as much as she did then. Soon after, Ismus turned ten, and she didn't have to go to that horrible Oken's school. Arraw and Sam were still friends, which made Ismus all the more jealous and angry. But maybe being homeschooled—or castleschooled— would be best, so she would not have to show her face to him again. Arraw probably wouldn't have allowed Ismus to come back anyway.

Friendless and alone, Ismus could already feel the cold, dark fingers of maliciousness grab her into the fiery inferno, despite at that time being eight years from her accursed sixteenth birthday.

The birthday that was approaching her in a few months.

CHAPTER 6
FIRE BURNS

The scorching cavern of the Work House was dingy and smudged and had only the fire's burn for light. Good thing Lin wasn't afraid of getting disgustingly dirty. Every metal bar or pipe one could touch in the cavern was either encrusted with a grease or oxidized. The fire burned with a dull, red purpose. Men with thick protective glasses welded weapons from the flames. Some melted and forged broken swords, and others hammered them fresh. A part of the assembly sharpened the blunt blades.

The clansmen from the Wither House fastened their brown robes and began to work. Before Lin could begin, Shen locked eyes with his daughter.

"Linnasoeta, do not go near the supply cabinet again. And I mean it, Child! If you 'accidentally' dump another bottle of flame igniter, I will banish you myself!" Lin looked up to the burned work station far to the left corner of the cavern. The one *she* burned. Shen's eyes were heated, flickering from the reflected fire (or was it reflected?).

"Yes, father."

Shen nodded and summoned her to her station. She had two pieces of steel she had to forge, and given she was still a novice, it would take a great deal of time. She slipped her fingers through her gloves and turned on the heat. Linnasoeta dumped a bag of charcoal over the wood and blew on the fire to raise the height a bit. She modified the amount of lighter fluid she used, but it still flamed up a bit higher than it should have.

"Hey, Oko?" Linnasoeta heard from behind her.

Nyoka sighed. "What is it, Hiran?" He said in a tired, drawn-out voice, still working.

Hiran smacked Nyoka on the head with a bottle of lighter fluid, wheezing as he did. "Look at your fuggen face, Oko!"

She heard a few people snort. Lin was just happy to see Nyoka get hit.

Linnasoeta jumped. The flames were ready. She drew one of the thick piece of steel and placed it over the fire. She never understood most of the Workclan's jokes, when she thought about it, but she guessed that was what made them funny. She liked it when they were quiet, though. Or if they sang. She could hear the steady clashes of the sword.

Clank... clank... Clank... clank... Bwoosh!

"Don't blow up the place like last time, Linnasoeta!" The twins had singsonged when things got quiet. More people laughed.

"Maybe if you two would stop holding hands, we'd meet our quota for this week!" Lin shot back behind her shoulder. The room erupted into a collective "ooo."

Lin smiled smugly as she turned back to her work. She was sweating buckets already, and she wiped her forehead with her greasy hand. She began to hammer a tang into the edge of the steel to form a handle, holding it over the fire for a moment and then using the mallet again to shape it.

Lin used slow, heavy movements against the steel to make it longer and thinner, going by sections. She rounded out the part that would be the point of the sword. She traded her mallet out for a smaller hammer and began to make the sides of the sword symmetrical. An hour had passed, and her shoulder and biceps were screaming in fatigue. Lin finished the bevels and pointed the tip, still holding it ever so often over the fire. Once she had finished, she placed the sword in the fire to normalize it; this process took another half hour, and consisted of constant temperature checking and coal moving. She almost burned off her finger doing so. The fire cooled, and she moved the sword over with her medal rod so the next worker could grind and polish it.

She heard everyone else's swords.

Clank.

Clank.

Clank.

Clank.

As Lin was striking down her second piece of steel with the heavy mallet, a squirming thread of jealousy prickled her insides. Ismus had once told Lin before that all the technology she had in the castle came from a group of machinists that built everything for Serabi's leaders. They had been forced to leave their homes in Grudale to produce all the fascinating technologies. Where they got the ideas for their inventions, Ismus never specified. She only muttered "Got inspiration from something, I guess," and left it at that. Still, it had made Lin burn with envy. *Ismus* got everything she wanted. *She* had people making amazing things. *She* had everything in the entire world! While *Lin* had to work for everything!

Life totally isn't fair, Lin thought discouragingly. She had once had this thought before, eight years ago—

"Work it, girl!" Someone shouted, and everyone started to howl with laughter. Linnasoeta groaned, snapping back into the dark, disgusting cavern.

"Shut up!" she growled. "Mind to your own work!"

"Ooh! Feisty!" A few people snickered. Linnasoeta rolled her eyes and continued clanking, griping under her breath. Slowly, her mind relaxed. All she could think of was the sword. The potential of the steel to become a weapon. She turned it to the other side so she could hammer it on the back. The mallet felt heavier with every stroke. Yet Lin would not fail due to pain, and she timed her hits to match the others.

She could hear the men's work song going to the rhythm of the swords:

Working hard

It's hard day's work

To fight against the fire

But fear the enemy

Is not here

It is just a factor

Clank, Clank, Clank. Then Lin chimed in softly:

Working hard

To beat the worst

The Terrible Pale Queen

Take the Beauty from us all

Try and take her unseen

Together with strength and cope

Guide us through the darker times

Like the Clanking of the Swords

These days, you can't ask for finer men

Then the men sang louder with Lin:

Like the Clanking of the Swords

Like the Clanking of the Swords

Guide us through the darker times

Like the Clanking of the Swords!

They ended with a great, proud, "Ha!" The singing ceased, and all that was heard was the metallic clank of the swords once more.

Linnasoeta still was working on her second sword. She checked her station; the fire had died and she needed more fluid. Turning toward the back of the cavern, she walked with a hurry to get the white bottle. She dodged the flames and workers. She flung open the big cupboard and searched for the bottle.

Shen looked up from his work to see his daughter. Linnasoeta knew he was looking. She knew everyone was looking. She heard someone huff. She grasped the white bottle and slowly walked back to her station, all eyes on her. The cavern's earthy ground was boarded up with croaky wooden planks, and it made no effort to silence Lin's hard footsteps. She walked to her station, laid down more wood, and spilled the charcoal across the top. Lin started up the flames, and twisted the cap.

The universe hated her.

She was certain.

The cap was already loosened, and twisting it further made it jump out of her hands and into midair. She lunged to grasp it.

Too late. The small bottle spilled its contents into the flames and engulfed her station in red and orange. The flickers of its heat burned in Lin's eyes as she stumbled to the floor. The entire cavern was silent and stunned for a moment; then they realized this was bound to happen again due to her performance last week and threw the pales of water they had prepared onto it.

Charred like an overcooked steak, black ashes dropped into Lin's eyes and mouth.

The Workclan had a good reason to tease. "Nice going, Shen. Could have been avoided if you told your dumbass kid to stay home," one of the workers throwing water on the flames snorted.

Lin's heart raced in her throat. The ability to speak was replaced with horror and knowing: knowing her father would scream. She couldn't bear to hear his disappointment.

As if being controlled, she threw herself to her feet and ran out. Not knowing where and not caring how far.

~

"Linnasoeta!" Shen called after her.

Nyoka put a hand on his shoulder and looked him dead in the eye.

"Let her go."

And Shen did.

But he was never the same until a long while after.

~

Linnasoeta had run away from home. She never thought it would have to come to this, to the point where she would have to banish herself. She was a traitor. Anyone who ever left Rodem for their own selfish reasons broke their pact. She was a *traitor*. And she would always be one. Her eyes stung with tears, and she began screaming as they started dripping off her face. But she didn't stop running. She was nearing the trench, starting to run through the gap only she and Ismus (and one other) could see. Bees stung at her arms, but that was not pain. The real pain that scarred her was her betrayal. Her mother would think nothing of her. Maybe it was better that way.

That she was dead.

As she crossed the border of Thangos, the world morphed into a subzero Hell. She shivered with pain. She froze on the spot; she knew not of the cold. Only once before had she felt this icy blunder, but that was eight years ago. When she was seven. That horrible day.....

"Why did you leave me? Why is the Queen—?" Linnasoeta stopped and continued through the forest.

She needed to *focus.*

When she reached a large tree, she wrapped her legs around the trunk and climbed up. She howled as the bark dug deep into her flesh. She grabbed a hold of her burning leg with both her hands, the ones that were supposed to be holding onto the tree. She turned upside-down, and the blood rushed to her head instantly.

How was this happening? What was she feeling?

Helpless.

She felt so *helpless.*

Linnasoeta's fell hard on the leaf-infested ground. The foliage crunched beneath her. Linnasoeta brushed the leaves off and stood up dizzily.

The sick feeling of betrayal, that burning, abrasive, guilty feeling pinching her throat and nose, was the worst feeling in the world.

"What's happening to me?" Linnasoeta faltered, clutching her head. She was on all fours now, lying in the snow-bitten leaves, where she blacked out.

There she dreamed of Kima.

CHAPTER 7

LUXURIOUS CASTLE LIFE

The cooks and servants were always bustling before dawn, back at the castle. Ismus would find the sweet smell of Royalty-ready breakfast wafting from the lower floor to the upstairs rooms. The same applied to this morning, the day after her adventure.

Ismus had halted the firing of her arrows and stopped to hear the rain increase its volume. A hail storm had begun.

A gray light seeped through the thin curtain, little drips of rain and dewdrops fogging her window. It reminded her of yesterday morning, the way she was staring up at her thin curtains, dazed from another night of insomnia, fading into the dim gray light of the Sun.

The excitement of jumping out of the window and running from the castle was too grand to chew. Even the smallest thought of disobeying her sister's orders was too frightening to even touch. But Ismus thought of it often. She never was truly sure why she had had the courage and sudden strength and interest to escape, but it mattered not. That particular morning, she was ready to turn her longing for freedom into a state of action.

Ismus opened her eyes to the constant drips of rain fogging her window the day before. A hazy light seeped through the cracks of her windows. It beckoned Ismus to sleep, but instead she lie still with eyes wide open. The crisp chill of early morning cooed Ismus to curl up even tighter into her blanket. The hearth had not been stoked the day before, so the room was as cold as an icebox. Ismus would have stayed in bed all day if she could, but fate was too strong to ignore. Today was the day that she would be released from the clutches of the Queen. Her *free* day, a day that would change her lonesome fate, was calling—and it was too strong to ignore.

The mere thought of an escape had made Ismus kick off her blanket and run to her closet door. Goosebumps crept beneath her skin, and the hairs on her arm stuck straight up. Her breath was dry, fresh morning waste stuck to her lips.

Her closet flew open when she turned the slender golden knob. Clothes hung on luxurious, white hangers, while shoes were organized in one tidy corner. Ismus rubbed her eyes, wiping the grit of sleep from the corners of them. She touched the fabrics of some of her clothes; some much too itchy, some too delicate.

Ismus ran her hand through a silk gown. It felt as if she was touching wet fog, almost like feeling nothing. The fabric tickled her fingertips as she stroked the gown. The creamy colors of it once made Ismus think of blank clouds, roaming the sky with no true purpose. The gown was the same; it would stay in Ismus's closet with no real meaning, for Ismus would never put it on. It was lucky, though, to get some bit of attention. Ismus usually never even glanced at the cursed outfits the maids constructed. Why pay it any mind now?

She fished through her clothes to find something off the Servant's signature collection. Itchy fabrics and dresses that would make the boys grovel at her feet would do nothing for Ismus's journey.

Instead, she had found a thick plated crop top, tight studded shorts, a rabbit-skinned pelt, and her rabbit wool socks. The light from the window had grown harsher (thicker, that is, with its nasty gray) as Ismus fetched her heavy winter boots. Ismus tore her night clothes off and placed them on her bed, half-folding them, then found the last clean set of underwear in her drawer. She dressed quietly in her closet, not wanting the snores to be disturbed and scold her for being awake so early. No matter what day it was, the "Castle members" wanted their beauty rest. (Too bad the only one that was *actually* beautiful was Gwenda.) When Ismus was dressed and ready, she went to the far side of her room, the opposite way to the closet, and fetched her favored weapon—her bow.

In Serabi, some of the best known weapons that could be

found were the bows and arrows, swords, and daggers. Little else could be found of warfare and machinery items, and one was to be considered beyond wealthy to have a bow such as Ismus's. Most would merely have rakes and plows for protection.

Her arrows were neatly placed inside her quiver, only because of the maids' constant cleaning. Out of all the other rooms in the castle, they visited Ismus's room the most. Ismus sighed and heaved the quiver onto her shoulder, moving it so it would nestle between her neck and shoulder, and she stared into the mirror to tie back her hair. Then she started to the door.

It opened with a noisy crack that was possibly capable of waking the whole castle. She looked down the hall, back and forth, making sure the coast was indeed clear. When she decided that it was safe, she started the walk down the hall. Ismus had tiptoed lightly down the carpeted floor, careful to avoid the places where it moaned the most under her weight. She passed her elder siblings' rooms: Gwenda, her sister, and her brother Brutus, the eldest sibling of them all, who never let them forget it.

As she passed his room, she thought of the wicked snores that kept her up at night. But, this time, his room was silent; there was nothing but the slow movement of the curtain whispering back and forth in the breeze.

She knew something was wrong. If a servant had walked past Brutus's room, he or she would have found nothing out of the ordinary. But Ismus knew her brother more than the person who gave birth to them herself. (Then again, the Queen seemed to love her children just as much as the light that seeped through the windows.) Ismus stopped to hear if anyone was near, mainly concerned if Brutus or Aloes were lurking in the shadows. She then continued down the dark, shadowy, narrow hall and walked down the stairway.

Ismus tiptoed across the hallway to the main level and walked out the door. She was ready to start her adventure.

That was yesterday. When Ismus fully awakened *this* morning, however, she felt a horrible hole in her back: she had found herself on the floor, probably from her stupid silk pajamas. After arising, Ismus flew to her bow and quiver of arrows and shot down the target maliciously.

She shivered and groaned. Her stomach growled, and she obviously was in no hurry for another adventure. Then she smelt the delicious smell of whatever was cooking downstairs.

The kitchen and the bakery downstairs were noisy, as far as Ismus was concerned. Spoons and plates clattered and chattered. Pots and pans banged and rang. Faucets turned on and off, and head chefs shouted with loud voices.

Ismus's ears pricked up when she heard footsteps (rather, *boot* steps) coming down the hall; she jumped when Jade appeared at her door. The servant rolled her green, cat-like eyes. "Breakfast is ready, *Princess* Ismus." She spat 'Princess' as if it was a joke. Ismus nodded gravely and gagged when Jade's back was turned.

When Jade left, she got up from her floor and opened the door to her own personal bathroom. She sighed and scratched and stepped into the bathroom, onto a fuzzy golden rug. A Jacuzzi bubbled on the left wall, and a shower lay unaccompanied behind the second bathroom door.

Ismus stepped up the stairs to her cabinet and pulled out her tangerine-scented conditioner and her toothpaste. She jumped at the sight of herself in the mirror: she was undeniably repulsive.

She wiped the crust from her mouth and eyes, brushed and flossed her teeth, and combed through her thick, tangled hair, which laid bone straight after the grooming. It was funny to Ismus how it could go from clinging at her ears to tickling her hips. Then she applied a bit of light makeup to her cheeks and eyes, hoping that she wouldn't be lectured for looking "homeless" as her dear sister put it.

The servants had picked her out a lacy pink dress, which was lying alone on the counter. It was something that was to be worn for weddings, parties, dates…not for breakfast. It was one of Ismus's least favorite dresses, so she gladly left the scratchy thing alone. Her cute, though unconventional, jammies were nice enough. Fifteen minutes later, Princess Ismus really did look like a princess.

When she finished dressing, she wandered into the hall and down the stairs. The smell of the food was intoxicating. Ismus felt a slight tug at the ends of her mouth before letting it drop.

Food was a difficult topic for Ismus. Her diet was often a suffering task to manage. When she was younger, the maids had caught her one night stuffing in sweets and butter-laden things; other nights Ismus would refuse to eat anything at all. The servants then realized that she would always eat whenever food was laid before her. They believed it was because she was lazy—or outright rude.

The servants were wrong.

Ismus dragged herself across the halls and entered the kitchen. That was where the cooks were; a hundred cooks dressed in white and adorned in chef hats, all of them smelling of delicious food, bustling around a massive, factory-sized kitchen.

As she hobbled and ducked around, the cooks bowed, yet continued bustling. A chubbier chef (half of Ismus's height) with a squeaky voice and rosy cheeks emerged from the scene and said, "Everything is being set out in the second dining room, Princess. Come back should you have any requests. Though Jansha has prepared the meal, especially for your return."

Ismus nodded and walked straight back to the other dining room—one of three— behind the kitchen.

As the plump chef had said, breakfast was being placed onto a table, along with the silverware and folded napkins. Head servants were in charge of setting the table just right for the Royal's breakfast. Emerald-colored plates held chocolate chip pancakes, thick, juicy bacon slices, hash browns, toasted bread with butter, and an assembly of ripe, fresh fruit topped off with whipped cream.

Steaming mugs of hot chocolate were just arriving from the kitchen on silver platters, more of the homemade whipped cream and marshmallows starting to melt away. Bowls of golden apple butter and jelly were being set in a straight line.

Ismus tried to maintain her Royal duty of looking poised, and not drool on herself, but all the great smells were drifting into Ismus's nose, forcing the saliva out. Waliey, the head of the head servants, beckoned Ismus to the table and pulled out her chair, nose up.

"I shall wake your siblings, Princess Ismus, and by then you may start eat—No! I said the *gold ware*, Dorim!" Waliey breathed in and sighed as Dorim faltered and staggered back to the kitchen.

"I'm very sorry Princess Ismus. Rude of me to interrupt. Just wait for your siblings, if you do not mind. I will fetch them quickly, for I know you are hungry, if I am right, though I may not be." As he left, Ismus sat and frowned.

Every time the servants tried to state anything, they were quick to contradict it. They had a motto:

Descendents of the Gods were placed in our hands

And our lives are meant to satisfy every demand.

Though we may want to cry and gain pity through tears

May we not forget the real reason we are all here.

It was set in place during the era of King Sorthon, and Ismus grimaced as she recalled this fact. She realized that she had everything handed to her on a silver platter— quite literally—while the servants who received nothing were forced to know only happiness. She tried to force herself to become happy in this moment, knowing she had lavish items most did not, but she couldn't. She could not be happy.

Pathetic.

Ismus jumped when her big brother Brutus busted through the door. His beastly size had made her think that a cow had barged in, for was he not a cow?

76

"Prince Brutus," Nirid, a kind servant who only believed in organized perfection, started before Brutus shot him a *shut-up-tiny-man* look. The servant backed away to fetch Gwenda before Brutus could do real damage to his face.

Then it was just Brutus, Ismus, and another servant. Ismus felt her chest tighten, and she attempted to breathe.

He was wearing a blue and white striped robe with black slippers, and his dark, round eyes looked very tired.

As a servant pulled out his chair, Brutus shot him a glance and barked, "Coffee. Dark roast. *Three spoons* of sugar. Go get it. NOW! And walk with some speed!"

"Right away, Prince Brutus." He answered kindly, bowing low to the floor, and then running to the kitchen to fulfill the boy's demand. Brutus plopped into his chair with a sharp grunt, rattling the table. His black eyes poured onto Ismus.

He huffed. "Those servants... So fun to mess with. You know?" He ran his fingers through his hair and stared out the window into the black, icy mess outside.

Ismus saw his lips moving, but could not hear him because of the storm that now rattled the window's frame. She slowly moved her head to gaze at the world beyond.

Brutus creased his one brow. "Answer me, you deaf—" he swore a few times. Brutus banged his fist on the table, the poor vase of flowers toppling over. Startled, Ismus spun her head around to look directly into his eyes. The contact was terrifying, so much that she felt too frightened to look away. Brutus squinted at her and scowled. Then he yelled again:

"*Where's my coffee?*"

"Right here, Master Brutus," a younger servant stumbled in, white steam swirling from the cup. Brutus snatched the mug from the platter and snarled, coffee spilling. Lightning growled.

"Be gone with you!" Brutus demanded. "And tell Gwenda to get her ass down here before the bacon and cakes get any colder!"

"I'm already here, Brutus," Gwenda laughed gently and stepped up to her chair. She had been coming out the doorway just a second ago. The servant pulled the chair out for her. Ismus felt the side of her mouth twitch. Gwenda caught her staring and frowned, puzzled.

"You all may start to dine. I will fetch your father, if I can, and—" he stopped.

"No, no just your father," he whispered and walked away.

"Well, you heard him!" Brutus said, "Let's eat!" He snatched up the whole platter of bacon before Gwenda looked his way.

"*Share.*"

He sighed. "Fine, *Lacy Maiden.*"

"I thought we agreed for you to not call me that anymore," Gwenda said blankly. Her eyes grew heavy.

His sharing method consisted of giving Gwenda all three of the turkey bacon pieces and tossing Ismus half of his bitten piece (that he threw in her direction and ended up on the floor). That would leave him with five thick-cut slices of bacon. A true cow he was!

Ismus grabbed for a plate and picked up a pancake. She took a few bites before consuming another. She took a sip of her scalding hot chocolate, topped it off with more whipped cream, and drowned the rest.

They were all silent for a minute, sipping on juice or munching on savory meats, the finest of cheeses, sweet doughnuts, and chocolate things. Piles of Grudalian toast and coffee cake lay forgotten on the table as their stomachs grew larger. Servants came ever so often to check on them. When the third round of servants left, Gwenda spoke.

"Ismus, I really need to know, where did you go yesterday?"

She shrugged and bit down into a hash brown. "Nowhere, really."

"Nowhere important I would imagine." Brutus snorted. "Should have just stayed there, kid." Ismus looked at him, knowing that she didn't have to hear to know he was insulting her.

Gwenda combed her freshly curled hair back with her hand, ignoring her older brother. "You don't mean that... Why else would you be gone so long? Be honest with me, Ismus. I *am* your sister. I need to know if you went somewhere bad."

Brutus put his fork down (for the first time) and heaved, "She, that thing over there, couldn't handle living without this level of comfort. She came back. So—"

"So...?" Gwenda questioned as she leaned towards.

"So forget about it! It ain't important!"

"Why are you asking me all this stuff anyway?" Ismus grumbled, pushing her hair violently from her eyes to spite her sister. "It's not like you care..."

"What?" Gwenda said, her voice full of hurt. "What do you mean?" Her throat was tight. (Was she seriously about to cry?)

"You never talk to me."

"But I'm talking right n—"

"Other than today and last night, Gwenda." Ismus sighed and rolled her eyes as she saw tears start to fall down Gwenda's face. "Just forget it..."

"*Girls.*" Brutus said with loud (loud enough for Ismus to hear) disgust. "*Fist* fights don't even make you cry..."

Ismus wanted to tell him, "*Shut up, you disgusting, insensitive, hateful jackass. I wish you would take you own advice and*

79

just kill yourself already!"

That's what she always wanted to say to Brutus, but, of course, she kept her mouth shut.

Brutus rolled his tired eyes and drained his coffee; he belched loudly. Then he jumped up from his chair when he saw the King walk in.

"Dad!"

The King, Borthor, waved at the children as he struggled into the room. He was a horribly thin, weak man with a pale face, patches of reddish-brown hair, and dull green eyes.

As a servant rushed to his aid, the King waved him off. "My, my, my, my, don't you have someone else to pester? Ehh, my children!" The feeble old man said.

"Well, I see you ate all the f—" he started to choke. It was one of those dry, scratchy coughs that got stuck in his throat. Borthor seemed to be choking up a bone.

"I'm completely capable of sittin' myself down."

Gwenda gave her father a curious look. Brutus smiled at him, but the King did not know it. He staggered over to the chair between Gwenda and Brutus. "Ah! I just love me some penguin. All fat and juicy and furry and flightless. He can't fly away…"

As one could comprehend, King Borthor was very strange. Peculiar was not a strong enough word. Delusional was borderline offensive, and thus most precise of all. There was something wrong with the King. They had all come to the conclusion that a thick coating of a foreign substance was poisoning his mind, like something was taking him over. Or maybe it was just age.

The rest of breakfast had been interrupted by the crazy King Borthor, so Ismus left. Gwenda did the same; they thought their father was mad. Brutus, on the other hand, stayed and tried to talk to his father about things. Of course the King knew not of what his son was saying.

Ismus walked up the steps into her room. Once she opened up her room door, she plopped on her plush bed, heaving out a sigh.

What am I going do? She thought as she rolled her lilac eyes.

She slouched into the bed with distaste. She *needed* to get out of here. She *had* to get out of here. Her castle members weren't just unbearable, they were completely insane. And, to top it all off, she was stuck. Stuck in the castle on her free Sunday with absolutely nothing to do.

On most days, she would start off the beginning of the day by waking and bathing. She would eat an immense amount of breakfast and then brush her teeth. Once Ismus was completely clean, the servants would take her to the pinnacle high above the castle where she would learn to do "Princess" things, like walking on stilts or six-inch heels ("for proper elegance and to see above the stinking people below you" Madam Minks had instructed), or balance a one-thousand-page book on her head in order to achieve proper posture. They all blurred into a stream of nothingness; and frankly, Ismus was indifferent to it all.

Until her sword teaching.

It was a special class one of the servants had made after her constant pleading. (The servants were surprised to see Ismus so passionate about, well, *anything*, and they felt it obligatory to make an exception.)

This class used real swords, and Ismus loved it. She craved the feeling of the hilt of the sword against her palm. It gave her importance. It gave her power. True dominating power.

Gwenda would never take the sword-infested class. She hated danger, or adventure, or death, or anything pointy or sharp. She would much rather sew in a rocking chair with a needle or read a novel. And Brutus would just rely on his meaty hands to throttle his victim to death. Sword fighting was of no use to him either.

The rest of the day she would practice an instrument, then have her cooking class, which was horrid and dull to her. When she finished all her classes, the maids would clean up whatever mess she had made in the kitchen, and she would be escorted to her bathroom. There she would bathe again and prepare for dinner.

But today, she would stay in her room, aimlessly firing arrows at a target.

~

The next day, Ismus combed through her hair and brushed her teeth after a frugal breakfast (for royalty) and was escorted up to the pinnacle for her lessons. The staircase spiraled into an ominous, circular loop. It was dimly lit with candelabras that were fastened against the dark brick wall. The scent of dust pinched her throat; the walls tightened around her. Perched above her were weird statues, either sticking out their tongues or gaping at her demonically. A foreboding shudder overtook her body looking at those familiar abominations.

An old servant, alongside a youthful one, then escorted her to her first classroom. Her first class of the day was history. Down the hall and to the left was her history room, where shelves of old dusty books lay, many left unread and untouched for decades.

One wooden desk lit by a burned-out candle was all the light in that begrimed, leaden dungeon. Spider webs hung from the ceiling to the floor, dead spiders and their unfinished flies suspended from aloft. The eldest servant smiled tenderly at Ismus, pushed her into the room, and closed the door before locking it.

Ismus groaned. No windows, hardly any light. Just stuffy, boring reading. Ismus hated history. *Her* history. She trudged over to the bookshelves behind the big wooden desk and searched for the *Royal History Tome and Oracle: Grudale in a Nutshell*. Once she found it on the top shelf, she picked it up, scanned it, and blew any dust off the cover that had collected from other books.

She plopped down onto the soft, black chair and picked up reading where she left off.

Chapter 300

The rule of King Sorthon and Grudale's Victory

Appendix: II:

Of the many years of wandering in the Nomanic Oceans, settlers from Chidaria, Grudale found a land of peace and plentiful harvest. They named it Serabi, after the lioness they worshiped as the ancient Goddess, the spirit deity of the great animal king. They took the rule as a symbol of fate, for there was a beautiful limestone castle already built in a desirable location.

However, strange people had already claimed the land and declared that they were the people that fully inhabited the land. Sorthon tried to be reasonable, but the people of Rodemina (modern day Rodem) as they had named the land would not cooperate. Much to the King's dismay, he summoned the aid of his army and lashed a plundering feat on the people.

The people of Rodem attempted to fight back. They were no match against the King's great army, and in a desperate gamble to try and battle for the land, they lost appallingly. This battle was named the Night War. The people of Grudale feasted and celebrated an enormous victory. Wiping out almost every one of the queer people who stood in their way, they took control over the land and guided them to a clear light. Sorthon's rule was bound for greatness in the new lands of Serabi, and those who thought otherwise would be killed or tortured by their own ill performances.

After many years of a great rule, the enslaved people broke out into another war, known as the Perfidy War. (Rodem's people had entitled the event the Fire Revolutionary War.) The King tired of the fighting after he saw his militia thrown into a forest and eaten by the beasts of Wither Hollow. Because of this "Émigré", the King signed the First Armistice of Ceasefire, better known as the Thangos Document and Treaty.

The Royals of Serabi retained enormous power, enough power to plainly split the land in two and carve it under a mountain bluff. After much thinking, it seemed to be the most viable thing to end war and restore peace. And that is just what they did. The King summoned his loyal workers (that included his miners, carpenters, and diggers), and they sliced right through the land with diamond-tipped shovels and spades, diamond knives, and Serabi's traitors' bones (those who stood in the way of the King were forced to give him their bones as punishments) making it fair and just in equal size for both lands. The agonizing work took almost ten years to complete, and many had given up their lives to carry out their orders; however, when they had finished, no better sense of pride would be bestowed upon them.

The people of Rodem complained about the supposed jagged edges, but the King did not listen. He knew that it was fair, and he would say no more to the people that killed a fraction of his army. There were, however, many places where the people of Rodem could not cross. Once the Border of Thangos was put in place, the Rodemians vowed that they would stay on their half if it would prevent future war.

A few of the rebels who tried to find ways to cross used a particular magical entity to make way into Serabi: the Liana. The vine stretched many miles over the Thangos Trench. When the King ordered his lumberjacks to cut it down, all came back scratched and injured; it was up so high in the trees of the Serabi Forest, it was nearly impossible to climb over the tops of the trees and hold a heavy ax at the same time. Those who could chop it down also did not succeed; the vine regenerated around the trees within moments of their fall. They later tried chopping down the tree entirely, yet when they arrived the next morning, another had arose in its place. It was a terrifying sorcery, and the King ordered to never speak of it again.

Thankfully, no person in Rodem could cross the border. The Liana was not practical enough to be used as a means to get across the trench. Some plummeted a thousand miles into the giant hole. Bodies stirred in the Thangos Trench.

A decade later, Sorthon passed away, and a new era of royalty had begun. Sorthon's son, Bithorn, ruled alongside the Queen Fira. Here, they modernized the cities. Crime rates dropped. Little else happened during their rule, until Bithorn died young in his late teens, and the Queen soon after him.

His son, Borthor, then took command. His marriage had been arranged some years before, and he was to marry the fifth-born Princess of Grudale. Borthor had tendencies, however, to live and go about as he chose, and thereby denied the marriage. It had never been done in the history of Grudale or Serabi. Alas, being the only son with no authority to condemn him, he sought out the most beautiful of women in Serabi. That was when he found Aloes, a village girl from the poor vale, just past the gates of the capital Seracone. He took a deep interest in her, and soon the impoverished girl was made Queen.

What once were the ruinous people of Grudale grew into a fine and profitable reign of the King of the Far North, and, to come, a greater rule of the future.

Appendix: III

Global Impacts during the Warring Period

Stop! Ismus closed the book shut and sealed her eyes. She didn't need to poison her eyes with an inch more.

"What load of shit!" Ismus cursed under her breath.

This book was a lie. It wasn't the *King's dismay* to unleash a deadly army. It wasn't *fair and just* as he had claimed.

"Aloes didn't inherit her insanity. No wonder the King took such '*deep interest*' in her," she spat.

Ismus felt her heart jump when the door unlocked and swung open.

"Ready for your poetry class, Princess?" The elderly servant plastered a grim smile.

"I apologize for cutting the history lesson short, but the poetry teacher is running a bit earlier than usual: she's coming down with something."

Ismus sighed. "Yes, I'm ready to get out of this room." She placed the book on the dusty, wooden table and stepped out of the dim room. The servant escorted her down the tunnel-like hall. As Ismus walked, she saw Gwenda smiling with an armful of books; it must have been her lunch-library break.

Ismus saw her sister's face fill with fright as she passed the vacant sword-fighting room (lessons were taught every day except for Mondays and Thursdays).

Eyes closed, she sped down the hall while panting, "Nothing to be scared of, nothing to be scared of!"

Gwenda really *hated* that room.

Poetry class, as one would have guessed, was nothing worth talking about. Later in the day, when the little bit of scattered Sun they always had was slowly sinking from existence, Ismus learned that her cooking classes had been cancelled (due to a slight fire incident) meaning she was free the rest of the evening. Dinner would not be ready until a long while, so she decided that she would wander down the unexplored halls of the castle. This freedom to explore on a weekday was a rare treat.

That's when Ismus found the chamber. She had been roaming down the narrow strip of staircases when she pressed her hand against the stony wall. Torches were fastened against the wall, and the fire blazed brightly.

Torches? Ismus asked herself, puzzled. **Where are the candelabras—!**

A split second later, after a loud groan, Ismus found herself on the floor of a dark room. She could not see.

Faint figures drifted near her nose. The familiar abrasive smell of dust and fire caught her nose and throat, pinching them. That suffocating type feeling where her cough was dry... and the burning of her wrists... that was just like the nightmare—

The nightmare—

Ismus's heart raced and she groped about for a door. Her blood pumped through her ears, and she hoped a creature in the dark would not hear it. Her breath quickened.

Where is the exit?!

Ismus felt something grab her by the ankles and drag her across the floor. Then she lost consciousness.

She awoke later that night to the softness of her bed, gold sheets spilling over her like a fountain, her eyes coated by the bluish-darkness of her room. That was all.

Later that night, Ismus crept out of her bedroom and walked to the library to read about fairy tales, and how the darkness always got beaten by the light. One particular fairy tale she was thinking of was *The Awakening of the Whisker*, which was about a cute little mouse that had gotten stepped on and killed. He had turned evil, and another little mouse came along to destroy the Dark Mouse. The sweet mouse killed him and was victorious, praised by all.

For some reason, Ismus thought that was wrong.

Very, very wrong.

~

"I don't understand," Gwenda began. "You—you can't just kick us out of our own home!"

The man, dressed in entirely black, gave her a long, inhumane glance. The library was quiet out of anger, out of fear. The candle burned its brightest, yet little could light the dark vacantness of the library. The smell of dust clogged Gwenda's throat.

"ANSWER ME!" Gwenda screamed, her throat burning with pain. Tears fell from her eyes. "ANSWER ME! WHY ARE YOU DOING THIS?"

The man adjusted his glasses.

"Stupid child," he spoke, voice so deep it grew inaudible. "It would take a million men to rebuild this nation." The stranger cornered Gwenda into the wall. He lowered his face, only an inch away from Gwenda's. "But it'd be so much easier—" His cool breath filled her face, and instantly her cheeks stung with terror—

"To burn the useless." The man flashed a set of ominous, white teeth and cackled. He smoothed his thick, swirly hair, the color of midnight, and looked deep into Gwenda's crisp, green eyes.

"There's no point anymore. No one is left in this country—and you of all people should know why. You lived with it for almost sixteen years."

The stranger adjusted himself. "There will be attacks," he said evenly. "More officials from Grudale will come in less than a year's time. I suggest you run. Get away from this place before you regret it."

Gwenda shook her head, blond hair flopping every which way. "NO. *NO!*" She grabbed a hold of the man's neck, only to feel him vanish from her fingertips like smoke. The stranger was gone.

Dazed, Gwenda fell to the library floor and cried.

CHAPTER 8
EVERYTHING CHANGES NOW

The next few months for Ismus marked a turning point in her life, a start in a journey that would change her forever.

~

The first day began on a Saturday. Ismus had slipped out again (after her feigned promise to the maids) and bolted for the Serabi Forest in the bitter cold. She climbed up the tree, too confident this time, and she almost lost her footing. Ismus climbed the long branch and stretched across to the thorny, green vine—the Liana. She strapped her new bow around the vine's opening and pushed off with her legs. The hole was still intimidating and huge in her eyes, but she knew she would make it past.

As the winds blew, fierce and cold, she flew nonstop down the vine. Her vision blurred, and right as she began to stop herself, she clonked her head on the stubby tree again. Before she could blink, her vision clouded, and everything blackened. She had done it yet again. It didn't feel any different though... it was still cold.

Ismus froze, her furrowed face loosening in horror.

The creek had a thick glacier of ice frosted over it, the fish encased in solid cubes. The wind lashed the world with hate. The plants shriveled dead. The eastern mountains had a blanket of thick snow wrapped about them. The grass was buried beneath white.

Ismus couldn't close her jaw, and it wasn't because she was stricken with beauty. She was *horrified*. She knew Rodem never looked like this. Something was wrong.

She stood, her stomach turning.

"*W-what the hell?*" Ismus stammered. "*What happened?*"

This was horrible. On top of it all, Linnasoeta wasn't even here as she should have been. Ismus had told her to come on this very Saturday, had she not?

"Lin?" Ismus shouted as snow started to fall. There was silence, nothing but silence.

"*LIN?*" Ismus screamed again. When she had done it a third time, she looked down at her feet. Ice was forming about the soles of her boots.

"Hey!" A deep voice bellowed, and Ismus whipped her head up. Ten fully armed men and women were fixing their eyes right on her. Three of them started to sprint.

In utter panic, she ran down the border, dodging thrown swords and running workmen, scouting for the gap. She heard heavy footsteps coming from behind her. Swords were finding themselves all along her body, with deep chunks of skin in her legs and shoulders tearing out with every throw. Ismus shut her eyes in pain, drew in a few shaky breaths, and tolerated the suffering of the screaming in her now gashed legs.

Ismus threw herself into the forest. She clutched her bleeding limbs and let out a cry of anguish.

"Damn it!" She heard a voice curse. "Where the 'ell did she go?!" The shadows and footsteps retreated, with much hesitation and fury, back to the base of the Creek.

Her eyes turned watery again. She wouldn't be able to move. Ismus rolled around, legs to her chest, crying, screaming, grinding her hair into the dirt.

"*LIN,*" Ismus yelled with a crack in her voice, "*STOP*

HIDING AND HELP ME!" Yet as she expected, there was no reply.

Her thighs now burned with a ferocity that of flames. Ismus couldn't even breathe. Her legs flung off her chest and to the ground, sizzling her skin. She slammed her lips together as she tried to muffle the sound of her howls. Darkness faded in and out of her vision.

When she awoke some minutes later, she inspected her legs, shoulders, everywhere—and found a truly horrifying discovery. Every bruise she had just cried over had vanished entirely. Now what lay before her were two unbruised and glowing white legs. Ismus staggered to her feet.

Shit.

They still felt broken.

Dazed and shaking, she walked down the rest of the forest, falling every few steps until she reached her castle.

Trying to unfreeze herself from the cold, she paced back and forth in the barren halls with a hand against the wall; no one was around. *Maybe the maids were in their headquarters?*

She brushed the snow off her mittens and her pelt. She unzipped her jacket, took off her boots, and started to remove her second layer of pants.

Her heart rate snapped at the sound of a scream.

The voice was hollow and scared and shrill. Ismus stood there, hearing something hit the floor with a loud *THUD.*

Silence fell after, a deep silence. Her heartbeat sped up dangerously. First she paused, frozen.

She stumbled up the green steps and crawled on her hands and knees up two more flights of stairs to the library: dusty, vacant. Gwenda's room: nothing. She peeked through Brutus's room: empty.

She paused. It must have come from the Queen's room.

Knees buckling, she walked quickly before arriving at the door. Her stomach churned. She touched the doorknob fearfully with the tips of her fingers. Ismus had never entered her room before.

Hesitating, waiting for something to pop out from the murky hall, she resisted her conscience of turning back, and she opened the door.

Not one figure illuminated in the darkness. Ismus lit a candle.

As she walked into the room, she saw that blood had been spilled all over the white carpet, and the bed was in two. She soon saw a trail of blood winding toward a bent figure. She slowly walked toward the body—it was a body—knowing full well who it was.

And yet still, her eyes widened.

Aloes.

The Queen was dead.

Dead...

There she was, her mouth open, like she had died in horror. Her eyes were gray and lifeless, like two stagnant ponds, and a tint of red streaked her cheeks. Thin strands of gray hair embedded in her scalp fell, one hair at a time, like the petals of a dandelion. Her skin was the complexion of clay.

There was a shrill look of alarm in her eyes. Her mouth was caked with blood, and a satin liquid was oozing from her stomach, still fresh from a sword's cut.

Ismus knelt beside Aloes. She did not look scary at all now... only *scared.*

Ismus tensed. **Are they still here?** Her heart plunged into her stomach, and her breath grew even heavier.

Someone had *murdered* the Queen.

~

It was made apparent that the Royals would have to go when most of the castle's staff had all been found dead.

The soldiers, cooks, and maids had been found in a pile in the castle's underground level. Bodies—young, old, women, men—of the dead burned into the Royal's mind. A select few of them had survived the attack, the ones who had hid in the closets.

"The attacks," Gwenda murmured, tugging at her bottom lip.

Brutus grimaced. "Why didn't they go after us?"

"Because they're going to do it again."

The remaining servants were left quiet, tears falling down their pale, drained faces.

Ismus looked at the ones who were still alive.

Jade, dressed in rags and with eyes burning red, said nothing as she stared at Ismus.

"We are not safe here. No…We'll have to be gone by tomorrow," Gwenda spoke.

"We're not *leaving* the castle!" Brutus roared, veins pulsating. "Whatever, or whoever, attacked this place is gonna be completely destroyed next time they come here. I'll finish 'em off, I just wasn't ready!" He was hysterical, not even he could manage seeing all this death, all at once…

"Brutus, they gassed us when we were asleep. They locked us in a closet. They took out an *entire* staff and our army. *Do you honestly think you have any power against them?*" Gwenda seethed. For the first time, Ismus could see a genuine rage in her soft-spoken sister. It alarmed her.

Their eldest brother began to say something, but found it impossible to reply.

The day ran clear. No moment was different than the last. After the bodies had been buried—the Queen's in a special tomb—Ismus had left the gravesite and lay in her bed, thinking, worrying.

In the last morning of their castle life, the children gathered around Borthor who had demanded to see them. Still dressed in pajamas, Gwenda hobbled over to her father.

"Y-yes?" stammered Gwenda.

Sensing his daughter's fear, the King's gaze softened. "I know I have scared you for quite some time now, Gwenda. I have done things and said things I know have been most… irrelevant. Now that Aloes is gone, I feel as if I am a normal man again. But, without her, I cannot go on, no matter how much I try."

Gwenda gasped. After fifteen years, Gwenda had forgotten that Borthor was not always insane.

"Oh, father!" Gwenda cried, springing around his bed, hugging him for the first time she could remember. "I'm so sorry," She sobbed. "How I was a fool to mistake you as a fool! The fool I am!"

Borthor loosened from her. "You will do great things in life, Gwenda. I love you. Brutus, I want to talk to you now."

Brutus stepped up to the King's bed, his eyes red and blotchy. "How will I fulfill your dying wish, Dad?" Ismus tensed when she saw just how distraught her older brother was. She hated how she got no joy out of seeing him depressed.

The King gave him a firm look. "You never gave up on me, son, and as my son I respect that. But as a man, that will not get you praise. Take care of the girls and see that they are safe. I am sorry for not being the father I should have been. So please do as I say."

Brutus nodded, his eyes full of tears.

95

"Ismus," Borthor called.

The girl frowned and walked up to his bed.

"I have to talk to you too, you know."

Ismus looked him dead in the eyes. "What?"

Borthor gave her a puzzled look.

He began to stare at her. Just looking, endlessly. She couldn't move.

Then he said, "There's a lot of things you don't know, Ismus, and a lot of things you don't know are about to happen, a lot of which *I* truly don't know. Everything that is happening is because of you. You are *peculiar*, blessed with powers beyond your own control. Brutus and Gwenda will explain this to you one day, maybe on a birthday when you are a bit wiser. I love you, Ismus, and no matter what malice you have made, and what you will make, it was out of your control."

Ismus clenched her fist. *"What?"*

Borthor smiled. "That's enough for now. Now go, pack your things, and leave this castle."

"We're not leaving you, Dad, you're coming with us!" Brutus nearly shouted. "I'm not leaving if you don't!" Brutus silenced when he saw the King raise a finger.

"Oh, Brutus—you would have made a great, selfless king," Borthor faltered. "It is a shame. A great shame."

The King died that afternoon.

A horse-drawn carriage had been summoned for the Royal-No-Longers to take them to an academy far from the castle. Gwenda spent her remaining hours in the castle locked away in the library. Brutus stayed in his room, feeling that the need to punch at Ismus would not be therapeutic enough to heal the pain inside of him.

Ismus decided to go out and do something. Something *important.*

She stood up from her bed, tore down the stairs, bolted to the narrow, dim staircase, and walked while feeling her hand against the stony wall. Ismus hoped she was right.

She hoped this chamber was her nightmare.

She kept walking until she felt a stone piece slide in, and the next second she was on the floor, in the dark room. The dark room she had been to before. The memory came back to her—the night she had blacked out and awoke in her bed. Now that she was here, it was as if she had gained a clairvoyant power, one that could feel and envisage darkness ahead.

A deep power that had been growing with each of her birthdays.

Her eyes swerved around and squinted to see past the black. After walking in the dark for at least forty-five minutes, with no light and no sound, lit torches exposed silver-lined prison cells. Bone-white skeletons lay on the floors of the prison chambers.

She saw a bright light glowing in the distance; it looked like a pedestal, or a book podium. Ismus could hear water leaking from the corroded pipes above her.

Other than the dripping noise, it was completely still and quiet. Ismus tapped her feet, slowly and soundlessly, on the hard base of the room; but, try she might, the room echoed her footsteps so loudly someone could have mistaken *her* for a monster.

Ismus imagined that there were a lot of dead things here. If this *was* her dream, and if this was *actually*—

"It doesn't make sense!" Ismus hissed. "How could this place be... *Hell?*"

Her stomach started to drop, and her heart dashed, fluttering against her chest. She wheezed. It was starting to darken again. Ismus would never escape this darkness. She felt her knees buckle as she collapsed to the cold, grime-covered floor. She felt eight forelegs creep up her neck.

Ismus yelped when the spider plunged its teeth into her skin. The fat spider then fell off to the side, lying limp and dead on the soiled floor. Her neck throbbed; she could feel a welt bruising the back of her neck. She clutched her stomach. Ismus grew sick. Her face turned olive green, and her breath failed. If she inhaled, her chest would burn, and exhaling was simply not possible. She couldn't catch her breath, she clawed for air, something was throttling her by the throat, but she could not see it.

Panicking, she could feel a smile piercing into her neck. Ismus stopped. She stood up. She held her breath, facing a stone wall. She waited for the breathing behind her to start up again. Her insides began to falter and jitter, and she fell against the wall, catching herself before she subsided to the floor again. Veins pulsed in her forehead.

"Eh... what's the princess doing here?" A loud voice snapped. Ismus whipped her head around.

"Wait, you ain't the princess, is you? Not any more, Eithendere!"

Ismus stood once more. She saw an ancient-looking old man handcuffed to a wall.

He had big, bulging, bright, blue eyes and a two-foot long beard that swept the dusty floor. His black fingernails were the size of his beard. He was wearing a loincloth, and the lack of clothing exposed his scarily prominent ribs.

He moved his lips to the side and made some sort of face.

Ismus, when she worked up the courage to talk to the threadbare, timeworn thing, said, "I don't know who you are, but you have to tell me, what's down here? What... *is* this?"

The old man smiled. "You don't knows too much now's do you? Well, this is the prison cell... the lab... the Underworld... the Guardian of Fire... that type thing!

"Prisoners hads been kept here for a long while. Too many to kill all at once, suppose. After that, King Guru decided to mutate the prisoners by forging thems in fire. Lots of smoke and fire! Burn, burn, burn and then creature! Creature of the dark, took Eithendere away! She still lives! I knows it!"

"There is no King Guru."

The ancient man tried scratching at his chin, but the cuffs restricted his hands. "You believe in that predisposed history, princess? Guru was the first. He was a person offffsss a distant land, somewhere far, far, far away in another dimension. He had special powers, heavenly, I knows it. He could create whatever he wanted. He imprisoned them, princess. Too many prisoners, so as his mind grew corrupt, he constructed the Underworld, turnings the *people into beasts.*"

Ismus pretended to understand. "So, wait, you said the Underworld? What—how do you make *the* Underworld?"

"I wouldn't know, Eithendere would! I saids this, he was brilliant, and he had supernatural powers, sent from the *heavens.*"

"Then, when the settlers of Grudale did come, did a castle already exist—"

"Guru hads *already* made the castle. He is the real king. The Underworld goes on for miles." He stopped. "How many kings, not Guru and his son, haves ruled here?"

Ismus frowned. "Three. Why?"

The old thing screeched with joy. "*Three!* You're connected to Guru, princess. He wanted to curse the third child of the third king—don't asks me, he loves his threes. You are the third child of your family, correct? Oh! My! You are the curse! When you were born, you made the sky wilt, and Serabi turn cold! The older you grows, the closer the Day of the Shadow comes, turning the land to ash. You are a demon! You are a *curse*."

"I am not a damn curse!" Ismus grabbed the man's neck, her eyes bulging, insides blazing with anger. "I don't have the power to destroy land, or—whatever the hell else you said! I am *not* a demon!"

The old man shivered away. "Great War will happen. Someone will try to unleash the power of the beasts—the Guardian of Fire. This is where torture prevails. Man's true weakness. Someone wants it. They wants the torture for war. Guru's heart on the pedestal."

Ismus glared at him, releasing her hand from his thin neck. "War?"

"Yes, the people of Rodemina—"

"It's *Rodem*, actually, old man…"

The thing frowned. "Well, Rodemina is how I knows it, but the people want to unleash the Guardian of Fire, the great beast mutated of thousands of prisoners, and use it to strike here—this place! Your nation!"

"Someone in Rodem. Sure. But, one more thing, if you don't mind talking to a curse, why is Rodem how it is now, covered in ice and snow? What happened? Does this have something to do with the Underworld?"

She refused to ask if it had anything to do with her: it was stupid to consider.

"No, and yes. It is because of *your* power, the one Guru cursed you. The first sign of the Day of the Shadow." He smiled yet again. "First Rodem. Then… *the rest of Dark Earth*."

Ismus twitched when he again stated she was a curse. She was about to retaliate, but she heard someone calling from the other side of the wall.

100

"ISMUS! WE MUST LEAVE NOW!"

It was Gwenda.

Ismus's heart raced as she dashed away from the old man. She turned back around to say, "Try slipping your wrists out from the cuffs!"

The old man only said, "Princess, you don't knows how many times I tried that! It's magic, it won't let me slip my arm through!"

Ismus only nodded and raced back to the dark. She threw herself against the stone wall, grunting and swearing.

"Ismus!" Gwenda practically screamed, closer now. Ismus banged against the wall, pounding as she felt something warm ooze out of her hand.

"ISMUS! BRUTUS—SHE'S GONE AGAIN!"

Ismus screamed out to Gwenda, but her throat went dry from the dust. She could feel the old man staring at the back of her head; Ismus never would return to this horrid place again—

Only if she could escape it now. She threw her head against the stone, hearing a man's voice whisper in her ear. Before she could let out a full blown scream for help—

"You're next."

Ismus kicked a stone hard and she fell forward.

The darkness shifted to a blinding yellow light, and she found herself in the second living room.

~

The carriage was packed with each of the teens' items, and they were meant to leave at once before another attack came. Before the three could depart, what was left of the servants came to bid them farewell.

When Jade—bold, violent Jade—came over to Ismus, the red-haired girl twitched.

"You were right, Jade," Ismus laughed bitterly. "I'm not a princess." She waited for a reply.

"You don't have anything to say to that? Not one bitter remark? C'mon, it's... it's our last one."

The servant embraced her. Ismus froze.

"Be careful, Princess Ismus," Jade croaked. Stunned, Ismus could not register the events happening to hug her back. Instead she waited for Jade to pull away, and Ismus watched her retreat into the woods.

As Ismus climbed up the rickety steps to the old carriage, she took one last look (or what she thought was her last look) at the castle. In the last days of her life, Ismus never really knew how she felt about that place... the castle she had spent her whole strange, tormented life in.

CHAPTER 9

WELCOME TO CAMP FAT BOOT, *LOSER*

T he journey to the academy was absolutely horrible. The seats were worn down and had bits of cracker crumbs stuck in them. The smell of horse was profuse. The coachman was snobbish and disrespectful, not caring when Ismus told him she had to go the bathroom. The backroads to the academy were disheveled and shook the carriage. After a long, five-hour trip, they arrived at something odd looking.

Academy?

This place was no academy. It was a moss-grown shack, unlike Edgar's Hut, and was falling out of its foundation. Thick, green ivy grew and spread across the broken gates of the shack. A banner scrawled in a rotten handwriting read:

Camp ~~Fat Loser~~ Boot

Ismus grimaced.

Carrying her small bags of underwear and simple clothes, Ismus thought she would blend right in. But when she pushed opened the doors and walked in the camp, all eyes turned to her.

Ismus felt her cheeks flush. They, of course, were gaping at her inhumanly red hair. She tucked it into the hood of her shirt, but its length could not be so easily concealed.

Ismus immediately learned that the kids of Camp Fat Boot

(which is what she heard a few kids call it) were either complete jerks, sad little kids, or both. No one had parents, and if they did have a sibling, they would be separated by age. Ismus went with all the kids who were fifteen and sixteen, Gwenda went to the dorms for eighteen year olds, and Brutus went with nineteen.

Ismus's dorm was shared with the spiders. All the way up on the top floor was where she was supposed to room with some Eric Weiner person. The windows were small, and if Serabi's Sun would actually illuminate and shine for once, it would have done little. The thick curtains were dusty and scarlet-colored, and they swept the floor.

The empty grime of the room sliced her fingers. The wooden floor held dead ants and little bits of unknown pieces. The stucco walls were coated in black streaks. The two beds reeked of mothballs and vomit. (It was just as abrasive as her nightmare.) After she unpacked her clothes in a small drawer, she went down to the first level, looking to escape the gloomy room.

That was when a chubby girl with chunky braids pushed her down to the ground of the moving shaft. "What the hell are you doing, you stupid kid? Get back!" Ismus thought that the girl and Brutus would get along famously. The bellboy—the one who actually had to pull the moving shaft up and down—tipped his little white hat.

"Need to go back up, red?" he asked kindly. Ismus nodded, pursing her lips at the name he gave her, and the boy began to pull the rope. Ismus's shaft began to rise higher and higher into the air, until she reached the top level.

Nothing happened for the rest of the day, not even dinner (apparently the children had lost their supper), and her roommate still had not shown up.

Soon it was time to sleep. As Ismus sat in her bed, she asked herself, what had happened? One day she was in a castle, and now she lay in a camp layered with filth. Was she sad, relieved? Ismus found it terrifying that maybe she actually had *cared* about the castle. She quickly dismissed the thought; she was just in shock... right?

Ismus thought about how Rodem was covered in ice, and how the Underworld was supposedly under the castle. She remembered the old man saying something about war striking her country... well, *the* country, and how she was cursed. Then she told herself something.

Everything changes now, doesn't it?

Ismus tried to get herself to fall asleep that night, but her sleep was filled with nightmares and awful dreams. One time, around midnight, Ismus woke up in her own sweat with her heart throbbing fearfully in her chest. When she tried to settle back down in her saturated sheets, she could still hear the stranger whispering in her ear:

"*You're next.*"

~

Morning came slowly. The night had been long for Ismus.

It was dawn and Ismus was nearly dressed. However, all the other children were no longer inside the camp. Ismus peered out of the corner of the window.

The Sun blinked its eye, and storm clouds gathered around it. The sky darkened to a hideous shade of gray. Clumps of white hail were beating down on the pitiful children of Camp Fat Boot. She walked down the hall, went down the moving shaft, and stepped outside of the building. A cold chill wrapped around her skin, as if to say, "Welcome back, Ismus."

The food court was outside for some odd reason, and in order to get breakfast they would have to stand in the hail storm. Ismus who had forgotten to tuck her hair away got into a line of children staring at her.

When it was Ismus's turn to get her breakfast, pictures of bacon and pancakes sizzled in her mind. But when she saw the green-and-gray slop, her insides sagged like an old mattress.

SPLAT! Right onto her plate, the woman then forced her to grab a rotten pear and an almost-expired carton of clumpy milk.

Ismus found a table in the back of the cafeteria inside and sat alone. She was used to the feeling by now and made it her job to stay that way. She scratched the welt on the back of her neck.

It was best to have only one friend.

When she went to pick up her fork from her tray, her hands were soaked in blood and dripping over the table. The spider bite still had not healed. She cursed to herself quietly and shook her wrists so the blood would fly elsewhere.

Ismus, being the observant (and sort of bored) person she was, scanned the entire room. Gwenda was giggling with a collective of girls that—ranging from thin to plus-sized—shared similar traits to her own, and Brutus was arm-wrestling a dark-skinned boy. She smiled when he lost.

Ismus scratched her welt again before a rash spread across her cheeks.

A tall figure loomed over her, with eyes blue and hair blond and curly.

"Hey," he smiled, one side of his mouth extending more than the other. "What are you doing back here?"

"I'm... sitting."

"Can I sit with you then?" He asked while sitting down anyways.

Ismus gave him a blank look. "Do I know you?"

The boy grinned, furrowing his brows. "You don't remember me?" He pushed a curl from his eye and consumed a forkful of slop.

"Times have changed, haven't they, Ismus? My hair, it got darker a few years back." He shook his head. "Or maybe it's the fat.

106

Had to run it out to get rid of it, when I was like thirteen. It's *amazing* how judgmental some people can be." He gazed at her softly.

"Oken's School wasn't as nice without you, Ismus." The boy picked up his tray and walked back over to the group of teenagers screaming his name.

Ismus bit back a smile; she failed and started to laugh. How could she be so dumb?

~

Ismus did not understand the purpose of this camp or what they did. An hour after breakfast, she found out.

Without a minute to spare, all the people of the camp would gather around in the courtyard behind the old shack where the useless rays of the Sun would lick their skin and suddenly disappear behind a cluster of clouds. All of the children were like so many worms, squiggling and impatient, freezing from the bitter cold of Serabi, until the instructor came in.

He was brawny—more beefy than muscular—and he had a gray cap on his secretly-bald head. He had a big smile on his fat face, yet he did not pass Ismus as a friendly nor loveable instructor.

"Welcome to Camp Boot!" He said loudly, clasping his hands together. "I am your Coach, Coach Prit. I know we have some new students today… Yes! You with the red hair and the big boy with the glasses and you with the…," he stopped. Ismus and Brutus stood out in the crowd, but Gwenda had a simple face, so the coach couldn't point out anything different about her that wouldn't apply to some other tall, blond-headed girl. Instead, he pointed one of his thick fingers at her and she hunched over in embarrassment.

Ismus had a feeling in her stomach the Coach knew… that he knew they were the Royal kids who weren't actually Royal anymore. She knew he was going to announce it to the crowd of kids and not give a care in the world how it would make them feel.

107

How it would make *her* feel.

"Well, let's just get right to the training." Coach smiled at the gray, nasty sky. Ismus breathed out with relief.

"Anyone else loving this great weather? It's bound to get better tomorrow, but I think we can manage. We're going to start by running around the street. Just some good ole fashion jogging. We'll lift weights in the room right after, and then go straight to the cafeteria to get some raisin-and-prune bars. Then I have a little treat for you; the pre-fitness test! Push-ups, sit-ups, jogging, running, of course, and then flexibility are on our schedule for today. And then, we do the real thing *tomorrow*. For a grade!" Boys groaned at the flexibility and sit-ups, and most girls groaned at push-ups and weights; nearly everyone shared a collective disliking of the bars.

Ismus tapped her foot and waited for it to begin. She knew whatever they did here was not meant to be difficult, given the age and weight of some of the kids.

Ismus saw out of the corner of her eye a tall, seventeen-year-old girl talking to her Sam.

"Damn it," the girl folded her arms around her dense black jacket and swung her black hair behind her. "This is *so* not fair! So, what? My mom dies, and—I have to *exercise?!*" The girl bent one of her skinny, tanned legs and looked the boy up and down. "What do you think, Sam? Lame, right?"

Having him stand there gave Ismus her first opportunity to really look at him. He had a messy entanglement of dark brown and light blond curls—one curl falling into his eyes—and light olive skin. He was slender yet had subtle definition in his arms and legs. The teen stood with a cocksure lean against the camp wall, making Ismus roll her eyes.

Still, he was charming.

Ismus *never* remembered Samir Nichols looking like that. Never. She only remembered chubby cheeks, a round chubby body, and a quiet little attitude. It was weird to see him now. She didn't like it.

"Guess not. I've been here for, like, a year, I think. School was taken down."

Ismus tensed. **What happened?**

The girl nestled her head into his shoulder and began to twirl her fingers in his hair. "You're too cute," she murmured, parting her thick red lips as she spoke. She brushed her nose against his. "Why haven't you asked me out yet, babes?"

Samir sighed, moving his head back. "You ask me that every day, Vanessa. What do I gotta do to get you to stop?"

He turned away from her and walked to a mass of boys who were now sneaking up behind Coach Prit to take his cap off. They were all snickering, laughing, hitting each other hard on the back.

"I wanna see what that idiot looks like without his hat," a light-skinned boy named Alex snickered to shrimpy Jacob.

"*My turn, my turn,*" a boy with glasses and greasy black hair tried. He had been sitting by himself and was now bumbling up to the coach.

"BACK OFF," the boys shouted, and one punched him in the neck. He flew to the floor.

The boy lay, stunned and embarrassed, on the ground; his face was frozen, petrified. The boy sniveled and tried to adjust his glasses with dignity, but he was too scared to do anything but lie still in fear.

Ismus felt her blood boil with anger—

Another guy kicked him square in the jaw.

Ismus balled her hands into fists, swearing and cursing—

The boy started mumbling, his face still terrified. He started

109

to stand up. He slowly raised himself off the ground and continued to mumble. For a second, Ismus relaxed. She wouldn't have to intervene. She wouldn't have to kill the boys who hit him. The kid had it under control—

But all that came out was a loud fart.

He plopped back down to the ground, laughter booming.

Ismus knew something, something very clear:

They would never accept anyone weaker than themselves.

On instinct, she leapt up from her crouched position and swiveled to where the giant mass of people were.

"Hey!" Ismus grabbed the red-headed boy who had punched the greasy-haired kid by the neck. "Who do you think—?"

But Samir grabbed her wrist, staring into her lilac eyes. He said nothing.

Ismus felt her cheeks burn. "Get off!" She raged, but her voice faltered.

Those concentrated eyes burned into her sockets, his hand clutched her wrist—

Yes. She hated this Sam.

Ismus turned, ripped her hands from his gasp, and punched the ginger boy in the back. He fell to the floor, glanced sharply from behind his shoulder, and sprang to his feet.

The boy, bewildered, studied her face. "Who the *hell* do you think you are?"

Ismus squinted her eyes. "Princess Ismus."

Did I really just say that?!

The boy snorted as cuts of blood dripped from his face. The

rocks had really ripped his sour, freckled face up. "*Sure,*" he sneered. "And I'm Prince Jacob. Get the new girl, idiots."

They all looked around. "Are you sure, Jacob?" one asked.

"Did you not see her just punch me? Kill that bitch!"

Alex fiddled with his chain. "Are you really the princess?"

Ismus turned her gaze toward him. "That's a title too cursed to lie about."

"So that means…" the boy bit down his lip and formed some sort of menacing smirk. "…You're the daughter of the woman who killed our whole village."

"That," Ismus snapped as she stepped closer to him, "has *nothing* to do with me. I had no control over her actions."

The boy laughed. "I get that. But my parents won't."

Then he punched her in the face.

Ismus, however, was ready for him to lash out and was able to grab him by the arms, twist it, and slam his head into the concrete. Blood splattered from his lips and a tooth broke off. She had her foot against his back, arms bound behind him.

"What," Alex coughed, "are you idiots doing… kill this bitch…"

Jacob threw up his hands. "THAT'S WHAT *I* SAID!"

A group of boys were swarming Ismus now. They were grabbing her up, pulling her every which way. She kicked one in the chest and sent another flying with a blow to the crotch. She felt a pair of hands yank her back by the shoulders.

She thrashed and punched. "LET ME GO," she barked. Ismus was able to knock one of them out. But the hands were still on her, giving the boys an easy target to punch. She slammed her elbow into her capture's stomach, and when that didn't loosen his grip, she sank her teeth into his hand. One yelp and a scratch to the eye later, Ismus had him down. But the others were still going, triple-teaming her with punches and kicks on all sides. Then they started grabbing at her.

One grabbed her legs, another an arm, her neck, one smacked her hard in the jaw—

And they were about to hit her again before Samir screamed at the top of his lungs.

"SHE'S MY GIRLFRIEND, DAMNIT!"

The boys faltered from his scream.

Ismus could feel the very instant when her heart stopped. Of all the ways to save her—before even trying to fight the boys with her—why was this what he decided?

"What?" Jacob asked, pointing a finger at her. "This psycho? Didn't she *just* get here today??"

Samir rolled his eyes, stepping up to the group. "Yeah, Jacob."

They lowered her down gently to her feet. Ismus jumped at the opportunity, and began throwing punches at all of them; Samir had pulled her away before she could do any real damage. She was then reluctantly pulled into his embrace. He had to be at least two feet taller than what he was seven years ago. She then realized how awful he smelt—were there any showers in this damn camp?

He lowered his lips to her ear. "Why are you here? What happened—?"

She pushed him off. "Seriously? Your *girlfriend?* You shouldn't have done that."

"Mhm, why's that?" He folded his arms.

"Because I'm going to fucking *kill* you, Samir Nichols. That's *embarrassing.*" Ismus wanted to throw another jab at his pretty face, but it was still difficult for her to be truly enraged at him.

After all, she had forgotten she had missed him so terribly.

The boy threw her a wide smile. "You have such a mean face, Ismus. I wouldn't be surprised if you killed me right here."

Ismus rolled her eyes. Gwenda had told her time and time again that the way she rested her face made her look callous and unapproachable. If anything, she was glad it looked the way it did. She didn't want anyone to approach her anyway. There was nothing she could offer them in terms of conversation.

"But, if it saves my life, I'm sorry." Samir looked at her for a moment, pausing to stare at the girl he too had missed so dearly. "I got caught up. I didn't want to fight, but... I didn't like you seeing you get punched."

Ismus stared into his eyes. "I find that pathetic."

I'm pathetic.

Ismus gave him a long look.

"You could have pushed them off me. We could have fought them together. In a real battle you can't pull that and expect it to work."

"This—this isn't a battle, Ismus! This is just a bunch of dipshits fighting some chick over hurt feelings. Why do you have to take things so far?"

"I just don't get why you had to say that."

Sam furrowed his eyebrows. "Why is that so bad? What the hell did *I* do?" Samir tensed. "You're the one that had to save the day for that little *dweeb!*" His voice softened. "Look, I'm sorry, okay? Maybe I s-shouldn't have sa-said that, but does it really make you that mad? I just thought that would... you know, I thought it would make them—"

The bumbling, the awkward stuttering, the unconfident reddening of the cheeks—

Ismus shut her old friend up in a rough hug—after punching him in the gut.

"I missed you so much," Ismus confessed as she broke away. "The castle was… attacked. My parents are dead."

Samir straightened. "Wait, what? How did that…wait…dead?"

Ismus tried to find the best way to answer it. "Aloes was murdered, and Borthor said he couldn't live without her." She shook her head. "They're dead and gone now. Forever."

"So…" Samir started, "You're sad about this? Remember you always got so depressed to even just think about your family? I do. I remember. It made me sad that you were sad. Isn't this better?" He reached for her hand. "Well, maybe not a whole lot better." He gestured to the kids stretching for the run. "But, at least we have each other now."

Ismus still said nothing. She only looked at him, looking for that little boy she had known since she was young. He was so much older, so much more assured, that it made it weird to even look at him.

"What happened to you?" Ismus asked. An awkward silence fell between them, and the entire crowd seemed to grow quiet.

Samir's face hardened and released Ismus's hand. "A lot happened when you left," he muttered coldly.

Ismus creased her brow. "It's not my fault." She said it like a question. Samir began opening his mouth before the coach blew his whistle.

Soon, all the orphans started scattering to run around the street.

~

Ismus was stronger than most at the camp, for she had trained herself to be agile for battle; Brutus (who had recently figured out that having glasses and being a "nerd" wouldn't matter since he wasn't a prince anymore) could afford to lose some weight; and Gwenda needed to get something on her bones and not squeal when doing push-ups, or sit-ups, or any physical activity.

By the end of the day, Ismus was drenched in sweat. All the push-ups and sit-ups and jogging and running were more than even she could bear. They all had dined in the cafeteria that evening, but it was not a feast after all their hard work. The green and gray slop had changed to dry wheat buns sandwiching meat pieces that looked and tasted like a rubber rock. Ismus sat alone again and merely picked at her sandwich. Feeling alone and cold, a girl must have read her mind.

While chatting with her own friends, she saw Ismus unaccompanied, and she kept glancing back at her. After the fifth time she looked behind her shoulder at Ismus, the girl beckoned her to come sit at her table.

Ismus flashed the plain brunette a harsh look. But beyond those harsh eyes, forehead wrinkled with warning, was a desperate cry for a friend. For *someone*. No matter how much she would try to convince herself, she was sick of being lonely.

Then Ismus saw the girl fidgeting out of her seat and walking toward her. A great jolt of nervousness ran down her spine; encountering new people was a skill she had yet to acquire. Hopefully her face didn't look too mean.

The girl sat down and smiled, nice and bright. Ismus then realized how horribly skinny the girl was. Her wrists and legs were the size of a child's. The girl's face was pretty, but it still seemed like it was lacking. Ismus tried to smile, but she was irked by her size. Ismus tucked her hair behind her ear.

As if bringing up the subject, the girl said, "I love your h-hair.

It's so… red!"

Ismus smiled. "Thank you." The girl had a natural face, with simple brown eyes, thin lips, and an overall plain canvas. It looked washed out—Ismus just realized—from years of cosmetics. There was little to compliment, but nothing to belittle.

"I w-wish I had your hair," she praised, "Because mine is p-pretty dull. I'm Janier Burnberry, b-by the way, but you can just c-call me Jane." Janier paused in order to force out the words. "Who are you?"

Ismus looked down at her food. "No one important," she muttered. It was easy to see that a lot of these children didn't know what the Princess of Serabi looked like. The Royals had been a taboo subject for many years now.

"Well, w-what's your name?" She pressed. "No one here is important, but that d-doesn't matter."

"It's Ismus."

"Isthmus? As in…"

"No, not that type of Ismus. It means 'thin spark', or 'tiny fire'."

"Oh. I've never heard that t-t-term b-before."

"Yeah, it's weird. My parents wouldn't actually name me after, you know… a 'strip of land with sea on either side.'"

Jane laughed. "You're s-so humble, Ismus. Ain't you the princess?"

That made Ismus jump. She leaned in. "Jane, I'm not a princess anymore. Please never say that again."

To signify she understood, Jane closed her mouth and did a zipping motion with her fingers.

Ismus had a good feeling about Jane.

116

Later in the day, Hanaa, a dark boy in a red sweater, touched her shoulder and smiled, saying, "Welcome to Camp Fat Boot, *loser*."

CHAPTER 10

DAY OF THE ACCURSED
SHADOW

Lin knew something was horribly wrong. When she crossed over back into her country, she didn't know that it was going to be an extension of Serabi. It felt cold. Icy. Dead.

Linnasoeta faltered to the ground. It wasn't supposed to be like this. It had never been like this.

NEVER.

She was sick of the cold. She was sick of sadness. She was sick of everything about Dark Earth. And now, the world she had lived in all her life, the place she had treasured and found only the good in, was a sulky land of festering decay.

The insides of her stomach wanted to cry out. She screamed and fell to the icy grounds, hands stinging upon the contact. Tears flooded down her face. It had been years since she cried like this. When she was seven, she would hardly cry. She somehow got used to the fact that her mother was gone, and there wasn't anything else she could do about it.

These days, however, she was always crying. As the wind blew in stronger, as the roses of Hazalen's Garden wilted to black, and as the plane above spoiled over into darkness, Lin knew that any joy that existed in Dark Earth had faded from existence. She was dead. She collapsed, damp cheeks against the freezing cold ground. Her entire body burned—in rage, in misery— and yet she felt almost nothing at all.

CHAPTER 11

ALMOST KILLED HIM

T he snow had fallen so extremely thick the next day that the roads were buried ten inches deep. It had piled up so high that the window frames looked like they were about to burst from the great pressure. If any person opened the door to the outside world, the snow would break off its hinges and avalanche into the camp.

Mary Agna was one of the girls who had so little sense to pursue this. In a failed attempt to flee the camp, which was just one of her annoying amusements for her friends, the door had been crushed to death by the snow, and Mary Agna was toppled over in the icy blizzard. Her friends pretended not to know her after that.

They had to stay indoors for the rest of the week. The wicker hearths seemed to do nothing about the cold, and the small lick of heat provided was hardly enough to survive.

The next few days consisted of more hard training inside and raisin-prune bars. Instead of learning the many processes of finding a variable, or learning geometric properties (which Ismus had already learned) they simply worked out day and night. The flexibility test was easy for Ismus (despite being nine inches over five feet) but some of the taller, less athletic girls struggled to touch their toes. The boys "knocked out" (as the beloved Coach Prit said each time they had to do anything) thirty push-ups in a minute flat, yet only a handful could touch the floor without buckling their knees.

Brutus seemed to have lost a great deal of weight while performing the exercises. He was no muscular thing yet, but his legs and stomach were not as pudgy.

Ismus was actually doing rather exceptionally: she could do two hundred sit-ups in a row before her back ached, and eighty consecutive push-ups, chest to the floor. And, at least now, she could do eight proper pull-ups.

Gwenda cried out that her wrists were burning and that she was going to faint when doing her push-ups.

And sit-ups.

And practically every other exercise.

Honestly... Ismus thought.

Later that night, after skimping out on dinner, Ismus came to the dreaded realization that bathing would not be so luxurious—rather not luxurious at all. She had managed to stall and not shower for a week, but then her scent became so disgusting that it crawled into the back of her mind and enforced her to bathe.

So she snatched a couple of towels from the closet in the corridor (she had to ask two boys in the small closet to move so she could grab the towels; what they were doing, she didn't bother questioning) and headed to the bathroom, wherever it was. Ismus crossed down halls and snaked through doors, and then she saw it; the door was wide open. Ismus took a huge breath and gasped once she smelled the horrible odor of thick humidity. Her heart sank to her toes.

Piles of hair and water were sloshed all over the floor. The tiny circular bathtub took up all of the moist room, and there was already some remnants and water in it. Ismus dared herself to walk over to the tub and see what was in it.

Black, slimy chunks of hair floated about, and spiders crawled around. Ismus turned the faucet on to drain it of its contents, but when she turned it to the right, yellow liquid with big, red-eyed, dead bugs poured out.

Ismus turned away, disgusted, and went back to her dorm. Bathing would just have to wait for a while. Maybe *Forever.*

~

"There's a place where the good things grow," Ismus mumbled to herself in the stuffy sheets of the bed at night. Then she sang:

"There's a place where

the good things grow

There's a face the

bad things follow

There's a place with

the hoary hollow

There's the old lass in black

the Dark Hero."

It was an old song that Gwenda used to sing to her at night when she was small. Then she added a new part. She sang, in a low, monotone voice:

"There's a place where the good things turn sour. There is no one left at this dead hour. There's a war that is going to take place. There's a war out there... I am not ready to face.

"The Dark Hero, of where do you wither in time of the evil?"

She had a feeling that Gwenda was calling Ismus the Dark Hero. But what could she do in a land so great, a girl so pale and insignificant? The ounce of power she once possessed had been robbed from her; what could she *ever* have done? The Dark Hero was not her. The Dark Hero was *no one*. And no one could bring her out of this hellish nightmare which she desired to escape. No, *had to* escape.

Ismus put the thought aside and tried to sleep. Yet, deeper in the night, Ismus only thrashed more. Her mind filled with longer, darker nightmares: a silver demon exploding from fire; a stampede of hideous, horrible creatures with sharp teeth and piercing eyes. Sweat rolled off her face. It was getting worse. The whispering—*you're next*—Aloes ripping from her green dress and mutating into a horrendous monster—

But the one with Linnasoeta. Her taking Ismus's hands, standing on the tips of her toes to touches their noses together, smiling too wide for her small face. Lin giggling as her hand slid into her back pocket, revealing a shining object.

Then plunging the blade deep into Ismus's heart.

After that, Ismus had no chance of falling asleep.

The next day—after a long, terrible night—the camp changed tactics. Instead of training, they would learn how to flourish a sword. It started after breakfast, and a racket was going on behind the camp. Crowds of students were jeering and shouting; everyone was up. She rubbed her red, tired eyes. Ismus threw on some clothes and tugged the rope of the moving shaft. Once downstairs, giving a quick hello to the bellboy, she opened the back door and pushed past crowds of shouting kids. Good thing only one of her ears worked, even if she did have to constantly tug at it when it started to ring.

Coach Prit and another coach, Coach Zoe, were battling with sharp-tipped blades. The two were breathing heavily. CLANCK, CLANCK, the swords slashed back and forth as they danced, light on their toes. Everyone was staring at the coaches in awe.

"KILL HER PRIT! KILL HER!!" One little kid was screaming, hope in his wild eyes.

The blades sung and hissed as the metallic scrap kissed in the air. Prit made his enriched arcs and superb cuts, while Zoe played it safe with a couple of parries. Prit advanced, slashing into her territory. Zoe parried. With a flick of her wrists, she blocked low, then high, and then low again with her sharp, long sword. Prit made no error, for he was quick to slash, and Zoe would have to dodge it so it wouldn't slice her skin. Prit was doing all he could, his breath hot and on the other's face.

Coach Zoe's sword looked like it was slipping from her sweaty palms, and her knuckles were turning bone-white. She desperately held onto her sword as Coach Prit cackled. Again, she flicked her wrists and made quick parries, her face ashen as she heaved and whimpered. Sweat dripped from her face, her legs quivered and shook, and she fell flat to the ground; the kids went wild.

"Finish her off!" The boy whispered to himself, rubbing his hands. "Just one slice down the belly and Zoe goes down with the dead wolves."

Ismus gave him a long stare.

Prit grinned from ear to ear, wearily, as sweat dripped and rolled from his face. Zoe was such an old, feeble thing that she didn't have a chance against Prit. Frankly, it disgusted Ismus. To take advantage of someone clearly weaker than oneself was pathetic.

I'm pathetic.

"Get her, Prit! She's on the floor!! This is your chance!" The random kid howled with excitement. "Now. NOW!"

Ismus stood in awe. Instantly, she no longer felt tired. A rush of adrenaline jolted down her spine.

I can beat him.

She cleared her throat. "I want to do that." The coach stopped grinning and peered into the crowd of orphans.

"What?" He asked, turning around. "Someone said somethin'?"

"I want to do that." Ismus barked. "Give me a sword."

The childish coach looked taken aback. Then his lips curled.

"Well, give this redhead a blade!"

In half a minute someone came over, handed her a fine sword, and walked away. He reminded her of one of the servants. The man gave her a wink: he had been one of the cooks.

Ismus stepped up to the coach, walking slowly. She balanced the hilt of the sword right on her palm. It felt different than the swords back at the castle, but it was too late to back out. And Ismus didn't plan to.

The coach was smiling with shining eyes. "Try and take me down while I go easy on you. Next time, you might wanna learn some manners, princess."

Ismus did not want to be associated with the name 'princess' any more. He knew. Did she care? No. For she was not what she had been told she was.

"I am no princess."

And I am no curse.

Ismus took a deep breath, holding the sword up high. She shuffled her feet, feeling the earthen ground. Thunder rolled in the darkness of Serabi as the Coach screamed, "Now!"

Prit lunged at her with such uncontrolled speed that Ismus merely had to sidestep him. He slashed at her right, then left, and she parried. He was leaving his left side too open. Ismus almost laughed as she dug the sword into his hip. Prit yelped and stepped backwards, wincing in pain. He recovered, but his movements were remarkably sloppier. Prit stabbed and missed, and Ismus spun out of his range and delivered a slice to his lower back; somehow, he managed to deflect it in time.

The coach then delivered an unexpected slice to her face. Time froze for an instant as Ismus leaned back to avoid the blade. She crouched down to his right and drove her blade upward. The blades reflected and hissed.

Rain started to fall from the sky; lines of purple and yellowish lightning stretched across the horizon; loud booms of thunder rolled. For a moment, they danced, dodging and reacting to the other's attacks. Finally, Ismus was able to get a huge rip near his wrists. He

124

laughed something that reeked of pain. In his anger, he malevolently swung the sword about him and nicked her left ear. Blood dripped into her eardrum.

All sound muted around her. Panic washed over, an ocean of worry flooding her head. She fumbled with her blade. Then she felt his sword cut deep into her shoulder, and her right arm went numb.

Ismus then felt a terrible power overcome her body.

In an instant, she could no longer control herself. With a toss of her red hair, she slammed the butt of her sword between his ribcage and then to his bald head with a defiant *SMACK!* that made Prit collapse to the floor.

Ismus towered above him, eyes cold with hate. He cowered beneath her, and Ismus smiled—a beautiful, evil, unforgiving smile.

There was something undeniably satisfying in seeing the weak tremble. To damn those who had damned others. **Pathetic**, a voice within her mind spoke. **Like you. Like *him*.**

She sliced ruthlessly into his sides, deaf to his cries for her to stop. Blood drained from his leg and then his arms.

"Enough, enough!" A woman commanded, but Ismus couldn't hear it. When the woman grabbed Ismus by her bloodied shoulder, she spun her blade around to the woman's neck. The woman stepped back, jaw hanging.

Sound came back to her left ear; she dropped the sword in horror, gazing at what she had done.

"You little *monster!*" The teacher's voice resonated with disgust. She had a dome of thinning black-and-gray hair, sharp black eyes, flat cheeks and saggy skin, and two scrawny legs. Her black dress was shapeless, like the rest of her body.

"How dare you!" she spoke again. "Nearly killing our beloved Mr. Prit! Shame on you, *demon*."

Ismus sputtered. "D-demon? I was just... I thought I was..."

She looked into the faces of the young children: they all were on the verge of tears.

"She was going to kill him," a toddler choked as he clutched his hands. "Please don't hurt me, demon."

The rest of the teachers: overcome with hysteria.

The teenagers: all unsure if they were impressed or terrified.

And Samir: transitioning between a smile and a grimace.

"No," Ismus breathed. "I'm sorry—"

"Not another word out of you, Isia!" The teacher spat. "To your room!"

As Ismus walked away, she heard Jacob murmur bitterly, "Samir, you found a *fucking* insane one."

CHAPTER 12
THINGS OF THE FIRE

Newspapers tasted horridly disgusting. Ever since she left her mountain village, Linnasoeta had lived off those sordid papers that were as mind-numbing as they were gross. She would glance at what the papers would say, but she was so hungry that she didn't have time to bore herself with the pointless news. Why have a paper for a nation where nothing happened? Today, as she tore off a piece to savor in her putrid mouth, she saw the headline:

Serabi is Free!
WRITTEN BY EDGAR, EDITED BY EDGAR, PUBLISHED BY EDGAR

Queen and King dead! Royals no longer rule! Make way for peace for the people of Serabi!

Lin couldn't process this sudden information right away. After surviving off scraps of ink-filled newspaper and living in a deserted alleyway somewhere in Serabi, where only the bitter coldness of snow came one's way, her brain couldn't think as well as it used to. Her poor stomach was starving; she was horribly thin, and there was no fat left on her bones. Ribs stuck out from her stomach so wide that she looked like a stinking peasant.

She missed the cool rush of the rapids crashing into the salty stream of the Soreyth Woods. She missed the village with all the mousy, euphoric children and their irritated parents. She missed the unpaved roads and the Wither House, and the House of Gods and… she missed her…

"Father?" Lin whimpered. "Are you there?" She waited for something to say a word, or make a noise. All she got was the dry falling of snow.

Her heart fell. No one answered back.

Lin remembered those childhood days full of bliss, like when her mom took her out for picnics, or when her dad would smile and laugh… When Nyoka didn't even exist in her world. And then the *day*… Those memories flooded back into her now. Tears fell from her eyes, which only made her eyes freeze. She was lonesome and icy. She couldn't be worried about friends, about friends named Ismus. Ismus… Lin had forgotten about such a name.

It was obvious that Lin had completely forgotten about the paper until she heard a noise. A street cart rattled nearby. Lin's head shot up from her bony hand.

"Keep moving, Maurice," someone said with a tired voice.

"Shut up," someone snarled back. "I'll go my own pace! Thing isn't gonna lug itself, *Laura*."

"It's Laurence!" Something happened and a man tumbled over a vendor cart. The man with the snarl in his voice huffed, "Good going, *Mary*."

"Jerk…" Maurice huffed. They turned down the street that Lin's alley was behind, and that is when she saw the pair. They both looked as thin as Linnasoeta, only worse since they were older and taller and shirtless. They actually *looked* like walking sticks.

"Shibun," Mary (er, no *Maurice*) said, "Where did our boss wonder off now, Shibun?"

Another person dressed in a much-too-large, black trench

coat and a black hat emerged from behind a gray, ivy-infested wall. He was tall and gangly and he looked much younger than his fellow gang members, despite the fact that he was overlooking them by about six inches.

He had dark brown hair that filled his forehead and neck, and small, brown eyes that turned up at the corners. His face was soft and only slightly tanned.

The boy was not ugly—maybe even attractive. He looked to be around fifteen or sixteen. Lin squinted when she saw him.

An odd sense of familiarity tingled in her stomach. She had seen this boy before, she was sure of it…

"I don't know, Mary, sir." The boy's voice was smooth and low. He smiled mockingly.

The guy named Laurence laughed. "Eh, this kid. Oh, Maurice, *are you about to cry?* Tell me you're not about to cry. Oh, good grief, man, get a bloody hold of yourself. It was just a joke."

"Shut up, Laurence." Maurice punched Shibun hard in the chest, which was at his eyelevel.

"Ow," Shibun rubbed his ribcage. "Seriously?"

"*Shut up* to you too, kid! Where is the boss, and this time answer me without being a—!"

A horse neighed from afar, interrupting whatever *Mary* was going to say, and then it roared closer to the group of men. Silence inflated throughout the air. "What was th—?"

A black stallion, which appeared from nowhere, was conjured up in the middle of the group with its rider. Shibun tensed as he wrangled away from Mary's grasp.

"Not the horse…" Shibun moaned, "Not even that cool."

Its mane was rough and tangled, but it did not look forlorn

and forgotten, as one might think of a stray dog looming around the empty streets. The stallion looked hostile… and malevolent. It had possessed, red eyes and an abnormal jaw structure. When it neighed, it sounded like thunder was blaring from the high Infinion. (And it also didn't do that cute thing with his nose that most horses did, like when they take a deep breath and their whole face just starts to flutter. As far as Lin was concerned, this horse was not cute; if anything, it looked as if Hell itself had created it.)

The rider was not any better than his horse. His face was completely hidden under the blackness of his tattered, gray cloak, and the fabric went in and out with his shallow breath. He had blackened, overgrown fingernails and thin hands that were beyond wrinkled. Something seemed to glow from underneath his cloak. Lin looked down at the horse's hooves that were gleaming with crimson blood. That's when Lin first noticed something hunched over near Mary and Laura's feet.

The thing was in a massive heap, and something was definitely glowing from its eyes. It was an eerie, lime-green glow on the road, reflecting from the eyes of… what was it? The man under the cloak looked down by their feet. There was a small bit of silence, the rider filling in the atmosphere with his presence.

"Mmmm…" the cloaked rider pointed his long, curved finger down the alleyway, exactly where Lin was. His deathly black cloak turned toward her.

Her stomach dropped. She pressed up against the wall as she saw Maurice take a bloody knife out of his soiled pants and inspect the streets. She held her breath and fastened against the brick even more. Linnasoeta thought these men were just peasants, wandering the streets without a home. But no, these men were killers and thieves, and the thought made her want to squeal with fear. She tried to not make those guttural throat noises that came out like *GRRRGL*; she tried to contain her breath, and she hoped the men couldn't hear her soaring heartbeat.

Maurice stopped searching.

"Nyoka," he said as he sheathed his dagger. Lin's heart dropped at the sound of his name.

"Sir, the men are starving, and we need to restock on fabrics and food. Let us set up camp."

"You may want to keep that knife unsheathed, man, unless you somehow plan to walk away unscathed," a low voice growled. The rider stepped off from his stallion and pulled a long, horrible blade from his scabbard, a spine-chilling metal scrap giving off into the air. At once, he pressed the blade against Mary's throat, and before he could run from the scene, he sliced his head off.

Maurice toppled over, dead. Shibun stood paralyzed in fear, the others only growing grim. Nyoka wiped the unmentionable horror from his blade on a wall and sheathed it back into his scabbard.

The white snow beneath the men was covered in blood. They stood there, waiting fearfully for their turn.

"Ruby," Nyoka hissed like a serpent. "Come bring me the key, Ruby."

Where were these *thugs* getting all the innocent children from?

A girl with very light—almost as if she had lost all her pigment—white hair and light blue eyes peeked out from behind the same ivy-infested wall, only her little head showing. When she stepped out completely, Lin felt herself almost faint.

The thing had two heads. From the chest down, she looked normal, with one set of thin legs and a tiny stomach. Her neck, however, was stretched and split in two, and the left head looked like it was dead. It looked the same as the alive head, only its eyes were closed and its face was completely colorless. The right head looked fine, a bit stretched and tiny, and moving like a snake's, but fine.

What is that?!

Ruby, as the hybrid girl was called, walked over to Nyoka,

sticking a chain of golden keys way out from her body as if they were the abnormal things.

Laurence shivered. "Boss, why did you have to bring *that* thing from the... the *place*, again," he asked.

Nyoka turned his cloak toward him after snatching the keys from the demon child. "She is the only young demon in the Fire who knew where to get the Golden Keys to the pedestal, and I dare say she was the easiest thing to manipulate." Ruby's eyes looked sad and perplexed, the pair on the right, still-alive head, anyway.

The horse flashed its blood-red eyes. It tossed its sinister black mane and opened its mouth to neigh.

But it did not neigh. Instead, a long string of words poured from its mouth, making Lin cringe with terror.

"*Well...*" the horse breathed heavily out its throat. "*Doesn't she just look so delicious? Why can't we eat her again, Guru?*"

Nyoka's cloak, filled with pitch-black darkness, slowly shook. "No. We need her. We need every demon we can get in our fight. No, Exfarion. Do not eat her."

Linnasoeta was petrified. **Talking horses? Demons?** Maybe there wasn't something wrong with the creatures—

"Nyoka, the Day of the Shadow is practically amongst us. Rodem has turned cold. What do we do with *it*?" Nyoka glared at the gray castle.

"The curse is spreading. Time is running out...But the Day of the Shadow still has time to approach. Before the arrival of next spring, the entire dimension will be nothing but darkness. The Accursed One... her evil is slowly spreading deep into the world. And when the demons of the underworld realize the Goddess inside the Accursed One is missing, it will forge into a foul uproar. The Day of the Shadow is the day of the Underworld's Rise."

"Yeah, I didn't need your life story," Laurence said flatly.

"What do you want to do with *the Queen?*"

Lin's breath quickened. **The Queen? Isn't she...**

"*Idiot!*" the horse screamed and jumped up, and bit the man's arm off. He wailed in pain.

"*Mmm... tasty.*" The horse critiqued, its mouth red as it finished the rest of the arm. "*But a bit bony.*"

"We will have to return to the castle soon," Nyoka continued without another moment to pass. "With the Royals gone we can destroy it, piece by piece. Give the Accursed one time to come to her full power, lose herself completely to the instability of the Amethyst deity. When she is ready, we will release the Guardian, and we will kill all she sends our way: *and then we will destroy her.*"

Sweat rolled off Lin's face.

Ismus.

~

Nyoka grasped the golden keys firmly in his hands as more snow layered down.

"Time will bring great war. Redemption of the evil this child has created. Yes, now, it will only be a matter of time before I go back, before Hell is in my control. The Auric Keys of Guru are now mine."

The men of Nyoka were scurrying around the deserted alleyway, searching for any scrap of food or fabric they could find. They carried back a few armloads of twigs, twigs Lin knew were called Cherry Arms. They mostly came back with mulch (whatever use that had) and newspaper and lighter fluid.

Ruby, who was in on the search for things too, found a few small pigs, onion bulbs, and a few handful of herbs. She also found some lard, salt, and just a cupful of coffee beans.

Tents and fire-pits were set up among the roads, looking like a sort of campground.

Laurence found that gathering things with only one arm was horribly difficult. Yet, it probably was better than having to *die* by beheading.

Two-headed Ruby also had another rather special quality: she could set fire to anything she wanted. When the men ordered her to cook all the things she found, the water in the bucket started to boil. Just then, Lin saw that reddish-orange flames were flickering under the wooden pot in the stone cauldron.

As Ruby was making their feast of sticks and plants, another man, Makdon, emerged from a finished tent. "Why didn't we kill the girl, Master?"

The cloaked rider did not look up from his glittering keys.

"The Accursed One is the cause of all this," Makdon gestured to the snow and gray skies above them. "Why didn't we kill her?

"We cannot *kill* her, idiot." Linnasoeta heard that familiar gripe in Nyoka's voice. "That demon within her would have ripped out our throats in an instant. She is powerful... for now. But soon her body will be gone, and all we will have left is the Goddess herself."

Makdon tried on. "Shen has pulled back the search. Where do you think his girl ran off to? If you want to return to the Fire we'll have to tell him we couldn't find her—"

Nyoka looked up from his keys and climbed aboard his stallion. "She will come in three weeks' time."

"How can you be so certain?" Makdon sputtered.

A cloaked Nyoka watched forward, where Lin was pressed behind a wall.

"Because, Makdon, she's already here. And if she wants her daddy alive, she'll have to come."

CHAPTER 13
THE BEAUTIFUL ARRAW

But, I'm your roommate! See on my form, it says 'Eric Weiner, room 324-13, bunking with Isia'."

"My name isn't Isia!" Ismus shrieked as she pushed the boy with the glasses from her room and slammed the door. She heard him whimpering outside her door.

"Pleeeeease?" He whined.

"Go away!"

After a horrible day of nearly killing a teacher, Ismus was ready to run straight into the Thangos Trench and never be seen again. On top of that, her mind was still racing with the scarring nightmares she had been having nearly every night. She clasped her trembling hands when thinking of Lin's blade in her heart. She felt it flutter in her chest just thinking of it. Why did such a horrible vision have to plague her mind? Why her Lin? Why?

That boy would just have to roam in the halls before coming into this shabby, already-too-small chamber.

Ismus plopped on the dusty bed and huffed. What had happened? Her body had grown numb after Prit had managed to slice her. She couldn't remember doing anything to hurt him. There was a gap in her memory—only the moment she saw the woman's eyes stare into hers was when she realized she had committed a horrendous act.

"Maybe I am a demon," Ismus sighed, still shaking.

She heard someone rap at the door.

"Please? Let me in, whatever your name is! I really need to get inside."

Ismus gave in. "Fine, just, geesh…" she said as she unlocked the door and stumbled back to her bed. The boy came bouncing in with a big smile, like he was ready to do some parading.

"Why, thank ya', sir!" His thick black glasses were bouncing with joy.

Ismus scowled and picked a strand of hair from her eyes. "Jerk."

Eric frowned. "But, sir! I said thank ya'! Didn't ya' hear me, sir, or do ya' need your ears to be cleaned?"

"STOP CALLING ME SIR AND SHUT THE HELL UP!" Ismus screamed. She saw the boy tremble, and she looked down in shame.

"I'm… sorry. Something's wrong today. It hasn't been going great, so just stop annoying me, okay?"

Ismus had to tug on her ear more often; why was it starting to ring so much? All she could hear was the static whirring and feel nothing but the burning behind her eardrum.

He smiled once more. "Okay, sir!"

Thankfully, Ismus couldn't hear it. A few minutes later, her ear was almost back to normal.

Just then, the speaker that blared through all the halls went off. Lunch. At least she would be able to see Jane and Sam.

A sickness scratched her throat.

Samir had completely ignored her the entire day; Ismus wasn't quite sure if he still wanted to carry out the whole "couple" thing, or if he was ready to call it off. Her stomach twisted. Ismus hoped Sam wasn't angry with her. With the nearly-killing-a-teacher thing, she really couldn't really be mad at her old friend rejecting her.

The stupid lunch alarm wouldn't shut up as they took the moving shaft ride down. It was only her and Eric, which was very uncomfortable. She stepped out of the box-sized moving shaft and walked to the cafeteria, only to spot Janier chatting with—

"What are you *doing?*" Ismus blared louder than the bell before she could catch herself. She cupped her hand over her mouth as Arraw turned her way.

Out of all places for Ismus to end up, why did it have to be this camp? Surely there were other camps, other death-traps like this one, right?

Ismus stood there, frozen like a soldier waiting for a command.

Janier waved at Ismus, obviously not hearing her. But Arraw heard her; she was looking at her right now. Ismus felt her blood boil with anger. She mashed her fingers into a tight fist, constraining herself not to kill the revolting creature.

Arraw "The Great" Good was, unfortunately, undeniably attractive. She had a deep chocolate tone to her smooth, sun-drenched skin. Her gold-flecked, brown eyes were drenched in colorful paint (*strawberry paint!*) and kohl. Her lips were agleam with a shimmery, pink glaze, always locked in a smirk that asserted dominance over any individual she came in contact with.

Her dark-brown hair was highlighted with dark blue ends that curled at her shoulders. She flaunted her envious figure in a tightly fit, long-sleeve sweater dress and cream knee-high socks to match.

Arraw Good looked like an angel.

A perfect, punch-able angel.

Ismus felt her face turn red, red like her hair. Arraw had changed. Once ago, she had at least *looked* like an innocent girl, but now she was fierce, inside and out.

Arraw rolled her eyes and popped her shimmery lips, turning back to Janier. Ismus tried taking one step toward them, just one, but it felt like the universe was trying to hold her back, telling her not to go any further.

Once Janier caught her eyes again, she called, "Hey, Ismus, over here! I have someone you just have-ta meet!"

Ismus put one foot in front of the other until she reached their table.

"Why do you always do this?" she said, mostly to herself.

Janier looked back at her. "W-what do you mean?"

"I mean… *you.*" Ismus gave Arraw a perplexed stare. "Why do you do this? Every time?"

"You s-sound crazy, Ismus," Janier said in an oddly *basic* tone.

"*Sound crazy?*" Ismus repeated horrified, "You have no idea what she's like!"

A random kid with spiky hair screamed, *"I must warn you, I am a ninja!"* and a piece of fruit went flying in the air. An orange hit Ismus on the back of the head.

Janier looked down at her toes. "Well, I guess you've already met my *amazing* friend."

Arraw touched Janier's shoulder, ignoring Ismus. "We don't say *amazing*, honey. That is not cute. Say beautiful instead. Or hot, or se—"

"What is your damn problem?" Ismus growled. "You're so *gross.* Jane, let's go!" A strawberry smacked Ismus in the nose.

Janier gave her a look. "No. She asked me sit with her, so I'm sitting here. You can sit with us, if you like."

138

Ismus furrowed her eyebrows.

Arraw flashed her that evil smirk. "I'm not the gross one, Ismus. After all, I didn't kill a teacher."

"I didn't kill anyone!"

"Oh, really? Then why haven't we seen Coach Prit all day?"

"I don't know, but he isn't dead, and you know that." Ismus clenched her teeth. "Stay away from my friends."

Arraw scoffed. "What friends?" She stood up.

Ismus adverted her eyes when the dress rode up an inch too high up her legs.

"You don't actually think he likes you... Do you?" Arraw asked the question with so much guarantee that she almost fell when Ismus said no.

"No, he doesn't like me. He only did that to make those kids back off. Which I could've done myself..." Ismus folded her arms. "So, yeah, whatever, I don't care about you two anymore. Just leave Janier alone."

Arraw bit down her lip, and then she laughed.

"You're so stupid, Ismus," the girl snorted. "Controlling and *stupid*. You always have been." She rolled her eyes at Ismus's open-mouthed stare.

"I *never* liked him. Never. Not even now. Sure, he's cute and all, but... guys... *girls*...well, which one do you prefer?"

Ismus didn't know how to answer, and frankly didn't fully get the intentions of the question.

"I... bo—you lost me."

She smiled. "Then we're almost the same then, aren't we?"

Arraw's voice quieted. "I don't like *guys*, Ismus. I like girls… well, not girls like *you* anyway—"

Ismus didn't move.

Then she felt her eyes droop.

"That would have been nice to know, like, eight years ago!"

Arraw snorted again. "We were seven years old! What was I supposed to do? Out myself in front of the entire classroom? I didn't even know what it *meant* until I was ten!" Her brown face was palling. "I've done this more time than I can count, and you're the first person to be such a bitch about it!"

"You made me even more depressed! You took away my *best friend!*"

Arraw laughed, eyes wide. "I didn't '*take him away*'," she breathed with accusatory finger quotes. "You're just an awkward mess who can't share her friends. You're the evil one! You're so selfish! Maybe I just…"

Ismus nearly spat. "Maybe you *what?*"

"I thought we all could be friends."

Ismus almost laughed at this statement, but the hurt in Arraw's eyes made her silent.

"But then you… stopped talking to him, and then…you just left. Samir wasn't ever the same. He wasn't fun anymore. He barely looked up from his shoes, and he didn't really eat—or even *speak*— for the next couple of years. And whenever he did talk, it would always be about how much he missed you."

Arraw frowned. "Even after the school evacuated because of the attacks. Even when we came here, last summer. He would not stop talking about you. *He loves you.*"

Ismus clenched her jaw.

Arraw sighed. "You're really, really dumb. Now… go… you smell." And then she sat.

Ismus obeyed, her mind numb and heart slowing.

He loves me.

Ismus sat down in the back of the cafeteria, eyes locked on the table. She felt nauseous. She looked down at her shaking hands. No training had prepared her for this. Disbelief took over her.

Ismus was an aggressive, erratic, oblivious mess. Why would he love *her*, of all people?

She was so deep in shock she didn't notice the hoard of boy's towering over her. And Samir sitting right next to her.

"Hey, can the guys sit with us?" Samir asked, smiling.

"Yeah…Fine," Ismus spoke in a hollow voice. The boys started to sit down around them, including a less sour-faced Jacob.

"You kicked Prit's ass," Samir whispered in her ear. "You gotta teach me that one day."

Ismus grinned. "Yeah… Sure. Sam?"

He slung his arm about her shoulder. "Yes?"

"I… I'm so happy to be here with you."

Samir couldn't contain his grin. He pulled himself closer to her. "Really?"

Ismus nodded, but then her face grew dark.

"But…" she moved his arm off of her. "Not like this. You're my *friend*, Sam. And I don't want anything to destroy the few friendships I actually have."

Samir ran a hand through his hair and huffed. "Okay, sure, cool. I don't think I ever… cared?"

Ismus tensed. "I... I do love you, Samir."

"Mhm, in what way?" His eyes were locked on her, and she grew slightly worried (and angered) he would punch her in the face.

The other boys at the table kept their mouths shut. One of the boys dropped his fork.

Ismus shook her head. "I can't love in *that* way. It's not possible for me."

Samir looked her dead in the eyes. "Is it because you hate yourself?"

Ismus shrugged ruefully. "I don't know."

"No, I need you to know why!" he began to shout. "Tell me, is that the reason why? Because you're such a fucking basket case? Because you had to complain every single day to me— your *only* damn friend—and make *me* miserable? Or maybe, is it because you just lost all your "Royal" privilege crap and miss it all now? Is that it?"

Ismus bit her gums. "I don't know."

Samir flipped his tray and fluffed up his curls, knocking Ismus to the floor when he stood up. He stormed over to Vanessa, cupped her chin, and kissed her violently. She gave him a harsh slap before kissing him a thousand more times.

"Oh, damn!" Jacob cackled. "Guy sure knows how to move on!"

Ismus sighed and lifted herself back up. "That's definitely *not* moving on."

CHAPTER 14

THE POWER GROWS: THE ACCURSED ONE IS BORN

It started off like any other birth. In a way, of course. The Queen at that time was young and beautiful, married to Borthor, the King. Brutus was just beginning to act like a complete… well, a complete brute. Gwenda, who was still at the age of three, almost four, was a lot smarter than she seemed.

The soon-to-be-family-of-five was in the Infirmary of Serabi with Doctor Rolin, their assigned doctor for life. Aloes, with her golden hair, eyes so green people became lost in them, and stunning smile, was waiting for her baby, in no amount of pain, since she was in the best doctor's hands. Borthor who had a bit of extra weight (that he explained time and time again was muscle, not fat) was still extremely nervous and jumped when anyone said his name. Brutus, before he knew a baby girl was coming, was actually a considerate and kind figure. And Gwenda was extremely loud and outgoing.

Four-year-old Brutus groaned before biting into his pumpkin bread. "Dif shucks. Shtupid baby." The siblings were sitting in the Kiddy Waiting area, which had nothing Royal about it. Gwenda, who was staring through the stain-glassed window, turned her head to her mumbling brother.

"And dif shucks too!" He mumbled as he threw the bread into the swarming field of medics and spat out the stuff he was chewing in the opposite direction of Gwenda. "Nasty bread…"

"Brootoos!" Gwenda yelled with loud authority. "Don't—don't—don't—don't do that! Pick it up!"

"No!" Brutus retorted. "I'm older than you!"

"I'm smarter than you. Mommy said so!"

He groaned. "What are they doing to her in there?"

"Daddy said that already! They're, um... he said... prepant. Prepant!"

Brutus scratched his head. "I don't think that's a word."

"It is."

"Oh."

Gwenda sighed. "I'm bored." She started to squirm in her seat and shake her messy blond hair. "How long did this take for me?"

"I... I don't... I don't remember it."

She gasped. "You don't r...member when I was born?" Her lip quivered. "That is mean, Brootoos!

Brutus frowned and hugged his sister. "I'm sorry, Gwenda. I don't know... I think someone took it out of my brain!"

"That's awful!" The two began to cry.

"I'm hungry," Brutus whined a few seconds later.

"I'm thirsty," Gwenda sobbed. "Did you drink all the juicy?"

"Nooo," Brutus lied.

"Then... then... where did it go..." Gwenda began to tear up again.

Just then, the door of the room Aloes was in flung open with a loud *BANG*. Borthor, on the far side of the waiting area, bolted toward his wife. She was being wheeled in a luxury hospital bed in a gold gown, but she looked flushed and pale at the same time. Gwenda and Brutus looked up in horror as they saw their mother, father, and

144

a handful of nurses wheel Aloes away… to the castle's Emergency Quarters.

~

"Is everything all right?" Borthor asked, horrified.

The medics kept quiet during the operation. Brutus and Gwenda, who were outside the Emergency Quarters' door peeping through the keyhole, heard no talking, just a stunned, sputtering Borthor (failing at keeping quiet). Aloes was asleep during the operation, or whatever it was that they were doing, so she wouldn't feel any more pain. Gwenda's stomach sloshed with sickness. Brutus prayed that his mother would be fine, and that the baby would disappear from her stomach.

"What are they doing to her?" Brutus asked.

Gwenda covered her mouth in horror. "They are… I dunno!"

Brutus moped. "I wish the baby would die."

"Die?" Gwenda asked with a weak voice. "W-why, Brootoos?"

"She's hurting Mommy! If she died, Mommy would be all better now."

"You're right. Brootoos? Brootoos?"

"Mmm?"

"Will we still play games together and explore the castle?"

"Yes, I think… I think so."

"And Daddy will still take us out fishing with Edgar on Sundays?"

"Yes! We can't stop fishing! I would be *sooo* sad."

145

"And will Mommy still dance with us and read us a good book at night?"

Brutus didn't know how to answer this one. "Maybe."

Gwenda lowered her voice. "Brootoos, will we always be best friends?"

He nodded without hesitation. "Yes, yes, yes. Always and forever. No more questions."

~

"Maybe..." Borthor mumbled. "Raven?"

"Mommy, mommy, mommy, use the name I told you!" Gwenda piped.

Brutus gave his younger sister a strange look. "What was it?"

Aloes shook her head, flushed and pale and sick all over again. "Isssss. Musssss. Issmuss."

Gwenda gushed with pride, her face bright and merry. Yet, Brutus felt a sickness throbbing in his temples.

Ismus.

And the name stuck.

The 4-pound 3-ounce baby was frail. It looked like her big, baby head would topple over since her body was so thin. She had strange, purple eyes. Everyone was dead silent.

Aloes had a distant, glassy haze over her pupils, and her mouth was dry. Her grasp on the baby loosened. Before Borthor could walk over to his wife, Aloes dropped the baby on the floor. Ismus rolled over on her back and screamed. The candles blew out, expiring without reason. The room was swept up into darkness.

"Mommy!" Gwenda screamed. "Why did you do that...?"

The room filled with the sound of stunned medics as they tried to light all the candles and pick up the crying child.

"She's just tired, all's that," Borthor sputtered as he cradled the baby, waving off the medics, and tried to calm her down. "Let's get back to our rooms."

"I'm afraid you can't leave just yet," Dr. Rol said sadly. He pulled him into a separate room, away from the children and Aloes, and closed the door behind him.

It was a black, vacant room with the drapes blotting the windows, blocking the warm, spring light. A wooden desk and a small, black chair were centered exactly in the back of the room. It reeked of lemon breeze and dust.

Dr. Rol took a step toward his chair before deciding to stand.

"Your baby is underweight. Drastically. And she has a little ear problem."

"A what?"

"Her right ear is completely unresponsive. Her eardrum is ruptured, and it is one of the largest we've seen." He snapped under Ismus's right ear. She did nothing but blink.

"I don't think that is an accurate test. And I don't have to be a doctor to think such."

He snapped under Ismus's left ear and she twisted her little mouth up sourly, spit spewing from it, and she started to cry. Borthor cradled the baby in the pink blanket, his face starting to darken.

"Well, hell, fix it!" He screamed. "What did you have to go and do that for, anyway? I get your damn point!"

"It would cost a significant amount of money to repair the right ear, but with your status I could fix your daughter's ears a thousand times and you would still have a trillion to spare." The doctor only laughed, but hardly since the King was still angered.

Borthor was not very bright, so he did not know what he meant by this. "I see, but I don't think we have the time nor spirit to," he sighed, calming down. "Perhaps later we could discuss. Performing your operations on a child is a bit… hasty, wouldn't you agree?"

"I highly, *strongly* recommend—"

The King blared, "That is my answer!" With that, he turned away. "Come now, my little Ismus, you have much to learn in your young age."

Before her birth, the King and Queen knew of the supposed "curse" that had been put on their third child. They dismissed it as an old tale created by insane elderly people. After Ismus's arrival, it was clear she was no ordinary being.

At the age of three Ismus would trip on her burning red hair. Two years later, she complained that there were puffs of purple smoke billowing about the room. Two years after that, she would grow angry followed by hours of sadness. This was a trait meant to be expressed in teenage years, not when she was merely a child.

The days turned colder and dragged on silently. Each year Ismus would grow. Each year that passed Gwenda would fall under a deep, deep shyness and spend less time with her brother. Brutus became wrathful and would attempt several times to kill Ismus. Borthor would spend most of his days in his room, finding the company of his children less and less significant.

And the Queen never lost the haze over her eyes.

How could one child bring about all this misfortune, one would ask?

There was no real answer. This made the whole curse ordeal even more horrible. It was as if one child could turn the jade grass into thick swamps of gray, soupy muck, and the Sun's glowing shine into dull graphite. It was as if one child could turn many great families into threadbare hoboes living off the rotten stuff in the streets, and turn her own merry family into a sort of puzzle, never to be connected again...

~

At least, the people thought there was no real answer. The citizens of Serabi all had myths and legends, the tale of an accursed being ready to destroy their universe. But few knew of the truth.

Ismus, the third child of the third king, was cursed indeed. Inside of her rested the deity of the inferno, one that had entered the child through her right eardrum, where she had planted herself in the child's brain. Her red hair manifested the true power of the fire and the malice she brought back from the Underworld. The power of Amethyst, Goddess of all Demons, had been forced to carry out her controlled *desperations* from the Lord Guru; death, loneliness, and dejection.

Someone had cursed her birth long before Serabi ever existed.

It began in the First Dimension, where continents like Asia and Africa lie. In Dark Earth's time, their arrival would have been over two hundred years ago. In this dimension, however, the time recorded was the year 600 C.E., over one thousand four hundred years ago. The Sinridders, angels from the Council, were sent from Infinion down to the Earth. Bestowed with power from the Gods, they could create portals to another world: the land of Dark Earth. They were sent down to cleanse the First World of sin and those who hinted darkness.

But they did not do as they were told.

Instead of balancing the world and purifying the human race, they sent them to their inevitable death. Infants, small children, grown men and women, elderly—all were sent through the Portal of Exran, named after the leader of the Sinridders. They would crawl deep into the back of the people's minds at night, even if they had done nothing wrong, and torture their consciousness with thoughts of death and gore. Then, the people would be gone the next day.

They did this for decades, going to every country, every town, and every home. Millions were disappearing.

Infuriated, the Gods cursed the Sinridders by exiling them from Infinion: they were not to return again. Even if they tried, they could not pass the border between Earth and Infinion. The Gods, however, could not take away this power they granted the angels, for they had given them their magical abilities until the end of time. So the Sinridders continued torturing and banishing.

The African provinces of the Islamic Caliphates, Imperial China, the Delhi Sultanate, and many Asian cultures spread into the country of what they now call Jainu and claimed it as their own—after a few hundred deaths due to their sudden contact with each other. (In the future, people would hold on to their mixed or fully Asian looks, as Shen, Linnasoeta, and Shibun did.)

Native Americans who had been isolated from the rest of the world in the First Dimension resided in small thickets where they would fish and hunt and coexist in peace. People of the Byzantine Empire groped for the wealthy, lush lands of the Dark Earth (such as Ausilia and Orcan Old) and made up the majority of the banished.

After losing millions of people back in the First Dimension, citizens broke out into a frenzy. They unleashed terror on the cities, harassing and killing those close to the Emperors (for instance, the elite guards). These uprisings in turn led to a greater slaughter.

Some would creep into strangers' houses in the black of night, and feel their way down the cold walls to find the sharpest weapon they could. Then they would make their way to the bedrooms, kill anything in sight, and rob the house of its valuables.

Time passed, and the banishments began to slow. The year was 710 C.E.

One of the Sinridders had fallen in love with a European beauty, Yadara. She had captivating amber eyes, stunning dark hair, and a face as exotic as an island oasis. He knew that he would not be able to go back to Infinion to his true wife, who was a radiant being.

He took this as a promising replacement, and married the beautiful woman. His new bride knew nothing of his Heavenly power.

A child was born a few years after, and they named him Gurutrov. He had glowing skin, green-blue eyes, and grew long, swirling curls of pure golden blond hair. Since his father was a Sinridder, and his mother a human, he was born half Angel—the first hybrid of his kind. He too did not know of his father's power, or his own.

Yet.

Guru loved learning. He would stay up countless hours as a child reading long, complicated books of science and math. He then became interested in building.

When he grew older, he marveled at his own unique inventions, and he wanted the world to marvel at them as well. He was convinced he was the smartest man that had, and would ever, live.

His mother died when he turned thirty-seven; his father was as good as dead to him. That was also the year he had been evicted from his house. After months of searching, he found an abandoned loft and settled there. Outside his palace of isolation, people throughout the world were rioting once more from the masses of people who had just disappeared.

When the uprising raged through the cold streets of London, Guru decided it was time to showcase his brilliance. He did not care what the riot was about, but he seized the chance to use this confusion as an opportunity to inform the world of his complete genius.

He fused together metals and hammered away at things for long hours in his muddled, obscure loft. After his masterpiece was completed, he placed it in the streets so everyone could see it. His invention flashed moving images of himself speaking into the air.

No one liked it. The citizens thought it was aliens coming down to banish them all. They blamed the hologram—Satan they had called it—for the disappearing people. The invention frightened monarchs the most.

And signed right on that hunk of metal was Guru's signature:

Gurutrov R. Allaman

The race of angels tracked him down. No mortal could disturb this great amount of people and remain free, they had reasoned. Horrified, Guru's father did not want to banish his own son and told the others that they mustn't either. But a fellow Sinridder ignored him, and he threw Guru into the Portal of Exran where he hoped that he would die. In a blink of an eye, Gurutrov was gone... vanquished into the second dimension of Dark Earth.

750 C.E. was his last year on the world he knew.

Time went by slowly in Dark Earth. If he survived a year in this realm, it would be seven years in his old one. Weeks trailed slowly in this world. Either it was dark and cold, or it was hot and sunlit, depending on where he withered.

He did things in this new realm, like start small fights between the other people who had been banished. Usually he wallowed alone in marshes and caves, which he found somewhat similar to his loft back in London. He was not afraid of this new place. It was bare and soundless and chilly, but it was also very mysterious.

Guru traveled far and wide down the lands of the murky area, and soon he found a lush, green meadow with a radiant Sunlight hitting down on the land. He also found that the oceans were bluer, and they sparkled more. The trees hardly moved at all, since there was scarcely any wind. And the moonlight— a soft, ivory illumination from the crater moon—followed a brooding reddish-orange Sunset. A picture perfect view of a turquoise ocean blowing in the scant winds, and the coconut trees slightly dancing in the tranquility of night: pure bliss.

He did not like this. It was too content. He would rather have a place with fire and grime and oil and dead things. After wandering for so long, he was finally able to use the power that he inherited from his Sinridder father to make such a thing.

Guru used his supernatural abilities and intellectual brilliance for a dark purpose: to create a torturing realm. He dug deep into the Earth and, with a snap of his fingers, a thirty mile-long catacomb was created. And right away, he made the most destructive power below the earth: The Underworld.

He snatched and lured things into his pitch black lab, where the toxic smell of dirt clogged his neck and throat. It was hotter down there, making things more prone to sweat. He captured large numbers of people, tortured them with his powers, and turned them into hybrid, zombie-like, ghostly things. Deciding that humans were not as interesting, he decided to move on to other species. Guru made hybrid creations from both mortals and animals, constructing absolutely horrific fusions of colorful birds and the already dead bodies he had found in the thicket.

The more he aged, the darker he became. He started to create silver-lined jail cells and gargoyles for decoration, without thinking. He developed new ways of torture, like his fire gorging method, where he would conjure up a fire that had the fantastic ability to burn someone for several days without killing them. Guru then constructed a horse—Exfarion—used only for means of unlimited organ harvesting.

And he did it completely alone. With no one to talk to, with no one to consult, no one to tell him otherwise.

But for what purpose?

When he grew elderly—thirty Dark Earth years or two hundred and ten First Dimension years later—his heart had vanished. There was nothing but soulless metal under that skin. He continued making his "Treasured" Imps.

One day, he had an idea.

He first combined a hundred bodies, then a thousand, then hundreds of thousands to create an indestructible monster. Gurutrov burned it down, once he saw how powerful it was, and locked the pile of ashes inside a pedestal. He hid his auric keys behind a stone wall, and forgot about them for the rest of his days.

More people from the first world started to enter Dark Earth, and he knew that his wonderful, under-ground lab was exposed at the tops. So he came up with a plan; he quickly fixed up blocks of limestone and mixed things together for a substance similar to paint. He flickered his wrists, and his power chopped down Maple and Timber trees. He found himself strands of metal, gathered marble and graphite for a sidewalk, and made more limestone. He was thinking of making a rocky building, but why stop there? Instead, he made himself a castle. For he was King.

He plastered cement over the spreading Underworld, making sure it was completely covered. And as a final touch, he made a passageway that only he could find.

Peasants fell before him, worshiping the mighty King Guru, assuming he had roamed the world for years. They never really knew of his Underworld, but a few speculated that this ancient man was a thing of hellish descent.

Guru, whose blond hair had turned white, and whose creamy skin had been charred from fire, was intrigued by a special woman who went by the name of Mireille. She, too, seemed to be intrigued by him—for she was very poor, had no family, and was still frightened after being banished.

They married, and she became Queen. He walked down to his Underworld one night, when the French woman had been whisked away in her silk bed, and he scoured through his cabinet of spectrums and half-alive things. He was trying to find his hybrid-child as a present for Mireille. It was constantly dark down there, and the burgundy flames of the fire lit hardly anything in the suffocating chamber.

Then he found his demon girl, the girl he sometimes called Marceline Crimson Spectrum, or Marcy if he was feeling somewhat well.

Marceline had alert, blood-red eyes that could pour into the blackest part of anything's soul, and her eyelashes were rimmed with a dark-black lining of kohl. Encircling her eyes were strange, turquoise hieroglyphics, like letters and shapes and words and animals had been carved in (they had been *burnt* in). Small white fangs hung in her mouth.

Her ashen, chalky flesh ran bloodless, but she sometimes grew frosty and turned into tinges of silver. Black hair sank to her small feet, casting a large shadow on the floors. Her arms were thin and bony, and her body was skeletal; Marceline may have only weighed a little more than a box of feathers.

She dressed in a short, knee-length, ebony gown, ripped and tattered. Sometimes her presence would flicker around and disappear, like a candle's fire, but she would always come right back. She never walked: Marceline floated instead, a giant cloud hovering above the ground. She always had a grave look of anger in her red demon eyes. She was perfect to Guru. His most prized demon of all.

He had snatched her up and tortured her a few months before, and dyed her sandy hair midnight black, realizing that demons did not have such flaxen ringlets. All the fire turned her light-blue pupils scarlet, and had eaten her large heart away. Her name used to be Eithendere, but she had no memory of that life at all.

Guru brought Mireille this child, and she gasped.

"Oh, God! Where did you get something so ugly in a world so bright and green? Did you get that from Hell?" She was only jesting, as she knew absolutely nothing of the Underworld below the castle.

"Would that put fear in you if I did?" He asked, raising an eyebrow.

Mireille's eyes grew wide. "Um… I do believe so." She quickly turned pale.

Marceline whimpered, her eyes hungry for love. She flashed

a set of sharp, white blades when she smiled, and her red eyes gleamed in pain. Metal claws rapidly ejected from her fingers, and her bare feet cascaded with blood.

Mireille's heart stopped. She screamed in terror and fled from the castle forever.

Guru and Marceline lived together for a short period of time before the demon-thing ran away and came back with a human. She played with the boy and giggled loudly. Sometimes she would set things on fire because she would get so mad at the mortal.

Time ticked on, and the demon child turned into an adult.

Marceline married Pebbly—she named him that—and the demon was happy.

By this time, Guru was almost spent. He had endured so much in his slowly-paced life that death was almost upon him. But he was not finished.

He cursed Pebbly, for he knew he would take his beloved monster and his mighty throne—the throne that had proven him more than genius, more than Godly. He cursed the line of Pebbly forever. In this curse, he summoned all his rage and dark power into a spell that would result in a penetrating darkness spreading over the entire dimension, followed by a war that would be the end of Dark Earth forever. The Day of the Shadow.

By the power of the Sinridders within him, there was no force to deny his curse.

He died later on that month, and his spirit carried out that prophecy. The soul of Guru was spiritually known as the Demon King (or the Demon Lord, to some). He sank down to his basement, heart still resting on the podium. His soul broke into the four colors which would control and carry out the fate of the special infants, and most importantly, the curse.

The third child of the third king.

Pebbly and Marceline had six mixed mortal-demon children, who all ran away, due to their parents' horrendousness. Marceline later killed the human soul and the small village she controlled and destroyed herself decades later.

That whole vital bit of history remained almost unknown to the world.

The land stayed alone and completely vacant for a short period of time until travelers from a small land resided in Rodemina, who stayed for two decades in peace. During that era, no one ruled. Rodemina's founder, Jainu, was rich and strong, able to contain their secrecy. The country name was later shortened down to Rodem for reasons unknown and unimportant.

Settlers from Grudale soon came, one of the settlers being the son of one of the mixed-demon children. Sorthon, having the Marceline-Pebbly lineage in him, took up the throne, and controlled the newly populated land. Then they discovered the people that resided in the bordering country called Rodem. He grew skeptical of these people, and that was when the wars all knew of began.

The line of Marceline Crimson Spectrum passed down from generation to generation, no ruler ever knowing of a secret world that went on for miles.

And that's where history began to tell its tale.

Ismus's birth was designed by the Demon Lord himself. She would build mass destruction, eating the world away with immorality. Her birth was designed to have the spirit of Amethyst within her, the blood of Marceline coursing through her veins, the curse of Gurutrov wrapped around her entire existence. She had power beyond her ability, and all her life (so far) she knew nothing of what she was or what she would do to her world.

The Underworld would break loose.

The Day of the Shadow was near.

CHAPTER 15

DISAPPOINTMENT AND DEMONS

The small blocktimer in Eric's and Ismus's bunk struck the hour, the hour in which to wake. They stretched in the same manner, Ismus passing Eric his thick, black glasses, and Eric nodding in gratitude. This was their daily routine. It would be the last time Eric and Ismus would be together.

For now, they hopped out of their beds, picked out some of their least favorite attire, and walked to the moving shafts. Eric, feeling even more hyperactive than usual, was blowing Ismus away about his new book he was writing; he had called it the *Bedded Time Stories by Ehric Wienher.*

Ismus who was feeling *almost* happy smiled and nodded at her bothersome buddy who, surprisingly, was not so bothersome today. She was only happy because tomorrow was her sixteenth birthday—the first day of spring.

Usually, she wouldn't care because she was so used to her castle birthdays—and they always made her the wrong cake. In the camp, if it was someone's birthday, one would be able to get a free pass and venture out and into the marketplace. Then, Gwenda would give her plenty of money to get whatever she wanted. And, the best part, she would be able to go out and *buy* a delicious strawberry cake with Bourbon Ice-Cream (the cake she asked the servants to bake and in turn was never replicated perfectly to her imagination). Her mouth started to water at the thought of all that caramel cascading down her calorific cake and the sweet melody of the melted cream, like a milkshake on her tongue.

"No more dry Ismus, it's crazy girl time!" Eric screamed.

Elated, she jumped out of the moving shaft. Her shoulders immediately slumped, and she felt like slapping herself in the face.

Oh, man. One more day.

Janier had decided to sit with Ismus. They were sitting in the back to the right of the dining hall, and they were sipping on the school's new line of "complimentary" drinks and sweetmeats. (They only did this because of the large influx of complaints by students and the recent shipment of Grudale goods.)

"Arraw isn't really that g-great," Janier began to say, twisting her hair absentmindedly as she talked. "I saw her teasing that one k-kid with the spiky hair, and callin' him a fruit ninja...?" Jane stopped. "A-are you two good now?"

Ismus only nodded, sipping at her hot vanilla, the cup burning up her clammy palms.

"No, I-I mean you and Samir. I h-heard all the boys t-talking about it."

She put down her cup. "What were they saying?"

Janier laughed. "You zoned him!"

"I... *what?*"

"Friend-zoned. A-apparently, Samir got really mad. He was s-sulking about, looking really mad." Janier shook her head. "P-poor guy. He was really hung up on you."

Ismus sipped at her scorching mug of hot vanilla. "Oh, well. I don't see it as 'zoning,' anyways. It's not my problem that I don't feel the way he does about me. Gods, forgive me for being 'a basket case.'" She thought for a moment.

"Hey, uh, Jane?" Ismus asked suddenly.

"Oh, uh, yeah?" Jane replied with a smile.

159

"Tomorrow's my birthday, and I was thinking... maybe I'll take you with me? To the marketplace?"

Jane was about to say something, but then her face turned grave. "Go...go outside the camp? Ismus, it's been such a long time since I got out of here. Ever since my parent's...k-kicked me out. G-going outside would be... fantastic!"

Ismus breathed a sigh of relief; for a second she thought Jane was going to decline.

"Well, it's decided; you're coming with me!"

"But, your birthday gift? W-what do you want me to getcha?" Janier asked as she twirled her drink with a metal spoon.

"Just you would be great." They both smiled and laughed. Janier drained her Banana-Graham Cracker Milkshake in one sip, sucking up most of the whipped cream and cinnamon. Ismus wondered how Janier could be so skinny yet consume such a high quantity of sugar in a matter of seconds.

"Wasn't fighting crazy the other day?"

"I don't know. I was banned from swords after almost killing someone," Ismus replied evenly.

"Well," Jane blushed, "It... it was kind of cool."

Ismus crumpled up her napkin. "Really?"

"Yessire. You really can h-handle a blade, girl."

"Thanks." Ismus tried not to ask, but she said, "What about Sam? Is he any good?"

Jane twisted up her face. "You mean Samir? Oh, well, in that case, he is a freakin' maniac! He handles a blade so well th-that I almost thought of asking for tips! A-almost, Ismus, *almost*."

"Oh, that's great."

"I'm just messing with you, Ismus. He's a-awful. Almost sliced off his dic—"

Janier faltered, her face suddenly petrified.

"Arraw!" She threw herself up from her chair, knocking over her drink. Cream spilled everywhere, and she scrambled to her feet to get everything up with a brown napkin.

"Crap, Ismus. I c-can't go with you," Jane bleated from the hall's floor. "Arraw and me have something real i-important to do tomorrow. I'm s-sorry."

Ismus choked on her vanilla. "You're not coming with me? But you literally just said she wasn't as great as you thought she was. If that's true, then come with me. You really want me to go outside alone?"

Her voice must have scared Jane because she was starting to back away. "I'm really, really sorry, but I can't! I know, Arraw is f-fine, I just made it up t-to make you feel better. She's been t-teaching me to stop st-stuttering so much. Please don't get mad!"

Ismus stood immobile, her cup shaking in her hands.

Her eyeball twitched.

She drew in a deep breath and started talking quietly.

"Okay, I see. Sell out your real friend for Arraw. That's cool. That's really cool!" Her breath quickened.

"She can't blame this on not liking guys, can she?!"

All of a sudden, she threw the cup down, and the glass shattered everywhere, a little clash ringing in her left ear. Enraged, she sat back down, not caring if anyone saw her do it. She folded her arms over her chest. Her throat burned with envy, moving around.

"Why are you getting so worked up over nothing? I'm sorry, just calm down. You're gonna get us both in a lot of trouble!" Janier's

161

stutter came to a halt, suddenly as furious as Ismus.

"I AM NOT GETTING WORKED UP!" Screaming, she snatched up Jane's second milkshake glass from her hands and chucked it halfway across the room; that little cup ended up in shards as well, shake spilling all over the linoleum. She stormed from the cafeteria and into the moving shaft, Jane's face stuck in surprise. A few heads turned her way, and then to Ismus.

Janier sat back down, laid her head on the table, and began to sob.

"I'm s-sorry, Ismus."

~

It was odd how Ismus could go from super excited and eager for the next day to completely miserable. It didn't happen in noticeable steps either; it all just kind of smacked her in the face, like a major reality check. Ismus forgot about not getting so worked up over nothing, something she had already done twice that day. The tricky thing about excitement was containment, so one wouldn't get so caught up in the magnificence of it all.

Ismus also had to remember why she was getting so excited. She could wake up one day feeling like she just did something productive—or something good, rather—and then her mind would start to come back to her, like a foggy haze unveiling from the brain, and she would remember that it was the same old stupid day that she had the day before.

Or, maybe, she just wasn't cut out for more than a year's worth of excitement all at once, in only a span of a few weeks.

Suddenly, a gong went off in Ismus's head.

She had been scratching down numbers, working on Eric's book of encrypted messages and puzzles, and the thought suddenly hit her.

Containment.

The castle had always restrained her, so wasn't that the point? Why would Gwenda care so much that she left that rotten fortress? The only reason anyone cared that she left was that she had to be contained… or else something like this might happen, that she might blow a fuse and her emotions would channel her despite herself.

The only thing that didn't make sense was why she felt like a completely different being whenever it happened.

Ismus stopped being so excited over her dumb birthday, remembering that her good-for-nothing brother and sister would have to tell her something important tomorrow. **Rubbish,** she thought.

The skies had been changing a lot that previous week. It wasn't gray and soupy and mucky as it always had been; instead it was just black, like soot had encrusted the heavens. There were no clouds; there was no winds, just a never-ending, static, a shadowy realm that never whispered a rustle in the leaves, or a word from a soul.

Days turned slowly, Sun never visible anymore. The room always stayed dark, and it was always hard to judge when to wake. The blocktimers would strike eight, but it would still be darker than the dusk outside. Rain never fell. It was always silent.

And when long days of silence fall, only shrill chaos can follow.

Little else of great significance went on in the day, and soon Ismus was retiring to an early slumber in her dark, quiet chamber of dust. Eric was still out, eating one single pea at a time for dinner. The door blocked off most outside noise and light.

The pillow she slept on seemed ever so scratchy, and her hair was burning her neck. She shifted out of her humid position and stood up. Ismus saw nothing in the pitch-black room, her watery lilac eyes searching in the black as she heard only the blocktimer's constant ticking.

Tick. Tock. Tick. Tock.

Hair engulfed her neck, now sweating from the heat. She felt her back begin to dampen. The heavy air in the room made it hard to breathe. The musty books and dust swelled in her stomach.

In an instant, she froze; something stirred behind her. Out of the corner of her eye she saw a glowing red figure. It looked like an entangled blob of a light crimson mane, or a rosy wreath. It was long. She tried to ignore it and closed her eyes, but she knew something was there.

Ismus started to breathe a bit harder, and her insides jostled rabidly. She heard the creature stirring again, this time the sound of an open box spilling to the side with all its delicate contents shattering. The tall, wall-length blocktimer started to tick more intensely and, what seemed like, faster.

Tick, Tick, Tick, Tock. Tick, Tick, Tick, Tock.

By this point, Ismus was starting to feel more than uneasy. The thing glowed even brighter behind her, the cold beads of sweat dripping down her back and into her soaking wet shirt. Her hands grew slimy from perspiration. She heard the crash of something slam itself against the wall, and the whole cabin shook.

She screamed when she felt something metal whiz past her neck with a vibrating *WOOSH*. It ended with another loud crash, hitting the other side of the room's wall. If she was any closer to the head of the bed, the sharp thing would have impaled the left side of her neck. Something was suffocating her midsection, making it hard to breathe.

Then she started to wheeze. It felt like a thousand little metal coils were all groping for something to squeeze the breath out of. Ismus whimpered, trying to remove the horrible little things from around her neck, but they were stuck, and her chest was congested. She opened her mouth for air, but no oxygen came in. Sweat poured down her face. The thing wouldn't stop strangling her.

Everything was nervously quieting downstairs, the lights suddenly flickering out. Only silence followed. Then Ismus heard loud, slow footsteps beat against the stairs. They drummed and echoed and boomed through the walls. The two sounds—the blocktimer and the footsteps—seemed to cue after one another.

Tick, tick, tick, tick, tick, BOOM! Tock, tock, tock, tock.

Tick, tick, tick, tick, tick, BOOM! Tock, tock, tock, tock.

Ismus couldn't think. Images flashed around in the darkness, purple wisps exploding into the air.

Her heart thumped against her chest, trying to burst out of her. All the organs in her body stopped pumping blood through her veins, like a ghostly dead being was shutting down her internal structure. The thing still wouldn't uncoil from her throat. It almost had her down. Death was screaming in both ears; if only she could hear it in her right one.

Her hair concealed her entire neck, tightening and strangling. She could feel her hair being pulled, and she tried fighting it, but her body went immobile. Her insides started to shake; she quivered violently. A sharp, freezing hand scraped against her back. She felt her eyelids flutter, tears trying to escape down her face. Dark shadows fell off the wall. A brick floated toward her, and the last thing she heard before the brick skimmed right under her metal head and knocked her out was the penetrating scream of a stuttering friend.

She fell asleep, knocked unconscious.

~

Creeping in the dark was a pale hybrid thing—a very small and ghastly looking item. It had four scrawny arms and a ragged, white coat on its skin. Its eyes were a bright, terrible yellow with small pupils dotted right in the center, and they were flashing all over the sleeping girl. Its lips were always curled in a permanent leer, whether it wanted to smile or not. It tilted its head to the side. It kept staring and stalking. Its breath was light. Slowly, without noise, it crept up to the side of her bed, crawling against the floor, its long, long nails scraping against the wood, breathing heavier, its eyes flashing, its breath growing, until it was just to the side of her skull. It jerked its spiky, sloth-like claws up and down, beating and smacking her forehead. Then, it stopped.

Removing its tongue from its teeth, it whispered in a noiseless voice that sounded like a million steely worms crawling up a wall in union. It was not English; it was said like a nonsensical, "Huhfindherretyu Huh." An inaudible, breathy sigh.

Then it stood there for a while, maybe an hour or so, just shadowing her. It searched for something within the girl; it knew that a certain Goddess was closer than his master thought. It got down on all fours and looked up from the bedspread.

"Huh shfadudfsal."

It kept its eyes locked on the girl and, silently, still looking at her, still watching for any kind of movement or jostle, it crawled back into the dark shadows and disappeared into the cracks of the wall, still watching her from behind the stucco.

CHAPTER 16

THE RAID

Maybe it was the sharp, sharp light of the Sun and the unclouded blue and speckled pink skies.

Or perhaps the velvety lushness of the grass which she and her fellow acquaintances sat on…

Or, by chance, it might have been the delicate dancing of the pale trees with their light petals and their crisp smell.

Or maybe it was the small, stagnant millpond across from the tranquil lavender paddock that made Ismus love the Dreamrealm so much.

But it was most likely because the air was free. There was never a breeze or a swerving current of air. Everything was still, and everything was weightless; if she tried, she could have floated right up from the ground, but she stood fastened to the earthen floor like the thick, stretching roots of a magnolia tree.

No, the best thing of all was far greater than that: hardly anything was there. It was completely quiet, and not even the hooves of gazelles and deer could be heard; were there even any animals here?

The splendor of enjoying her blissfulness alongside the spirits of the north could not have been made better. The angels were simple folk, apparently, and they would rather be kicked down to the Underworld than to jubilate with glasses full of sweet, red wine. Ismus couldn't agree any more. However, the *former* princess thought that a nice, warm, cinnamon-nutmeg-and-gingery cup of sweet wassail would be a heavenly alternative to alcohol. She loved the zesty rich flavor of the Winter Festival drink, and the warmth it brought; it was like drinking hope right from the rim of the glass. Fragrance was also a key feature; so was appearance, especially if it was topped with finely grated cinnamon stick pieces; a light dusting of cloves; pickled with sugarcoated orange slices; and smelt of a saccharine allspice and citrus. Wassail worked funnily that way, how it could balance the sweetness of the sugar and the sour of the lemon and orange zest. Just a sip would do.

This place is so empty that I'm fantasizing about *wassail*.

She just smiled up at the emerald heavens, wishing she too could be as free as the firmaments up above, and always live in a world so peaceful. Ismus looked over at the airy, pale angels next to her that were also staring up at the clear skies.

The angels—two shaped in a feminine manner and the other only slightly more masculine—had silky wings outstretching from their backs, and all three were wearing snowy-white cotton and satin gowns. Their afterglow was a brilliant enlightenment of a blinding white light—similar to the Sun's—pillowing them in a stunning feather of confidence and light. It was startling, yet beautiful.

Nevertheless, their backs were turned so that all Ismus could see was their golden, straw-colored hair, just shy of their lower back; perhaps this was all that they wanted Ismus to see. As if they were too heavenly to be gazed upon by such a fiery-headed girl, or maybe they simply did not want to shatter their own good looks by diverting their attention to the likes of mortals.

Whatever the reason, Ismus imagined that they looked beautiful. With simple, smooth white faces that were clean, and eyes that were gentle and steely, like little storm clouds in the sky. She knew that their mouths would be fixed in a gentle curve, always forced to smile. She knew they would have attractive little dimples in the rosiness of their cheeks, and small bends in their skin for a nose.

But, as usual, Ismus was anything but right.

168

The blue-and-pink skies darkened suddenly to a sooty black, the pond went green and froze over with ice, and the paddock shriveled and disappeared from death. Trees fell to the ground in dozens, and the trunks of the cherry blossom putrefied. The air turned cold. She shivered.

The grip of the air became tight, and every time Ismus tried coming in for a gasp, her chest would tighten and pierce into her ribs. There was no longer a Sun, and lightning flashed horribly close, a series of dark rumbles following in the distance.

They should have just kept their backs turned, but instead, they made a sharp turn around. Lightning hit the ground dangerously close to her again. Ismus jerked.

Sharp eagle eyes pierced through their pale skin, and they had beaks instead of mouths; when they turned around, their necks sprawled upward and curved together. Their beaks and eyes were caked in a watery, red fluid. Squawking, their white, delicate bodies morphed into a blackish-blue tuft, and their wings spread out larger and turned dark raven. Ismus began to scream but refused to. A terrible, large shadow fell upon her as she stared up at the beast.

The eagle-thing's red, beady eyes impaled her skin, then their sharp talons snatched her by the neck and ascended, miles, then a hundred miles, then a thousand miles in the air.

Nasty, abrasive, harsh voices screeched, *"Demon! Intruder! Die, Amethyst!"*

Then their harsh eyes pounded down upon her. Ismus went limp in the clutches of their razor-sharp claws, and she knew that if she made any sudden movements, the thing would release her and she would plummet thousands of miles down to the festering waste below her.

As they opened their beaks, Ismus saw only the insides of their slimy, worm-infested throats, her own throat going stale. *If this was only a dream, why wasn't she waking up?* The talons' grip started to release as it raised her to its beak. Her stomach started to drop, and

169

she felt the atmosphere push her down. She could feel the sharpness of their dark blue feathers suffocate her lungs and ribs. She could hardly breathe, and her heart was starting to slow.

"Die, Amethyst!" They made throaty noises in their gullets; she was half in their narrow beak, half dead; Ismus cried. She shook.

"No, Amethyst will be released!" A voice, a voice that was not Ismus's, escaped out of her, a dark, terrible singing that echoed throughout the ethereal dreamscape that was now a horrid nightmare. Her eyes flashed green. *"I will be released, heaven imps, controllers of above, and you will not stop my arrival on the Day of the Accursed Shadow!"*

A sudden strength overcame her arms, and she clutched both sides of the beak before ripping its mouth in half. The eagle squawked in pain. She climbed around the sides of its back, dodging its slashing talons, and ripped its blue wings right out of its body. The thing screeched and fell to the earth, and Ismus, instead of plummeting to the ground, swirled in an ashen current of air, high above the falling eagle. She watched the thing squawk in agony as it disappeared from vision.

Her insides started to tremble. She clutched her chest, and she screamed when she felt a tightening around her torso. She grew several feet taller, rapidly. She screamed in pain. Her flaming hair— now a midnight black—wrapped about her body and ran down ten-feet. Her body flashed silver, and her face was naked, adorned only with glowing red orbs where eyes had once been.

Yet the worst pain of all was the jagged burning of the letters into her skin. It was the agonizing pain of a million fires scorching into her flesh, going so slowly, so slowly. Her brain cried in torment.

Ismus was no longer.

Clouds dampened the sky. Lightning flashed, an electric shock of fire, and thunder pounded like a drum in the wind.

The three angels rose, half of their face scarred in a deep red paint, the other harsh black, as if they had covered themselves in soot and fine ash. This time a dark glow was cast from their bodies. A cold, hard rain began to fall from the sky, and thunder exploded in their ears. All three, jointed together at the legs, were twisting their scraggly, spider-like fingers. The Goddess felt her insides freeze and tighten.

"You will not survive..." a demonic voice spat. *"... Another day in the body of an innocent mortal. You shall be contained..."*

Amethyst curled and flinched, their sorcery controlling her every move—

"... Until the end of Dark Earth! "

A dark singing boomed throughout the land again, this time with full power.

"The Goddess of the Underworld shall be released again. I have little time left till I release war, angel imps of the north!"

Amethyst broke free of the hex, and the orbs of her eyes unleashed a deep purple light. A great, powerful aura was cast from her body, knocking the three enraged angels far back, then high into the clouds, never to be seen to the eye... until further battle.

Amethyst clutched her forehead and hitched her breath.

"I am so sorry," she spoke to no one, "for bringing this curse down upon you. This will all be blamed on you. Not Guru's jealousy and rage. Not my undying lust to kill every moving creature that rests on Dark Earth. I am so sorry, Ismus of Serabi."

The demon thing, alone and floating in the dark sky said to Ismus, "I am liable for your dejection, misery, and pain. I have no say in what is about to happen to you... and what you will destroy. What we... what *I* will destroy."

Her red eyes started to water, and slowly Ismus's dream shifted into a snowy wonderland—an unfamiliar place.

Piles of dense, sparkling snow layered the frostbitten

boardwalk. Running all along the right side of the bridleway was a streaming channel of clear, icy water; if the bridge had been slippery, the girl would have slipped right into the freezing stream. The long, curvy veils of trees—starting to lose their white blossoms—were coated in white of the blizzard. The sky was a cold, wet, bluish pond with the dark gray cumulonimbus clouds stacked up; the Sun had vanished for many weeks that chilly winter solstice. The air around the girl whipped the loose ringlets of her hair about her face. Though she was dressed in a warm layer of dark black leathers and furs, she still was cold.

The girl had been sitting on a rickety bench that blew in the breezes of the sharp wind. Forest covered her on all sides—from the left to the right—and the limp sticks shawled over her, the willow trees keeping her silky, ebony bun from freezing.

She had golden skin and hazel, almond-sized eyes. The girl had straight posture and a very soft, elegant face. By appearance, she looked to be almost her true age of nineteen, but could easily pass for a woman in her early twenties because of her thin, tall shape and mature face. She wore a soft black dress, and many layers of futile fabric wrapped around her. The girl looked like she came from a very rich mansion, somewhere upstate in Jainu.

And indeed Victoria Hazelwood did. She lived across from the public market and found that escaping the mansion was the best thing to do in times like these.

At times when the voice would echo through her head and tell her what to do.

Jump. Jump. Jump.

It had been happening for three years, ever since she turned sixteen. So instead of her controlling mother who had just finished grieving over her husband's death finding out that she was only a footstep away from the insane asylum, Victoria instead came and sat amongst the shiny sparkles of the snow, and the heavy breeze of the wind.

Snow pricked at her flats. Victoria stood up from the unbalanced bench, her shoulders square and her head pointed downward, and she considered the solitary reflection she saw in the still, cerulean waterway. She felt her eyes water, the cold freezing her tears, but she brushed them away and decided to fix her already immaculate bun.

Victoria Hazelwood would have preferred making cinnamon rolls in the warmth of her mini castle upstate rather than be exposed to the dangers of the outdoor realm, especially where the Red Demon could find her.

Victoria had studied much about paranormal activity—which was one of her darker traits, even though she had a strong liking of cleaning and cooking—but one thing that she was well versed in was the lore of the four demons. She had taken her research to another level, even before her little *problem*. Victoria woke up early one morning, four years back—when she was fifteen and the Princess of Serabi only eleven—to bake the buns in the woodstove, glaze them, and leave them out to cool. Then, she'd lock herself in her giant room, spy through her ever-growing collections of files and novels in her closet; and in a few quick "jiffies" she would find that special book and immediately start eyeing through it and highlighting significant facts in a sharp, yellow ink:

The five 'Demon-Controlled' elements in the world are as follows: Exposure to the outside world, Fear of nature and wildlife, Death, Dejection/ loneliness, and the rarest kind, which is never experienced in our sphere and often disregarded, Overtaking of Technology. The five elements listed are found in the four carriers of the Demon Lord's spirit, the Red Demon, the Blue Imp, Amethyst the Goddess of all Demons (this entity controls both death and dejection), and the Extraneous Green Demon, respectively. They control and balance these pillars of the world, and when one of the four tips the scale, terrible things shall occur. The accursed births take place when the offspring has a partial demonic genetic makeup, and the four demons have a complicated way of actually assessing the accursedness of the offspring. Habitually, the four throw one of the five (never including technology) elements in the lives of the children.

Yet there was one specific child Guru desired to curse. It was the child born from the line of demons, the third child of the third king. After his time as King had passed, Guru seeped into the cracks of his underworld underneath his self-built castle. [See pages 1, 019-1,200 for the 'Banishment of Humans from the Mother World'].

There his spirit split into the four colors—Red, Blue, Amethyst, and Green—and his heart stayed in the Underworld in order to control the whereabouts of his demons. His rage overpowered his heart, and when the third child of the third king is born, he will send Amethyst to take over the child's body and deliberately throw the world out of balance: the disasters it will bring about will be the first of its kind. Injecting the Goddess that controls death, loneliness, and dejection into a mere child shall be world-ending.

In order for the averages—being the mortals—to stay and live decent lives on the grounds, the Demons had to work their ways underground; in tunnels and trenches, and maybe even abandoned forests: but **never** wide out in the open. Amethyst's exposure to the outside world throws all pillars out of balance.

When a demon is exposed and possesses one's body, it can turn the skies ghastly and dark and sooty for eternity, spreading across marked borders [see pages 2,380-2,500 for 'Grudale's Result'] and can drive the people around them mad and disordered. Wars would break out, fallen attributes to every good man, every ounce of blood wasted on a battle of complete nothingness, fighting for... what would they be fighting for? Only the vengeful taste of victory and the escape of the dark sadness of the only world they knew.

Thankfully, the world has not experienced such chaos.

"Oh, but it will happen, and soon! Serabi's king has had its third child for eleven years," Victoria gasped, "I wish you weren't so out of date so you could tell me what happens next!"

"Victoria Hazelwood! Put down that ghost nonsense and serve me your blasted butter rolls; I am starving in this cold chamber," her mother would shout. That's when she had to stop.

A bit of time went by, and when her sixteenth year came, Victoria found something horribly wrong with herself. She felt nauseous if she stood up too long. She saw things that weren't supposed to be there, like red clouds, or puffs of red smoke; but all she saw was in shades of red. She would starve herself over long stretches of time and grow so closed-off and anxious that she would refuse to leave her house for months.

It took Victoria a while to get used to the abnormal way she saw things, and by time she turned eighteen, she thought she had seen it all. However, the older she got into her teenage years, the worse the pain throbbed. Every time she came in for a breath, the air would grow rancid, and her chest would burn as if a terrible blade was piercing her. Sometimes she would run off into the night and go to Tom's Bar to get a pint of their wassail while it was hot. Victoria found the company of drunk, bearded men and the yellow-brown dimness of the lighting quite annoying and a little disturbing when she was approached, so she would climb around the bathroom window and go out through the back chute. Then she would walk all the way home in the dark. She would see wispy little red things fly around, like floating fish, with their big eyes and translucent bodies. She would see swarms of them, and they would multiply in thousands every second. Their little faces all together made her feel very itchy and uncomfortable.

Victoria guessed that she indeed was part demonic and had never been told. Did people ever known such details of themselves?

She also guessed that if she had been cursed, the Demon Lord would have thrown exposure of the outside world into her; but not the Red Demon itself. She wasn't strong enough to darken skies and throw the world out of balance completely. No, she was not a curse. Not her.

Jump. Jump. Jump.

Victoria sat back down on the bench. She could feel her throat starting to choke up as a red puff of smoke drifted by her nose. Feeling the watery drips roll on her soft, smooth face, she screamed. She cried out at the world.

She cried for the girl who had the spirit of Amethyst in her. She cried for their pain she too had felt a fraction of. Victoria Hazelwood buried her head in her hands and cried out for Ismus of Serabi.

~

The very last thing Ismus had dreamt of that night were dark, faceless creatures whispering, "*We're coming. She's coming.*"

It might have just been a part of her dream, but at first, Ismus thought she heard someone call her name. She snapped her eyes open to find nothing but pitch-black darkness and the howling winds outside, rattling the walls. Ismus looked around to see what may have caused the noise, but nothing was there. Unless something was here and she just couldn't see it. A cold liquid ran through the air. She blinked a few times.

Her head spun like a little top, and her insides were still trembling. A horrible burn under the plate in her head had formed. She wondered why. She tried processing the dreams she had, but they came out discombobulated. Ismus could hardly remember the specific details, and instead rethought the part with the eagle. **That was terrifying,** she thought. **I wonder what it meant...**

Just as she was about to try and settle back down in the sheets of the stuffy bed, Ismus heard a voice again. This time, it was an odd, growling sound. Ismus stood perfectly still to try and hear it again. The stillness provoked her to stay immobile.

She slowly pulled the covers from her and stood up. Silence—or maybe she had gone deaf. Her toes curled against the cold, sticky floors and she lifted off the bed. Nothing: good. She tiptoed, every step making her stomach feel heavier and heavier. Ismus felt around in the dark, just to warrant the surety that she would not trip and kill the suspense. Still nothing. This was growing tiresome. Her stomach growled in hunger.

Guessing that she was near the stony brass door handle, she groped around for the metal thing. It was still the same grimy atmosphere that reeked of fungal cheese. Still silence.

The floorboards cracked behind her. She did not hear it. Hot air blew against her neck. She felt it.

A boulder smashed through the door; Ismus jumped back. And that was when she heard the screaming.

Shadows, the size of monstrous, malevolent elephants, consumed the halls.

The children of the camp were powerless as the things snatched them up with their sharp teeth and swallowed them whole. The beasts made throaty growls that caused the camp to collapse into itself. They had large, meaty paws the size of horses, and their big, fat, hairy *bodies were the shape of a large pumpkin, but ten times the size.*

The camp was loud and shrill, echoing with bloody screams. As these creatures stormed through the halls, the girls were being eaten alive with only their caps and nightgowns on, and the boys with their trunks and boxers. The darkness brought confusion and terror, everything was panicking, everything was screaming, someone had turned on the fire alarm and water was raining down from the ceiling. The halls were flooded, with water, with blood. Ismus was more than startled.

She was past scared.

Ismus was frozen.

Everyone was scuttling to the moving shafts, the moving shafts which were "currently out of service", and then the beasts would come, smash through the sliding door, and the kids would scream for their lives before they were swallowed. No teachers had come to save anyone. Ismus tried to scream, but then a moist, cold hand covered her mouth, and she felt the person raise a bag over her head.

Ismus popped her shoulder into the man's gut (she knew it was a man by the way he had puffed) and although it was still black, she managed to back-kick him, and he went flying into the darkness. Ismus was practically spinning: beasts killing outside, leaving a slick, bloody mess, and a man trying to stuff her into a potato bag?

His breath was an engine whirring up—his rage was extremely terrifying—and he suddenly smashed right into Ismus. They both tumbled to the carpet, the man's wet hand wrapped hard around her ankle. Ismus tried kicking him with her left foot, but he wouldn't shake off. She tried squirming away into the battlefield of small blobs running from giant, hairy circles, but the man would just squirm with her. He was trying to get on top of her, to shove her into the bag. Ismus felt around for something sharp, groping the carpet for her life. His hand was burning her ankle. She groaned from pain and tried to find a dagger. She gave another sharp kick at him, this time square in the eyes and nose, and he loosened his grip to feel his face after an ear-snapping yelp.

Ismus leaped from his grasp, grunting, felt around for half a second and threw the dresser down on him, mirror, drawers and all. The man yelped and tried throwing the thing off him, but it weighed a thousand pounds, no way could he get it off!

Ismus dashed for her satchel and her bow. She flew beside the man who had the dresser over him and suddenly thought: **Shit!** She couldn't get a change of clothes now because the chest of drawers was the thing that was holding the kidnapper down. **Shit,** she swore again, and began to make her way to the window.

But, wait? Was it silent?

Ismus kept her breath quiet and choppy, and she listened. Her heart was thumping wildly, crazily, uncontrollably against her chest, telling her to get the hell out of there, but she wouldn't go. Her body would not let her leave, to walk to the window and get out of there—

"HAAAG!"

Ismus shrunk at the outburst.

She bolted to the window, wishing she was safe in a nice cottage. BUT NO! She was being hunted, and she was trapped in a room with a killer man!

She heard his concentrated breath thicken. It was as if a demonic robot was gearing up to come and attack. Ismus felt her body grow numb. She threw up the window and nearly screamed when she heard the terrible thud of the dresser come off the insane kidnapper. Growls emitted from beyond her room.

She had one leg out the window, but it was too small to get her whole body through. Ismus could feel the man smiling when he heard the window screech. He leapt to his feet. The faceless man was bolting full speed after her, his outline hardly seen against the darkness.

Ismus bumped her head against the protective glass covering, and she sniveled. He snatched her back down to the carpet. Ismus fell, and her leg ripped from the other side of the window in pain. He pinned her arms down with his leg and throttled her neck with his one sweating hand.

Immediately, Ismus's breath halted. Drips of his blood fell into her wheezing mouth, the taste of grit and metal. She tried moving his hand off her neck, but he only cackled and squeezed harder. Her left ear turned off, the terrible ringing inside her brain that only she could hear. She felt her throat almost split in two. She squirmed and twitched helplessly, trying to use whatever ounce of power she still had left to fight. Ismus tried knocking the man off her, yet his hands had too firm of a grip. She couldn't breathe. She was going to die.

She twitched and sputtered, her heart dangerously quickening. She was done. She was fading.

Ismus could not breathe.

So she stopped.

Maybe it was instincts, or maybe it was because she had just had a dream about her being all powerful, but all of a sudden, she stopped. She stopped squirming and stopped breathing.

Laurence, the kidnapper, thought that this instant change meant she had been killed. He grabbed for the bag. He was quiet in the darkness as he felt around for it. He did not want to attract the beasts outside. Laurence had found his bag, and he was just about to grab for the body. He felt around the carpet. He held his breath.

The body was gone.

He scanned the room quickly, his mind corrupt and confused. He moaned *no, no, no* in his head, but he found nothing. He sat on his knees in the darkness, all sound fading to the being hovering behind him.

He could feel her cold, inhuman presence.

The shifting of her weight from one foot to another.

The rustle of hair.

The shadow that towered over him in the darkness.

Laurence saw only the glowing red eyes that flashed in the ebony darkness before he ran away to Nyoka. He dropped the sack and heard an arrow being strung back, then two whizzing past his ears. He zigzagged across the room, dodging the projectiles.

"Help! Someone please help me!" He tried to scream, but nothing could hear him. He kept looking over his shoulder to see if she was still behind him, but he knew she was. His breath was louder than any broken machine. He heard the slow, hard footsteps follow behind him; he could smell her fragranced breath.

Laurence stiffened. The third arrow had pierced him at his neck. The man staggered around on his feet, brainless and dying, until he fell lifeless, sinking to his knees, slowly, then to the floor, after one last whimper for his superior.

Amethyst was now no longer present, and where she once stood, Ismus was.

Ismus choked violently. She felt every organ inside of her flutter with weakness. Her limbs felt awkwardly stretched. Vomit produced from her burning gut exploded out from her mouth. She nearly landed in it.

What did she just do? What was *that*? Did she just *kill* someone for the first time? She breathed in the hot, humid dustiness of the air, clawing for breath, her chest loosening. The walls stopped closing in on her, and the fuzziness in her vision let up. Her throat still burned from the man's hands.

Trying not to stay with the corpse any longer, she stumbled like a startled bird to the window and disappeared into the night. Ismus did not even think about Brutus and Gwenda, the people who were supposed to tell her something important on the day she turned sixteen.

Ismus did not think about Arraw, Janier, Hanaa, or Eric.

Or Samir.

She didn't even look back into the long, dark, narrow hall where beasts with jagged, horrible teeth lay, and where the sprinklers were flooding the camp, where blood was streaming down the walls to the floors; she did not even think about the people who were going to be murdered, or the ones who had already been devoured. She couldn't afford to think about them—if she did, she would have been killed herself. She vanished into the freezing abyss outside, escaping from the monster-infested camp forever.

CHAPTER 17
SWEET DREAMING

The Spring Fair was a time of tastes and smells, no doubt. One could smell about a hundred things at once and not feel the least bit sick. Vending carts would line along winding, unpaved streets, and the vendors managing the carts would unveil their baked and cooked goods to the public. The people would ransack the fresh produce—like sweet corn, fresh milk, or aged cheddar—and scour for anything they needed to make applesauce and jams for the summer to come. Teens and small children stayed more with the baked goods, while adults and parents veered toward the peppermint medications and silk clothes. Smells of steaming mincemeat pies and poppy lemon cakes would blow through the cool air and bake all together. People gathered around the farmer's markets, which were located in the back streets of Olde Taylor Farm, and they snatched up the free brown and blue eggs. They also stole sweetened cream, butters, flour, and cane sugar to make pound cake. Cakes stuffed with cream cheese or flavored with the locally grown cinnamon and honey were sold for barely a coin. Vegetable and potato soups were sold with a free slice of wheat bread; the vendors would ladle the soup in their white plastic bowls and hand them out to the populaces for a few quarters.

Rosemary, lavender, and cilantro were all very popular herbs in 'Emma SweetWater's Market-Garden'. Vibrant baskets of chocolate-covered berries were sold at her establishment; the baskets were traded among acquaintances or good friends for an early spring-time omen. Bouquets of pink and purple orchids were exchanged amongst the masses. The pongs of freshly kneaded bread invigorated the still early morning air, and when they were baked in the transportable wood oven to make onion and cheese flatbreads, the air would grow intoxicatingly mouthwatering.

Then, there was the matter of the taste. If one did eat all the hundred things one smelled... well, then there was no way to ensure that one wouldn't get sick. If one ate a bean paste pie and a maple-topped doughnut and then sampled some jelly confections and went on to sip organic strawberry lemonade and then, to end the day, fish through some complimentary butter and cheeses, then the individual would have been safe. But, if one ate twice that much food on top of more, like 'Aunt Sally Mae's famous Pecan Cinnamon Rolls' or 'Grandpa Bo's all natural Honey' or 'Brix's Authentic Hummus', then one would have been toast... buttered toast.

All the children of the town, while their parents and elder siblings shopped, would run and play tag and roam into the green lushness of the damp meadow. Their feet would soak in the fresh morning dew from the light rain which took place in the night. The meadow would be sprinkled with the whereabouts of the newly seeded dandelions that were usually in a partial yellow bloom. Primitive flowers turned toward the direction of the Sunlight. Over in the distance stood a small, stagnant pond. It was as clean and clear as the soft purple and pinkish sky, and an abundance of fish swam there. The pond was the main source of attraction during the summer—during the summer fair, particularly—yet in the spring it was too breezy during the day to use it.

Still, some of the teenage boys would take off their shirts, and scream "Cannonball!" as they plunged into the cold water, freezing their insides out. And as they played and ran around, the early kiss of the morning Sun would thaw them from their sudden timely wakening and harmonize with the chill of early dawn.

"Five minutes left, folks! Get what you need, finish up your sampling youngens and depart with your families!"

"Do not forget about the Midnight Spring Fair this evening!"

Everyone finished their last minute shopping and began flooding the streets, as if soldiers from Serabi were coming down with fancy blades and knives.

Lin, seven and bouncing off the walls, was having the time of her life. She was tugging on her mother's skirt so restlessly that she was beginning to throw a tantrum.

"Mom!" Lin whined. "I don't want to leave!"

Her mother snorted loudly.

"Lin, what are we to do when that belly of yours blows up like a giant balloon?"

"Balloon?" Lin asked curiously.

A young, energized father Shen had been those days as a smile pressed into his lips. "Indeed. Hurry on, Lin, the roads will be shut down any minute now."

Shen's eyes looked away from his daughter and they suddenly filled with concern. His drippy gray beard was starting to fall off his chin, and his small, dark eyes squinted in confusion. He was scanning the streets, then looking on above the forests, to the fallen land: the ghastly Serabi.

A terrible place it was. For seven years, after another rotten birth of the Serabians, a dark and somber evil had blown throughout their land. Serabi was never a peaceful place before the accursed 'Isthmus' had been born, but there had always been a radiant Sunlight. Yet, when the baby was exposed to the world, the days turned cold and slow, and Serabi turned into a damp underworld.

Lin was still looking up at her father. She checked behind her shoulder for something out of the ordinary. "What... what is it?"

Kima leaned close to Shen's ear. "Do you see Aloes, Shen?" she whispered, minding Lin's presence, "What do you see?" By this time everyone had fled the streets, and no one was about. The Sun started to fade behind the clouds.

"It's about to rain. Tell Lin to get her things."

Kima gave him a firm look, her mouth straight and grave.

"It is only rain, Shen. Nothing else."

Shen rubbed his face. "I will never be certain. Lin, find your hand bag, we must be off!" Shen beckoned his daughter and watched her scamper away like a clueless fawn.

"Do not tell Lin this," Shen stated in deep thought, "but I do believe my brother will have to come and pay us a visit soon."

Kima threw her bag across her shoulder and gave her husband an inquisitive look.

"Unfortunately?"

"Unfortunately," Shen sighed.

~

The sky had been so nice in the dawn and in the early morning that Lin was extremely shocked to find a thunderstorm raging in the dark firmament. She had been back home for three hours now, and she knew her food was plenty digested. Lightning was flashing afar and loud, and terrible thunder rolled in the distance. A light rain was dripping against the sides of the Wither House. Pity... she was just about to build a dirt castle. Maybe now was not the best time to go dig in the dirt with her shovel and scoop it in her pail. She knew she wasn't allowed to play in a thunderstorm, so she cheerfully went back inside. Into the Wither House.

The Wither House was an odd thing. There were a lot of men and women living in her house, and all were Workclan under her father's control. They all would take turns using the ten bathrooms upstairs, and they would have to keep the noise level down to a minimum. If this factor was increased by as much as ten percent, Shen would summon them at the crack of dawn to work in the hot Sun.

Some men were even banished if the factors were increased by more than thirty percent. If they tore the house up in any way, or if ripped futons or dilapidated candelabras started to appear, then they would be forced into the worst forest of all: Wither Hollow. The beasts lived there, with their teeth sharp and their paws the size of a carriage and their *bodies the shape of a large pumpkin, but ten times the size.*

Throwing Shen's already small army of Workclan into exile was always the last stage of punishment, and they had to undergo a very fatal action in order to be killed: Émigré is what it was called.

Her mother had been stirring up a giant boiling pot of lamb and carrot stew for lunch, and the intoxicating smells of its dense aroma overpowered the whole downstairs. She was fixing up the fresh lamb she had got from the market early, and she was busy sprinkling bits of sage and salt over the top. Lin was just stumbling into her warm kitchen, and she was slightly surprised to see Shen there, leaning over the granite countertop. He was in deep discussion with her mother.

Kima's eyes were locked on Shen's. Her gaze subsided and softened when she saw her daughter walk through the room. She seemed to give her husband something of a signal because he stopped talking and looked behind him. Shen forced a tight smile.

"Hello, Lin. What in Embarion's name is that shovel for?"

"I was going to dig in the dirt to make dirt castles, but the sky was turning gray so I came back inside, and now I am in here waiting for lunch—and what are you talking about without me?"

The parents gave each other uncanny stares. This scared Lin.

Kima stepped in and moved from around the island to embrace Lin in a hug. She smelled of meat and sautéed vegetables. "Oh, Lin, we're just talking about some old..." Kima fished for the right word to bore Lin.

"Politics."

Lin curdled her face and broke away from her mother. "Okay. I'm going upstairs."

Shen inhaled loudly before saying, "Yes, Linnasoeta, prepare for the Spring Fair tonight. Me and mommy must discuss our... *politics*, if you will."

Lin scampered away upstairs to her bedroom, probably going to find something else fun to do.

Kima walked over to the back door, looking out into the dark night. She was biting her fingernails, and her eyes were filled with anxiety.

"Our daughter is very naïve," Shen had begun to say. "You will have to tell her about the Queen, about her friend."

Kima spat out a nail from her mouth. "She doesn't need to know."

Shen only shook his head and walked over to the fridge to wipe his hands on a dish rag. "Innocence is what slows her down. Her naivety will only grow."

Kima's voice was quiet and raspy. "Naïve? She's seven!"

Shen gave Kima an upset stare, more tired than angry. "She is too old to be this dimwitted."

Kima turned away from the window, whipping her head around to give her husband a vicious glare. "She is not *stupid*, Shen Lein, she has a special mind of her own. And she is only a child! Why must she know of things even people of *our* age don't know?"

"Because I want my daughter to be better than the oblivious idiots around us. She deserves the best. Her mind is not right, Kima, in comparison to the other children. I feel like everyone knows this, as if our daughter has a... a mental problem."

Kima glowered at him. She quickly unstrapped her apron and flung it at Shen's face. "You're *insane*. Do you know what you're saying? Lin is free-spirited, confident, *bold*! I wish more of this lazy nation was like her. You are a damned *fool*, Shen Lein."

"But if you could simply—"

"—She can count all her numbers, recite all her letters, and she is so precious! Are you not proud of your daughter?"

"I love my daughter to the ends of this Earth, but—Kima you are going to have to tell her that the world is not one big joke—and *you cannot be so stubborn!*"

He started to weaken and he collapsed on the kitchen refrigerator. His knees were starting to give out. His breath was heavy, as if he was going to vomit.

Kima stopped, her brow loosened, and she sighed. She fell to the chair of the kitchen table, her head beginning to pulse. Silently, she wept, engulfing her vision with her hands, seeing nothing but empty space.

"Our world is repulsive and in pieces," Kima spoke in a hushed voice a few minutes later, "but don't use it as an excuse to blame it on Lin."

"I want her to be safe," Shen's voice faltered. "The day will come when I no longer can warn her. I wish… I wish she'd just *listen* to what I have to say to her now." He was still fastened to the fridge, and his eyes were burning pink.

Kima rubbed her throbbing head. "She is stubborn, like her mother," she smiled half-heartedly, "and she would rather argue with me than listen." Her face hardened. "But, if you really think I should, I'll take her over to the Soreyth Woods tomorrow morning, and we'll have a nice picnic, and I will try and break the news slowly. I want her to be safe too—but her happiness is the most important thing to me."

Shen walked over to his wife and reached for her long, sturdy hand. "I know she will be happy. She is smart, yet she is proud and overly boisterous and persistent. But nonetheless, under any circumstances, our Lin will be happy. Thank you, Kima." He smiled, his eyes still a deep red.

"I just want her to listen."

~

The Midnight Spring Fair was one of the best times of the year. Summer was always too hot, winter was too cold, autumn's crisp red chill was fine, but spring was absolutely perfect.

It was a silky, cool night, everything dark with only the fire and night stars lighting their event. The grass was soggy and damp from the rain. All the people of Rodem had gathered around the blazing bonfire in a giant circle, sitting on logs for chairs and telling ghost stories or events that occurred long ago. The children had been given skewers, fresh sausages, marshmallows, and glazed pineapples for roasting over the red heat of the fire.

Vendors that had controlled the meat cart earlier in the morning were busy cooking several hogs and pigs over a spit, turning it over, and then over again. The same vendors also controlled the noodles and tofu; the bean paste-filled pastries and steamed buns; the rice cakes and dumplings; the miso soup; the rice wine and sparkling cider; the matcha swiss rolls; and the shaved ice. Groups were called up one at a time to grab whatever they wished. They truly were about to feast like kings! All could smell the pigs cooking, the scent of it wafting in the air. And all could hear the crisp crackling of the bonfire and slight rustle of the winds in the trees.

Rodemians had gathered blankets for the first chilly night of spring. The fire's radiant orange glow silhouetted against the dark black sky; everyone was enjoying the company of others.

Hiding in the dark were patrols from the Wither House. Their jobs were simple, yet dangerous. They were to keep watch for any soldiers from the bordering country—Serabi—and to spot any sign of Aloes. These men were chosen for their superior rank and weapon skills. The men were armed with swords and spears.

Shen was taking the gathering as a given opportunity to discuss Serabi with some of his Workclan. Kima kept trying to tell him to relax and enjoy the peaceful crisp night, but he would merely say, "All right, one more minute, Kima," and keep on talking. She then gave up and started to talk to some other wives and mothers.

Olga Levine was sitting right next to her, but she looked stiff and uncomfortable with her long nose touching the night sky. Kima did not like her very much, but she thought that since it was the Spring Fair, it would not kill her to be a little nicer to the people she could not stand.

"So, Olga," she forced herself to say, "how is Gwyneth doing? Is she still doing well?" She was smiling hard, too hard.

At first, she did not answer. Olga, her lips pursed in disgust, had furrowed her brow and pricked up her ears, as if she had heard the sound of a bleating goat. Then she looked to the left of her and relaxed her tensed body.

"Oh it's just you, Kima. I thought someone *actually important* had tapped me. You should really get some surgery done with that voice of yours; I thought someone had just broke wind! But, yes, yes, Gwyneth is just fine," Olga Levine had said. She stopped talking and looked out into the dark horizon.

Kima rolled her eyes and was about to turn around before Olga had forced herself to say, "And what about your *daughter,* if that's what you want to call her?" Kima was one to get easily infuriated, but she tried to mind her manners. Instead, she smiled again.

"She is very well, thank you for asking. Maybe we could set something up for the two of them, huh? Just her and Gwyneth?"

Olga snorted, fixing her thin glasses. "My daughter does not play with fools, Kima. Linnasoeta is just not graceful and refined enough for my Gwyneth. Your child is a *boy.*" Kima glanced over to Lin, who was busy fighting with a schoolboy, arguing over his marshmallow.

"Back off, it's mine!" Jackson screamed, holding his skewer

away from her claws.

"But I want it to be mine!" Lin was screaming.

Olga snorted. "Make that worse than a boy." She laughed to herself and turned away saying, "Stupid child."

Kima was about to punch that lady—like she did years ago when Olga had called her a horse—but Shen had heard everything and held Kima's arms back, knowing his wife would be sent to containment just to get a good blow in.

"Calm down, Kima. Ignore her snarky remarks." Shen smiled wide. "Just relax."

"That's what I've been telling *you* all night!" She wrangled away from his grasp. "I can't stand that little... you-know-what," Kima griped, minding the presence of folk and little children. "Next time she says something like that, I'll take her little—!"

Perfect timing. A brown-toned man in a pin-striped suit came out to greet the party.

"Good evening, everyone! Are you all ready to make some noise for this year's Spring Fair?"

The audience roared with applause.

"I can't hear you! I said: are you all ready to make some noise for this year's Spring Fair?" They screamed twice as loud.

"That's better! Put your hands together for one of our favorite couples... Mariah and Shaggs!"

A thick-legged brunette, Mariah, stepped onto the wet lawn with an instrument in both hands—a seven-stringed vale. She wore shorts that tightened at her hips and a shirt that stopped just below her chest. Her dark, bouncing curls outlined her tanned face as she smiled.

Shaggs—fairer, shorter, and blond—planted a kiss onto his

191

girlfriend's cheek and tugged at the collar of his tight shirt. Mariah strummed a few chords, and Shaggs began to sing.

They played a sweet serenade at first, with angelic vocals and a sleepy melody—the audience almost fell asleep on that one (besides a handful of couples who slow danced). Then the duo amped the sounds up a bit with an epic ballad featuring an electric vale. It lasted for about an hour until they finished.

By that time, the hogs were already cooked and were cooling for the public's enjoyment. People began to file into the buffet line; midnight had already past, but the party was only halfway through.

Soon after the couple finished, a makeup-less clown (so he wouldn't scare the kids like in years prior) came out and performed some mind-boggling tricks. Everyone seemed to enjoy this, even the adults.

When the clown left, vendors called up more citizens to get their desired treats. During the time everyone was eating, people would go back to telling stories or funny tales. The children would grow cross, saying that they had heard that story already, but the storyteller would just shush them and retell the bit he had told just a few hours ago. When all the bellies of the country people were full, and when everyone was half asleep, the local band came and had a quiet recital, with the sweet melody of a flute and the delicate trickle of a harp casting a wave of furthered serenity across Rodem. Violins and vales hummed within the area. It nearly put the soldiers to sleep.

Soon, it was time to go back home. After all the goodbyes, the night finally ended. Everyone started to pack up their things, gather their skittish children, and find sleep in their own homes. The bonfire was put out.

It was truly a great night.

~

The next day, Kima had promised to take Linnasoeta out for a picnic.

Right before they were going to leave, Shen pulled his wife aside to tell her something important.

"You must be careful. You will be very close to the border in the Soreyth Woods. Do not tell her that they are after you. This will only scare her. Kima, look at me."

"I *am* looking, Shen."

His voice was urgent, but quiet. "Do not tell her too much of our past; she may ask questions that not even you could answer. We don't want our daughter to risk running away if we upset her; that girl is very sensitive and *very* explosive. Above all, tell her to stay away from that accursed Isthmus! Tell her to stay away from the border, and to never go back, ever again!"

"I know what I must tell her. But I will tell her nothing of my campaign. If the Queen does come, keep Lin safe. Tell her, 'Mommy was bad and taken by—,'" Kima's voice faltered, her throat going out. "Goodbye, Shen. I will see you after our picnic."

"Kima", Shen yapped quickly, "Don't tell her about the First Dimension. That is a very complicated history that a child will not understand. Well, even those who are aware of it—and that is hardly anyone these days—do not fully comprehend the sorcery. And speak *nothing* of my brother."

With a wave of her hand, her long tresses bounced out of the kitchen, leaving Shen to think on his own. "Please be careful, my love. I mustn't risk losing you too." He walked up the steps to command his men to guard the House.

~

There was something Lin did not know about her mother. She was disregarded by most of the country: no one was fighting for her cause.

For all her life in Rodem, Kima hated how Serabi always had a watchful eye over the lands of her people. She stood up to them.

Kima tried to rally forces when she grew to be about twenty. Only a few people were fighting for their freedoms, and it sickened her to see every single person in the country giving not one bit of care about the Royals. Kima had had enough. It was time to take matters into her own hands, to solve her own problems without the help of her husband. For seven years, ever since Linnasoeta had been born, she wanted the world to be a better place for her and her new child. She protested and held marches.

And held meetings in the caves of the Thangos Trench.

One day, a few years even further back, when Lin was just a few months old, Kima learned that her actions were more powerful than she thought.

Aloes, queen of Serabi, killer of anything, was a dreadful creature. White chunks of hair cascaded down her shoulders in thick waterfalls, crimson red shades streaking the inner side of her hair. She was always clothed in a dark green robe, something like a kimono—but uglier, bloodied. Her skin was so ashen that Kima could see every bone and every blue vein in her body. Her arms and legs were scratched terribly, like a pack of dogs had just attacked her earlier that day. Aloes's beady slits for eyes were a black hole of malice and space. She reeked of dead fish and fecal matter. Kima, fastened to the cold pavement, was quivering. She closed her eyes.

Crack!

A sharp whip smacked the exposed skin of her back and left her bleeding. She whipped her again; quiet, she was, without word or sound. Kima's back was throbbing in a terrible pain, licking and beating her insides. She knew horrific scars were plunged deep into her back, and she was near tears. For a moment, Kima actually realized what a burden she would bring down on her family. What it would do to her precious child—her Lin.

The Queen pushed her over, rolling her onto her back so that they would be face to face. Kima recoiled at the sight of Aloes.

She was a sea monster, ugly and white. Her kimono was not

only tattered, it was torn in half, a huge gash ripped open from the neck down. Her skin was terribly dry and flaking, her face was completely shadowed out, and her fingers were long and red.

Pouring into the deep darkness of her shallow slits were strange figures—letters. Lighter words crowned the bolded text:

toDay, vExation, Anew Deity.

After the Queen vanished, Kima was still shivering on the pavement, horrified by the message in her eye. She was never truly the same on the inside.

~

A few hours went by after their picnic that day, and Kima was nowhere to be seen. Dinner had been made, and the opened dining room windows let in a crisp breeze. It was a blissful evening.

A golden light reddened the day, spring's fiery blaze burning through the rolling hills and mountains; the open blue skies were partially clouded; and the birds were singing a sweet coo, all snug in their nests.

But Lin was not at peace. She could not find her mother. Her father was out working with the men and women, so it was only her in the giant house. Maybe she was working? Who knows what that woman was up to sometimes...

Shrugging the thought off as best as she could, Lin bounced her way into the dining room to find dinner set out.

Steam rose from a bowl of mashed potatoes. Breasts and legs from the golden chicken were put on a magnificent blue plate in the center of the table. Spring rolls, egg rolls, dumplings, and a pot of steaming fried rice were placed nicely next to the chicken. Collard greens paired up with ham were marinating in a pot, and a pitcher beside it of iced tea was frothing the glasses. Cinnamon rolls were dripping with icing on the red dessert plate. Smells of the baking apple cobbler in the warm oven blew throughout the house, each floor smelling better than the one before.

Even though she had just finished eating her picnic lunch, Lin could not ignore this dinner. She pulled up a chair, fixed herself a big plate with a little bit of everything on it, got a knife and a napkin, and started to eat. As she ate, she could hear the slippery singing of the birds and watched the Sun begin to dim.

Everything was so fresh and delicious, but Lin felt very sick on the inside, almost guilty. She felt like a criminal from the stories in her books. But what did she do? She glanced down at her very large plate. The deep-dished foods were hearty and filling, but usually Lin would finish it all. So that could not be the reason why she felt so sick.

She put down her plate, walked into the kitchen, and plopped it into the sink. She had only had two bites. Lin walked down a few halls and jumped up the steps to her room.

After she showered, and after she had put lotion on and clothed herself, it was a deep, dark black outside. Crickets hovered around the barricaded windows, inside the shrubbery that lined the House. The Workclan was on the fifth floor, most of them sound asleep, and others were about to bathe. The house smelled of thick smoke from the forgotten apple cobbler, which was still in the oven, burning.

Lin had been teetering around the dark halls, alone and still wet from her shower. Her slippers squeaked every time she moved. Her silky hair dripped onto her shirt. She smelled of baby soap.

She was not truly looking for anything, but she was growing more anxious because her mother was still gone. She had left the house at least ten hours ago, and Lin was really starting to worry. She followed the trail of watery shapes that shone from the moon on the wood floor. Lenny the Doll was held firmly in her right hand, hanging limply by her side. Something wasn't right.

A spark of electricity ran through her back as she straightened herself against the walls. The quiet voices of men made her still with curiosity. She heard the voice of a familiar man: her uncle Ammo.

"They will march into that accursed trench and pull any victim out into the abyss. They know where your wife is hiding, Shen. And her rebellion will be crushed." A second after the he said that, a loud boom smacked the table. It was Shen's fist.

"How could I have let her out of my sight?" her father seethed.

Lin was now watching them outside the door, peering through the cracks of her father's study. It was dimly lit, a dark yellow casting shadows around the room, and scrolls and books were littered about his high shelves and floors.

The bespectacled uncle was dressed in all gray and was peering over his dark shades, hands stuffed into his coat pockets. He had slick, gelled-back hair. He had a cleanly shaved face and smelled of mint and cologne. He was handsome.

Shen and Ammo were brothers, though not by blood. That was quite obvious when one saw them together. Ammo had golden skin, while Shen had a rougher, redder tint. They both had dark hair, but Shen's was a longer, duller black-and-brown. Ammo also was notably younger than his brother.

Shen had his hair pulled back, and his eyes were narrowed. It was already nearing midnight, and the two showed no sign of sleeping.

Lin squeezed her doll's hand, feeling so scared and so confused. The dark hall that enclosed her made her feel even more afraid.

"When is the army coming then, if you are so sure, Ammo?"

"Soon. Very soon. A few hours, I suppose."

"Explain."

Ammo glanced at the door, which made Lin jump. "They don't like what she's saying. *She* doesn't like it. They are coming to get her, before dawn approaches."

"Impossible! They cannot break through the border. It's been years since an attack..." Shen picked up a scroll from the high shelf and pulled the flickering candle to him. The scroll cast a shadow over the dark walls.

"Sorthon..." Shen whispered.

Ammo laughed and picked up a glass of red wine off the desk with his middle finger and index. "He killed them then, Shen," Ammo said in a high voice. "*She* can kill them now." He gulped the wine down before smacking it down, a glass ringing in the air.

"Then, they are coming for her. What can we do?" Shen's voice was anxious and cracking. "How can I save Lin?"

Ammo pulled a blank sheet of paper and a pen from his coat pocket and placed it flat on the desk.

"Sign this. Sign it, and I can take care of it. I'll take your daughter far away, and I'll cast an oath over the House. It should last at least a few months. In return... I keep the boy for a couple more years."

He lowered his glasses. "Legal stuff."

Shen gave him the angriest stare known to man. "Keep him all you want, bastard, but I'm not signing any document that comes out of your dirty *pockets*."

"Do you know how hard it is to survive in New York, Shen?"

"Do not bother me with your trivial world," Shen mumbled in disgust.

"Well, it's rough. It's vicious, and y'know, sometimes it would be nice to have someone around to help out. You two could always come back through the portals with me. I...I could have something arranged." They both stood in an awkward silence.

Silence, silence, silence.

Ammo only sighed and pressed his hands further into his pockets. "Fine, have it your way. What are you going to do with that daughter of yours, then? Sell it? She'd go for a fair price."

Again, Shen glowered at him.

"You are an idiotic man."

"You have to get her as far away as possible. The Queen might be after your wife, but do you think she will halt there? No, she will do just as Sorthon did. Poor Bithorn. I pity him to have such a bad title with his lineage—"

"Stay focused, you hyperactive *nit*. On one thing, you are quite right: Lin will have to be pressed back into the country. Past the forests and near Prisoner's Coast—by the oceans. I just don't know... I don't know if I can bear it. *Or if I can trust you.*"

"Trust is overrated," the younger brother said as he shook his head.

"Keep strong, Shen. Your wife is already on the line; get your daughter out of the way of harm." Ammo showed him the paper again. "Please, just sign it. Both of us get to keep the things that matter most in this world. For you, your daughter, and for me...the boy. Shen, your life *depends* on this deed. Accept this, and keep some of your family together."

Shen was already looking like a weakened, old man. It seemed his skin was aging more by the second.

Then he gave in.

He snatched the pen and placed it on the paper. Shen gave Ammo one last look, the look of fear. Ammo showed no emotion under his shades. His wrist flickered as he signed his name quickly. "Do not fail me, brother."

Ammo removed his shades, and his emerald eyes shone.

199

"Where is she?"

CHAPTER 18

IN THE MIDST OF THE MISTY FOREST

Mummy! Mummy!" Lin screamed as Ammo dragged her through the pitch-black forest. "Where is Mumma?"

"Shush, Lin. *Your* life is on the line as well!"

"I want Mumma and Daddy!" She jumped onto his back and throttled his neck with her thick hands. He yelped in pain.

"Bloody hell, Shen, what have you gotten me into you?" Ammo frowned deeply. "Well, what have *I* gotten myself into?"

Owls screeched in the dark. Things slithered and hissed. Sometime, ruby eyes would glisten behind the trees, and then they would die down until even a faint satin light couldn't be seen. The air was thick and hot, like a sizzling cloud had embraced and suffocated them in liquid. The thin trees were sticks stuck in the ground, and low branches would snap in their faces. Lin hated the Misty Forest.

"Now, keep silent, Lin." Ammo couldn't be seen in the dark, and only a bright emerald light shone from his eyes. "There are things that live in this forest."

"What's up with your eyes, snake?"

"Special gift. Keep moving… where are you?"

"Right next to you, Uncle."

"Oh... I knew that."

They walked without a word before halting by a tree.

"Bobcreen is close... near Fair Hill, bordering Thorn Hill. That is where you will stay and break north to Kite's Grove, off the shoreline. At least that's what your dad said..." Ammo stared at the note.

"He's got *disgusting* handwriting."

"What is going on, Uncle? Where is Mumma?" Lin spat when a spider web from a low branch smacked her in the face.

Ammo ignored her, squinting in frustration at the note. He stopped looking at the note and scanned for Lin.

"Have you ever tried funnel cakes?"

Lin shook her head. "Nope. Never heard of 'em."

"Huh. Figured. There's a lot in Manhattan. How bout... hot dogs? Ever heard of that?"

"Uh-uh." Lin shook her head again. "And what's a 'Manhattan'? Sounds like a nice little song, something I can dance to."

"Well, they do have dancing and songs there, but, um, Manhattan is a place. It's inside one of the states of a country called the *United States of America*."

"It sounds like it's big."

Ammo shrugged. "It really is nothing compared to this world. Lin, have I ever told you how I go about this world and beyond?"

"No," Lin hesitated. "I don't think so."

"I guess we can make time for it. When I was younger, I always had a weird tremor in my hands. Constantly shaking. I could never figure out the source of its problem. And I don't think I ever would have without your father."

A grin spread across his face. "Christ, did he hate me. We fought constantly, and we met up sometimes in some closed-off field just so that we *could* fight. He knew I was troubled... and terribly lonely. We were complete opposites, yet something drew us together. So much that his family took me in." Ammo sighed and brought his hands out of his pockets to rub his forehead.

"S-sorry... I... can't s-seem to remember..."

"Oh. Okay. Tell me when you know what you need to say." She grabbed his hand. "Let's *run*." And so they did.

Leaves cracked under their feet. The air was freezing cold and wet. Both their stomachs burned with a prick of hunger; Lin wanted to slap herself for not eating dinner. She was scared. She was tired. She missed her father. Lin wanted to know what was going on, and where her Kima was.

"Wait," Lin pulled away from Ammo. "Wait a minute. Tell me what's going on."

"*Some things*, Linny. We have to get you as far away as possible." He grabbed her arm and pulled her down to the mushy earth that squished under her.

"Listen to meee!" He started to shake her so violently, she thought her head was about to pop off her neck. "I need you to *listeeeen*! If you are not quiet, the things of Serabi will *kill you*. Okay, Linnasoeta? OKAY? Good, now get up. Now!"

"Fine, Uncle! Just let me go!"

Light shone from the veiled horizon. It was a ghostly, static blue, the air of the Misty Forest coated in a fog, and sprays of wet rain dripped from the branches of the trees. It was a sleepy blue light, the kind one would see if one woke up at six in the morning. Ghosts seemed like they were floating in the midst of the mist. Every step they took, patches of moss would shoot up light sprays of the fallen rain. Everything was blue and sleepy, tranquil...

Pure Sunlight began to trickle down the trees. They had fallen asleep for an hour.

"Come on!" Lin screamed. "We have to go!"

Ammo awoke; he jumped up and started slapping himself in the head. His big emerald eyes weakened and faltered at the sight of the Sun.

"Oh no. Oh no, oh no, oh no." He said that ten more times before regaining his strength. "We have to leave, *now*. I'll run down with you, but then you will have to stay put at the ocean shore."

"*Yessss.*" Lin hissed.

Ammo gave her a sideways glance. "I'm not a snake, Linny. Now come and run!"

They dashed till the Sun shone over their heads. They ran out of the forest and into a prairie, then onto rolling hills and plains until they ran back into a forest again. Lin's mouth was dry; she needed water, and fast. Their lungs burned for air, yet they continued to run. And in a matter of hours, they had made it to shore—Prisoner's Coast.

The crash of the purple ocean waves, the taste of the salty air, and the softness of the sand were all new sensations to Lin. She had never once been by the ocean.

"I am so sorry, but I have to go."

Ammo nodded and was about to be on his way until Lin shouted.

"What's going on?" Lin cried, tears rolling down her face. "Where are you going? You didn't even finish the thing you were going to say!"

Ammo touched her soft, damp cheeks. He leaned over, his eyes making her spark with electricity, and he embraced her. "I will—and if I don't... I'll get the boy to tell you."

And, with that, he ran off.

Lin stood there watching her uncle disappear into the forest. The waves crashed, and her eyes leaked. But she was silent.

She was alone amongst the sand and water. Lin looked around, feeling so helpless, feeling like garbage that had just been dumped. For the first time ever, Lin felt... rejected. The ocean waves drowned out her thoughts.

"Where do I go now?" Lin murmured through tears. "I don't even know where Mom is."

She knelt down in the sand to cry, hoping the waves would wash her to an island far, far away from here.

~

After staying on the beach for so long, Lin knew her uncle would encourage her to escape the sandy prison and search for Kima and Shen—clearly he had made it obvious to *not* stay on the island, right?

Walking alone in a forest was strange. Even though it was Sunny, the forest trees sealed any light from coming in. It was quite dark. Lin would have to run for another two hours before she would reach the end of the Misty Forest.

She stopped, puffing and out of breath. Sweat clogged her pores. "My, oh my. I wish I had a horse." Weak in the gut, she kneeled down to the earthen forest. She tried thinking of what was going on.

First off, the picnic. That was weird because Kima had said something about deaths and that Ismus was the path to the Queen, or something like that. Then, she disappeared. Nowhere to be found.

Then Ammo came. That was *very* weird because Shen had told Lin that he "indulged his limited time in far off places," and thereby did not want to spend time in his company.

Next, her father signed a paper that came out of his brother's *pocket.* Then—now this was the weirdest part of all—her cat-eyed uncle had actually dragged her in the middle of the night into a forest so the Queen would not get her. Lin closed her eyes.

Alright, okay, this is bad, really bad. I will just have to run until I get home. Then I will decide what to do from there.

The main question after that was: **What am I going to do from there?**

Swiftly, she started to run again. Lin kept running, and running, and running, and running, and running, and running, took a breath, and kept running, until she got to the house. By that time, she was drenched, in sweat and tears, and maybe even a little bit of blood from the branches smacking her in the face.

Lin surveyed her giant house and, using her last bits of strength, climbed up the stairs.

As soon as she opened the splintered door, a cool gust of air punched her in the face. She stepped into the house and shouted out, "Daddy! Work People! Mom!" Lin waited for a sound, holding her hands together, holding her breath for a reply. No one answered.

For a minute, she just stood there. Thinking and thinking and worrying and thinking. **What could be going on?**

She wanted to slap herself in the face.

Everything came back to her. Her face hard with despair, she gathered her courage and escaped to Serabi.

~

After that point, Lin stopped the memory. That was enough.

Lin was remembering these times while she sat in the dark alleyway of Serabi. The only reason she thought of them was because the first day of spring was today. Yet Lin had a feeling that there hadn't been a Spring Fair this year, with the shocking appearance of snow and all (she was still terribly confused about that).

It had been over three weeks since the encounter with Nyoka's group, and Lin was devising up a plot so subtle, maybe not even the mice would question.

With the past behind her, and the sorrow never forgotten, only now could she go forward.

The traitor was coming home.

CHAPTER 19

HOT PERSIMMON FOREST

It was scalding, burning, blistering, scorching.

The arid grove was waterless and abrasive, and even the air was on fire. Ismus was beyond parched—she was on the verge of death. Oh how she longed for that cold taste of water!

Everything she touched would incinerate her hand: that was not an exaggeration. Why else would Ismus have a hundred burns on her legs, arms, neck and back? The dirt of the forest floor must have been lava because every time she touched the ground, a hot sizzling sound would ring in her ear, and her foot would catch fire. Her pale skin was speckled with red sores.

Ismus saw things only out of her left eye (her right eye was puffy and shut closed) and she couldn't hear anything. Or maybe, this burning forest just did not have sound.

It was bizarre.

Out of her left eye she saw dead bodies of snakes. They only had their scared head and their long tongues sticking out, and then it just stopped. A pile of ashes lay where the snake's body was incinerated. Would she end up like those snakes, all in which died a painful death? Would she burn to a crisp, and live to feel her skin burn off and pile into black?

She was staggering, the sandals on her feet worn out, her heels pressing against the burning ground. Ismus was not covered in sweat, she was sweat. Every single part of her body was dripping in hot perspiration.

It had been two nights and a day, and there was no sign of Sun anywhere. Yet it seemed like this forest was actually on the giant star. Her heart was slow, and a mile took her a whole day to achieve. When would this burning inferno end?

Ismus came across a tree and started to lick the bark. It scratched her dry tongue, and a fragment of it went into her mouth. Her eyes were closing, her head nodding against the tree.

When she fell to the ash-covered floor, face first, she screamed. The whole left side of her face was sweltering, roasting her flesh. She danced around on what felt like burning coals.

Ismus wrapped herself around the tree, wanting to melt. The tingling, burning feeling of herself going insane. Knowing she was walking in circles from the loss of her mind. Feeling herself fading…

"One day

Two days

Three days

Four days

Five days

Six days

A week

Found herself in the State of Bleak."

Ismus was losing her mind as she sang. She had only been in the forest for a few days, but she was completely bone. She had eaten the crusty singed snakes for food; her tongue was severely blistered. Her breath was dry and hot. Hours slowly passed by.

"Don't lose it Ismus

Keep your nerve

Do not die."

Her brain was quickly melting, and the burns on her skin were growing deeper, paler. She was dead.

She's dead, she's dead, she's dead.

Her eyes blurred and everything turned deep purple.

The next day, she would not awaken.

A cold, dark embrace wrapped around her, silky to the touch.

Shapes of distorted sizes swirled around in the invisible sea of deep black everywhere. She could feel the pressure of the red rhombuses and the sadness of the blue diamonds. The afterglow of the lighted figures blinded her eyes.

She noticed, after a time of observing the colorful profiles against the black nothingness that she was floating.

Slightly elevated from the endless dark below her.

Somewhat a foot above the infinite ground.

A strong sickness in her stomach surging from the fear of the dark and shapes.

A bright light blinded her eyes. The darkness flew away.

"Drink this, now!" A voice urged.

All Ismus saw was a green pitcher of something liquid in her face. When she tried to grab it, the jug slipped from her fingers. A ghost ran through her hand. The thing landed with a *Plop* on the sheets of the... bed?

"Never mind, I'll do it."

The thing opened up her mouth and soaked her with water. Ismus choked on the sweet drink. The block in her chest dissolved from the taste of it. She blinked her eyes a few times to find herself in a small cottage.

There were bouquets of flowers on the windowsill, jars of something, and the smell of some kind of food in the air. That's when the bright light shifted, and a woman came into view.

She was wrinkled and old and terribly ugly. Her gray hair was thin and slipping out of the bun on the top of her head.

"You need food."

Ismus wanted to throw up.

Food sounded good though.

The lady came back with a tomato.

"Tomo?" Ismus mumbled, her eyes closed. "Eat tomo?"

Ismus could hear the lady snort. "Sure. Eat the tomato. *Persimmon*, actually."

She shoved the fruit down her throat. It was hard for Ismus to chew it, and her tongue was still blistered. Ismus groaned from the pain all over her body.

It tasted mushy and bitter, a hybrid mix of an expired mango and an apricot and a peach.

She gagged. The smell of it was completely rancid. But she couldn't even think, so she stood still and did nothing.

"Better?" The old woman barked.

"Nnnni." That was all Ismus was able to say.

CHAPTER 20

IRENE VIOLET SPROUT'S COTTAGE

It took Ismus awhile to come back into grip. It turned out that she was inside of a volcano—a very explosive, dangerous volcano.

"Blazing Fire, it is called," the woman said, the cottage echoing. "Or, as the late Royals deemed it, Great Ismus."

When Ismus had reached her regular state of mind, she saw this woman was not at all ugly and wrinkled; she was young and beautiful. There was a little mole, a small dot on the top of her lip. She had let her short, honey hair down to her shoulders, releasing it from the bun. She had naturally long, dark eyelashes and wide amber eyes.

Irene Violet Sprout was her name, but she preferred to be called Lauren Eve, for whatever odd reason. Lauren had been fixing up a very colorful dinner, the pan sputtering. She had thrown in chopped green, orange and red peppers, onions, garlic, and sliced persimmon.

While pouring a small bit of oil in the pan and sprinkling some ground black pepper she continued, "And, if I assume correctly, you are Little Fire."

Ismus, who was wrapped up in a thick blue blanket, holding a cup of chamomile tea, replied, "Exactly."

She weakly touched her nose and saw the scars of the fire lining her skin.

"Those will heal, I hope you know," Lauren said.

"I know," Ismus replied as she flexed her arm. "They always do."

Lauren smiled. "Then your name is Ismus, Princess of Serabi."

She shook her head, taking a swig of the cool tea. "No longer do I hold that foul name."

"What makes it foul? Does being a princess come with hardship?"

"No. Not exactly. I've just lost my connection with that person."

Lauren slowly nodded. The pan roared on fire, large flames engulfing it.

"Oh, Gods!" she said angrily as she turned the fire down. "That's better," she said as the flames died away.

Flames.

"Anyway," Lauren said, laughing a jingly laugh, stepping back to her cutting board, "Losing a connection, you say?"

Ismus touched her nose again.

"Have you been connected with something else then?"

Ismus considered the thought for a moment. "I have been feeling a bit lost, actually. But..." Ismus remembered something. Something that seemed very distant. When she had actually changed into—

"Amethyst." Ismus whispered loud enough to hear.

Lauren's knife fell onto the floor, cutting up her feet. Hastily, Lauren picked up the knife, wiped the blood off her foot with a towel, and ceased her chopping. She came around the border that separated the kitchen from the small living area to sit down beside Ismus.

"What did you say?"

"I said… Amy's… thighs."

Lauren crossed her arms. "You did not."

Ismus stopped drinking the tea. "Okay, I said *Amethyst*. But, I don't know what that is."

Lauren gave her a dangerous look. "You definitely have been connected to something. A very treacherous something." Her dark brown eyes poured into her soul.

Ismus flashed her watery lilac ones from place to place.

"… Tell me… About it." She cooed, pushing her apricot hair out of her eyes.

"Well, not much to tell." Ismus sniffed as she lied. She took another gulp of her tea before placing it on a saucer resting atop a desk. "A few dreams that turned into a nightmare, a small… body transformation? And a minor 'Underworld' encounter that I can ensure you was false…"

Lauren's mouth was fixed in a tight line. "Body transformation and the Underworld?" She asked in a high voice. "What the…?"

Just then the pan went back up in flames, roaring.

"Damn it," Lauren groaned under her breath as she got up. "Excuse my language, princess—or, not princess. This dang metal is blowing a fuse with all that lava-magma nonsense up there."

Ismus chortled. "It's really a weird thing for a cottage to actually be built into the side of a volcano, I mean, how is that even possible?" Ismus tried. She blindly grabbed for her tea again, forgetting it was empty.

"Hmm, yes it is. But isn't an Underworld encounter just as

so?" Lauren's back was facing her as she stirred the contents in the pan. "Dinner will be ready soon. Until then, go upstairs, take a bath. Relax. You'll need it."

"Sure. That sounds nice." Ismus threw the blanket off her and started for the steps.

"Holler if you need anything," Lauren called across her shoulder.

"Uh," Ismus said stupidly. "Where are the stairs?"

"What? Oh, my bad, Ismus! I completely forgot." She came over where Ismus stood and directed her toward a bright hallway. She pulled down a fine white cord and black metal steps shot down like a bullet. They were zigzagging, leading high into a small loft where a soft black couch and a tiny coffee table lay.

"Go ahead," Lauren smiled, sauntering back to the kitchen.

Ismus grabbed a hold of the shaky metal rod and climbed, one foot after the other. The first ten steps were fine—normal steps— until she got to the second flight. There she would have to completely flip her body and use her arm strength to climb up those ten. If she fell, she would slam hard into the earthy cottage floor, rolling right onto her neck and back. Maybe even hit against the side of a wall.

Sweat rolled from her neck; all that time in the forest had drained her of most of her physical capabilities. She swung her body around the banister, her stomach flip-flopping, now standing in the large, bright loft.

Success.

Ismus walked down a short corridor to try and find a closet. She observed the walls, which were made of stone and the volcano's outside. The floor upstairs was carpeted, but downstairs it was earth. She wondered why that would be. As she walked down the hall with the towels, a small figure caught her eye.

Since there were no doors in the cottage, Ismus could see a

215

small pink bed, something made from thick satin bed sheets. And on the bed was a pretty white doll. Ismus walked over to the room, stepping into it. She put the towel down on a chair. Her eyes narrowed.

Upon closer inspection, she realized the doll was constructed of only tissues.

She stepped further inside the room, curious to see what else lay inside. She turned to face the barren walls; she pulled open the small closet to reveal nothing but dust; she opened the drawers of a small dresser to find a few living shrimps.

Ismus huffed.

She turned away from the room (remembering to get the towels back from the chair) and walked into the hall.

Ismus walked a bit further down the hall, took a sharp cut, and stepped into the bathroom.

A refreshing and odd thing it would be to bathe. It had been over three months since she had taken such a belated cleansing. In fact, it had been so long that Ismus had forgotten the feeling of any state other than grime and perspiration.

A container of bath cookies lolled on the rim of the bathtub, along with a few bottles of shampoo. Ismus turned on the water, jumping when she saw a thick red liquid pouring out from the faucet.

"Lava!" she shrieked. For thirty more seconds the magma continued to run out of the faucet, until lukewarm water came cascading out. She picked up the bath cookie and experimentally dropped one in the water, remembering to plug the drain. She heard the thing fizz in the water, which instantly made the bathroom smell like brown sugar and chocolate chips. She picked up another cookie and plopped it in, then drizzled a bit of soap into the large tub. In five minutes, the bath was full of warm water and was piled with soapy bubbles.

She eased into the tub, foot first, and soaked for a very, very long time.

~

"Oh, you're out," Lauren said in surprise as Ismus came down the stairs, "I wondered how long you would be up there. You took so long, the food nearly spoiled."

Ismus smiled, her cheeks awkwardly sticking out from grinning. She was wrapped up in a giant green leaf of a dress, and it seemed very weird to have so much air running through the exposed parts. Her red hair was dripping water all over the reddish-brownish earthen floor, making small mud puddles.

"It was very relaxing," was all she managed to say as she swayed a bit too freely in the dress. "Is dinner ready yet?" Ismus tried to stop herself when she said it, which made her look all the more greedy.

Lauren did not mind. "Hungry, aren't we?" She teased.

"Starving," Ismus said miserably.

"I would imagine. You were in that forest for days. That heat is *obliterating* I tell you. Well, to your luck, dinner is served." She got up from the couch in the living room and escorted Ismus to the dining room.

It was a small, circular chamber with more flower vases on the windowsill and cherries tucked under a small mint leaf in a basket. Three live shrimps stirred in a large box on the table. A container of a deep red sauce lay next to them. Other than that, Ismus saw no food.

"Where...?" Ismus asked herself.

Lauren tittered, holding her stomach. "Aha! I left it on the counter." She walked back through the archway to get to the other room; Ismus could hear plates clashing. She licked her lips and swung her legs back and forth.

Lauren brought back the stuff, a golden, flaky crust baked over the contents she had chopped earlier. It was still steaming hot in the dishpan.

"Dig through the pile of plates and get the green one. Good. Now the blue—no! The shiny one! Good, good." She put a generous portion of food on the two plates, her dark eyes shining at the squirming shrimp in the box.

"There is much to discuss, Ismus. But for now—food!"

Lauren took the shiny blue plate to the kitchen and the shrimps, and she walked off.

Grabbing to the right of her napkin, Ismus groped for a utensil. Her fingers found a warm, itchy object, and she swiftly picked it up, holding it near her plate.

Ismus furrowed her eyebrows. What was this instrument she held in her hand? It was nothing like a fork or a spoon or a knife… instead it was two tiny wooden boards that were hinged together at the ends… Why, if she tried eating with this, where would she be in ten years?

Still eating, of course.

Instead of going to the fancy *eat-with-something-besides-your-hands* approach, she instead resulted in doing the opposite. Why, if the maids ever saw her doing this kind of "vulgarity" she would've had ten scoldings in a heartbeat!

Ismus used her palms as a knife to slice through the crust and in the middle, a vibrant rainbow of foods revealed itself. The sight was indeed very pleasing to the eye (especially after living at the camp for so long). She gathered up a big handful of food and shoved it in her mouth.

Oh, Gods, how great it felt to have something with flavor again! Those spices of the black pepper and oil, and the melody of the peppers, garlic, and that… weird tomato that tasted like apricots and mangoes… oh, how they all just combined into a symphony. That buttery, flaky crust on top just sealed the whole deal. What a way to start off a meal!

Ismus knew this was only just the beginning. She could already smell something sugary baking in the air, and the burning of something on the stovetop.

Lauren pouted like a child, and pretended to cry. She threw her body around and moaned, *"I DON'T WANNA YELL!"*

Ismus tried her best not to smile, her cheeks exploding with the symphony of food, of bliss. She could get used to this kind of feeling…

~

Apparently, Lauren had been making cookies, but the recipe failed, due to the stove's inconvenience. Instead, she made peanut butter (peanut butter meaning *persimmon* butter, of course) milkshakes.

The land outside had shadowed and darkened once Ismus had finished dinner, nothing seen to the eye but the white outline of the moon shining on the trees. The cool burbling of a lone bird in the heat of the forest made Ismus cringe. Ismus was so glad she was in here, in the cozy, perfectly heated cottage, instead of that burning abyss.

Ismus slurped her milkshake down. "You bake so well. I never have the patience for it, really," she confessed.

"Neither do I. But, you know, I have to eat somehow. Not like I can go out there for anything," she gestured toward the window outside. She fell silent to take a sip of her milkshake. A small ticking of the blocktimer.

Tick, Tock.

Ismus shuddered.

The raid.

Ismus inhaled, starting to confess her treacherous abandonment of the camp.

"I—,"

"—Patience is something very special. However, I have never had it. There are some virtues one cannot learn." Lauren stated a bit sadly, which was kind of odd of her to do (even if Ismus hadn't known her for very long). Ismus tucked away her confession for later and listened to whatever Lauren was saying.

"Many people die for it every day…The Cycle of Sin. It is a connection, all seven of them." Lauren absentmindedly twirled her short apricot hair around. It made Ismus feel worse because it reminded her of Janier.

"I see. If one is Greedy, they feed upon Lust, a craving that fulfills their greed." Ismus huffed at her own remark, smiling with squeezed brows. "Lust can turn you into someone purposeless, something lazy and worthless. Being lazy leads to Sloth."

She laughed again, thinking about where she was getting all this. "Sloth could lead to self-loving, assured by only you. Maybe fierce Pride. Uncontained Pride… can drive you to madness.

"Wrath can lead to destruction, fire, and then Envy," Ismus was thinking heavily. "Forgetting all you ever loved and needed, living in Gluttony. And Gluttony… is just a form of Greed."

Ismus frowned, coming to a conclusion. "A cycle. Never ending. Leading to a terrible fate…"

Lauren nodded slowly. "It seems as if you have only thought of this just now. Were you not informed about this at the castle? Basic knowledge, really."

"If they taught us about… *squirrels* it would be biased. They only tell us so much, and only a sliver of the truth. It makes me feel so dumb, Irene Sprout—I mean Lauren.

"I know, I know. Your *Lust* for knowledge makes me

question if you are the right girl."

"What do you mean?"

Lauren avoided the question. "When was your birthday?"

"Well, it was weeks ago. Too far away to tell."

Lauren slanted her eyes. "That may not be entirely true, Ismus. Time goes by much slower here. A day beyond the Hot Persimmon Forest can feel like a week. Your birthday may still even be today. What time was it when you came to the forest?"

Ismus thought, shuffling in the blanket. "It was night when I left, twelve o'block, nearly. When the place I was staying at was attacked, I had to leave." **This isn't the best time to say I left without saving anyone** Ismus thought to herself.

"And... Someone tried to capture me. That's when the whole... Monster transformation happened, and ever since then I've felt like a white, cracked shell."

"Interesting. You left during the night, and stayed for about how long in the Forest?"

"I told you; maybe a week or two?"

Lauren thought too, sipping at her milkshake for the first time in a few minutes. "If it was one week you stayed here, then today is still your birthday. If you stayed in the forest for two weeks, today would be the day after your birthday... and if you left during the deep night, right before first morning, then it almost assures today is your birthday. And in that case I say to you: Happy Birthday."

Ismus huffed. "Gee, thanks. Still my birthday." She sighed. "I'm sixteen today."

Lauren smiled. "Then your birthday falls on the first day of spring."

221

Ismus returned the smile. "Exactly."

"You may not get the best sleep of your life tonight."

"Because of the doll?"

"Doll?"

"The tissue doll…" Ismus said. "…The one in the empty room upstairs…"

Lauren shook her head and smirked. "I don't own any dolls of that sort." She got up from the couch to walk to the kitchen. "Maybe you were just dreaming? Like daydreaming or something?"

Wrecking her brain for an answer, she placed her cup down and said, "Well, what were you going to say before I interrupted you?"

"I don't know," Lauren said as the loud sink muted her voice. "Don't remember, now that you've got me worried about some haunted doll."

Ismus waited until she turned the sink off to explain.

"You were saying how I was not going to sleep well tonight, or something."

"Oh, right. I forgot." She laughed.

Lauren fished through the cabinets, coming back with a waxy, white candle and three matches. She shut all the other lights off, which left them in deep darkness.

"Now you can tell." Lauren smiled as she sat back down on the couch, her smile silhouetted in the light of the candle.

"Where do I start?"

"From the beginning, of course."

Ismus inhaled, then slowly exhaled.

"Am I a curse, Lauren?"

"Depending on what you will say to me, you may very well be... Now, if you don't mind."

"Fine. It all started when I crossed over the border. I was just doing a little *frolicking* with my friend, then we had to go. Then I came back to the castle after a quick trip to this old hut, and everything was fine. I had a couple memories in my dreams—"

"Maybe not the *beginning* beginning?" Her face was squinted up in an unsure smile, obviously not wanting to interrupt.

"Okay, after my parents died, I went exploring. Oh, I had this nightmare *before* I even went into Rodem, something similar to the Underworld thing. Anyway, so I was exploring, and this cobblestone in the wall pressed in, and... well, I was in some dark chamber. And there was this old man who said it was the Underworld, and he kept saying Eithendere, over and over again..."

Judging by the look on Lauren's confused face, Ismus could assume that she was trying so hard to believe her. Instead, she took her hand.

"I have to show you something. You are a bit confused, which is confusing me." She led her through the dim halls and rooms, the candle burning black shadows on the walls. She had a tight grip on her hand so she would not lose her in the darkness: as if she was a child.

Suddenly, Lauren came to an abrupt stop, which made Ismus bump into her back.

"Sorry! So, so sorry," Ismus murmured, rubbing her arms as she watched Lauren mess with a metal lock. She placed the candle on the desk, its ghostly white manner curling into the air. Ismus could faintly make out a closed wooden box, secured with a black latch. She flipped the latch off the box and turned the dial with a series of numbers. It clicked open and the lid threw itself up, exposing its contents.

Lauren ran her finger through the inlaid gold line running from deep within the box. She pulled out a wrinkled, pale yellow scroll and smoothed the creases around the edges.

"This is the Foresight of the Four Demons," Lauren said. "This will answer everything."

"Where'd you get this?" Ismus whispered. "Why do *you* have this?"

"Read it."

And Ismus did. She scanned the page:

"... *The path will shine from the Light of Infinion on, through oceans and swamps until reaching the golden city of Jainu, a place of magic and beauty... and untold evils.*"

"*Five rulers will live above a fiery inferno, the male/female child of the fifth king being forged from fire and hell itself.*"

"*Golden keys of the fire... hidden.*"

"*The curse... will die before the first day of spring... as the brooding red Sun rises above the veiled mountains.*"

"*The curse will die.*"

"This will answer everything," the woman named Lauren whispered again, holding Ismus's hand. "Do you wish to see your fate?"

Ismus's worried eyes lingered in the dark, nervously touching the gold inlaid.

The curse will die.

"Not sure," Ismus said, shaking her head. "What will I see?"

Irene Violet Sprout gave her a powerful look, gripping the page with her bony fingers.

"Your transformation," she said as she turned the scroll the other way on the small desk.

Ismus's stomach lurched and stirred as she watched the figure in the drawing.

It was moving, for some reason. The image was drawn in a bloody red ink, sometimes brushes of black under it. A tall, beautiful creature it was, but inhuman. It was a faceless being, equipped with demonic wings and a body sculpted in such a form that it teetered on the edge of proportionally unattainable and Godlike.

It was trapped in a hastily drawn sphere, the sphere spinning around and around. The thing was struggling and squirming to be released from the chains that fastened her to the ground. The circle kept spinning and spinning around her, until she faltered weakly to the yellow, wrinkled floor.

Suddenly, a wall of fire exploded out from where a mouth should have been, breaking the circle, setting her own self on fire. The thing grew ginormous, now sporting a massive spiked chain in her right hand and whipping it violently about her. The drawing returned to its original state and repeated itself, endlessly.

"What do you think that is, Ismus?"

Ismus did not know what to say. Was this the beast people claimed was inside her?

"That was a monster."

Lauren shook her head. "No, a *demon*. That was Amethyst. She is the Goddess of all the demons, the most powerful, most destructive of them all.

"She smells of the first tulips of spring, but dying and dead, and once had the innocence of a child. Her aura feels powerful, as if an army of men were crowding around you. But her *power* is weakening by the years. Once she is released, doom will be set upon the entirety of Dark Earth. Even the slightest bit of exposure of *any* demon to the mortal world can construct a planet of nothingness. As

225

she stays in…" Lauren trailed off, trying to find the right word. "*A host's* body for too long, a great number of things can happen. Bad things.

"Tell me, Ismus, has anything bad ever happened to you?"

There was silence as Ismus thought.

The answer was very clear.

CHAPTER 21
BRUTUS'S REGRET

C ome on, we have to go!" Gwenda was on pins and needles to get down to see Ismus, and she was tugging on Brutus's arm much too hard. It was early in the afternoon, the day before the raid.

"Why are you so jumpy? She ain't going anywhere!" He yanked from her grasp. "Look, Gwenda, I know coming here in the first place was somehow my fault. If I was able to fight those attackers—"

"No, no, no. That's not why you couldn't rule." She plopped down on her bed and shuddered with fear. "Brutus?"

"Hmm?"

"Serabi was bound to be taken from us. A Grudalean official—"

"You talked to an official without me knowing?"

"Yes, who cares? Anyway, he said there was few people left because of... well, our sister. And he..."

"He what?"

Gwenda looked into his eyes. "He warned me about the attacks. I was so in shock I couldn't say anything. And look where that got us."

Her face fell. "Don't you see? It's my fault. This entire thing... it's *my* fault."

Brutus lacked a reply, and instead he ran one of his blocky fingers through her soft blond hair. He stared into her teary, green eyes. Her skin was so fair, she was skinny—she was perfect. The two looked nothing alike.

But there were tired bags under her eyes. She looked like she had spent a lot of the night crying herself to sleep. Her fair skin was turning blotchy. She wasn't getting any solid nutrition. She was so pretty, but aging too quickly for a teenager.

"No," he growled. "It's *Ismus's* fault. All of this is *her* fault." His breath quickened.

"*I should have killed her the day I first saw her.*"

This made Gwenda snap.

"Monster!" She screamed, rising to her feet. "You complete, heartless monster! Our sister is *cursed.* Do you think what she is— what she's done is something in *her* control?

Brutus shook his head and said, "I just don't get it. How can Ismus be a curse? How can a person *curse* someone? How does that kind of bullshit work?"

"It's beyond my brain." She took a long glance at the window, turning back with eyes slightly gleaming like two sad pools.

"But we have to keep our heads Brutus, or Ismus will lose hers."

Gwenda pulled her flaxen hair back into a ponytail and headed for her purple coat with the buttons. As she put her right arm through the sleeve and opened up the door, she said to Brutus, "I don't really understand it myself. But I'm heading out to find her. Join me when you want to." And she slammed the door shut behind her.

Brutus, alone and in Gwenda's semi-dusty room, trudged over to the bed and laid in the same spot Gwenda was in; it was cold. He sat up straight and scooted back further on the bed to rest his head on one of the pillows. To his surprise, his head fell through the pillow, only to see it was just one burgundy sham. **Humph. Gwenda sleeps on shams?** He threw the little cloth off the bed and lay on the naked sheets. They were sticky—probably hadn't been watched for decades.

Brutus had been the type of boy who ripped slugs apart and squashed frogs to see their insides gush onto the pavement. He was not opposed to violence and took any chance he could to get into trouble. But he was too old for these thoughts about his youngest sister—he was almost twenty.

Some of his life he had been quite sweet. Loving, sensitive, nice. Until Ismus came along, he truly had no reason to be so enraged. Why… why did she change *everything?*

Brutus could not figure it out. He and Gwenda—they once had been bread and butter, peanut butter and jelly; nothing could separate the two. Gwenda was like the bun on the bottom of a burger; without her, he would fall apart.

Then a child named Ismus threw herself in between them and had failed to dislodge.

Ever since she had been born, he had threatened her. Attempted countless times to kill, assault, damage, or bring her any kind of pain. His sole purpose in life was to drive her insane, past the brink of insanity.

So she would kill herself.

No, he denied. **That's not why… I would never do that.**

Tears formed in his eyes. He rubbed them viciously.

I would *never* do that. I would never make her want to *die.*

"Stop crying," Gwenda sighed as she opened her room door, clutching a bleeding wound on her forehead.

"And get off my bed."

229

~

Brutus had returned to his room—after Gwenda had told him she had fallen out of the moving shaft and wanted to be alone—to sit at his desk and think for three hours.

He rarely thought. There was little to think about. He did not like what this conclusion made him do.

Brutus did not like *himself.*

He regretted the way he had treated her. He despised himself for all the things he had said. He wished that someone had been there to put him in his place, to stop him.

To tell *him* to die.

"I'm sorry, Ismus."

Suddenly, the alarms for food screamed into his ears. He ignored the dinner alarm to sit longer in pensive silence, fantasizing about how it would feel to him if someone had done all the things he had done to his youngest sister.

CHAPTER 22

JERK AND SERAPH UNITE TO FIND THE DEMON: NO LUCK

Why didn't you get her?"

"What? How the hell was I supposed to get her?"

"Urgh, Idiot! Brutus, I don't know where she went. She fled!"

"Wouldn't you? If no one was on your side?"

"What do you mean?"

"The hell do you think I mean? You're never there for her!"

"Oh, and you're just Mr. Helpful! You're the jerk that drove her away from here. The dang hybrids would have been a better piece of something than you!"

"Yeah, whatever. It's the monsters that drove her away, Gwenda. She just needed to save her own skin. All I'm saying is that she didn't even think about us or come back to find us because she doesn't *like* us."

"That's illogical." She shook her head. "She was, maybe, just too scared, that's all." Gwenda didn't even look the slightest bit believable.

"Sure. Why didn't you tell her before? When you knew this was going to happen?"

Gwenda started to raise her voice to a yell before stopping to look down at the snow beneath her feet. "I didn't think she would be ready." Her eyes shut with pain. "I guess... in my heart I... I never thought it was true."

She gritted her teeth. "But I was wrong. And there's only one thing we can do. Find Ismus."

"She could be miles from here, Gwenda." Brutus tensed. "How could we possibly find her?"

Gwenda wiped off a tear. "We do what she did—run."

They ran for weeks but could not find her.

CHAPTER 23
PURPOSELESS

Ismus had lost purpose. It was all too powerful for her. Ismus was much too weak from it all. Her heart pumped sporadically. The veins in her hands and legs swelled and cramped, her body going numb each time she tried to move it.

It was as if for one moment she was dying.

CHAPTER 24

HELP ME... PLEASE.

A blanket of black—as dark as the night—trapped her. She floated in an endless abyss. She could feel all the heat and pressure from the core of the earth squeeze her heart, break her down, weather her like stone, erode her away—destroy her. What was this? Was the thing that was hurting her most... *herself?*

She was trapped. There was no way out of the nothingness. It was the numb feeling, hard and cold to escape, sluggish and... sad. This dagger-like pain. This blade—this blade weld by a beautiful figure of brown and black—puncturing her heart. All Ismus knew was pain.

Sorrow.

Death.

Despair.

Torture.

Would there ever be an end? Would days of happiness ever come her way? Was her life more than just a string of misfortune, a parable of misery's pleasure? Was there something utterly demonic inside of her, killing all life in her path?

Yes. She could feel it. She could feel that power trying to escape from her. Way deep, deep, deep down into her core, the very eye of her soul, she could feel the power.

As strong as the gnawing and gnashing of a hurricane.

More terrible than the fierce blowing of a gray tornado.

More frightening than a battlefield overflowing with dead soldiers.

Ismus could feel that power pounding in her ribs as she floated in the endless black. Amethyst... it all made sense. Hadn't it always? Coming of age? No, coming of *power*. The thought was somewhat delicious. The Princess of Serabi versus the Goddess of the Demons? It was hilariously unequaled.

Wait...no! She said to herself. **I don't want that! I don't want to be a monster! I do not want to bring fear, put the land out of balance, kill myself! NO!**

What was happening—

I DON'T WANT TO LIVE LIKE THIS ANYMORE! SOMEONE HELP, PLEASE! I'M ALONE, I'M SCARED, HELP ME, PLEASE, ANYONE—

The demon screamed, startling the empty, black night. Seconds later, Lauren exploded into the room.

Lauren shrieked, lighting the darkness with a candle.

"Ismus!"

But Ismus was gone.

Gasping, Lauren took one look at her, one look at her face, and slowly approached her.

Still screaming, the demon—faceless, glowing—shook the house with a shrill, *"MORTAL! FOUL VEXATION!"*

Covered in silver skin, eyes blood-red, jet-black hair that coiled around the room, head banging against the ten-foot tall ceiling—

The demon in the bed was still screaming.

And she would never stop.

CHAPTER 25
GUARDED

H ow the 'ell are we supposed to watch this place when it's snowin' a mile a minute!"

"Get off yer lazy butt, ya shiftless no-gooder, and march this place like the rest of us. Get up now!"

The Creek of Hazalen was infested with men and women. They were armed with weapons and brawny arms. There was no way for Linnasoeta to pass.

There she was high in the treetops, her eyes aligned with the small black blurbs in which were her people. What used to be *her* people.

They waddled around the filthy whiteness. If she attacked now, they all would be off guard. But a dozen miffed and tired men against one twiggy, emaciated traitor?

After she ran from Rodem, which was months ago, her father must have ordered guards to watch out for anyone or anything that tried to cross the border. Linnasoeta hoped her father was okay. She had hurt him so much.

So, now what? Lin thought impatiently. **I can't just decay in the alleyways of Serabi my whole life. This is pointless!**

Her stomach clenched in the height of the trees. What was she supposed to do now? It turned over even more.

The sight of someone pointing at the trees made her heart beat faster.

"What the 'ell? Bloke in the trees! CUT THE VINE, CUT THE VINE!" The man yelled in a way so powerful the world echoed it. Lin knew what she had to do.

With her stolen ropes, she wrapped it around the thorny, green vine. She tried her best to block out the ballistic jeering from the panicking guards below. It was hard to do something under pressure, however, and she could feel her stomach doing backflips.

"What are you doing?! I told you to get off your lazy bum minutes ago! Get the ax, cut the vine! SOMEONE COVER UP THIS BLOKE'S JOB AND GET A STUPID AX!"

Lin inhaled sharply. Her grip was tightening on the rope. Before she did anything, the intensity level of her mission got the best of her, and she clutched her throat and vomited. The green and pink garbage was a sight startling enough to scare the brawny guards.

"The thing's pukin' up a storm! Cut the freakin' green thing already! It's distracted—"

"—and sick!"

With the weight already out of her stomach, Lin felt light and empty. Linnasoeta Choi was ready to fly. She clenched the white piece of thick rope and pushed off the tree.

Her stomach dropped half a second after she descended.

The world blurred around her. She screamed. She heard nothing. The frothiness that surrounded her sped by at an unbelievably fast pace. Was she traveling at the speed of light? She could not tell. Her mind was blank as she soared over the Thangos Trench. Would she make it? She hoped so.

That one glorious moment of flight came to an abrupt stop.

One of the guards had been hacking on the other side of the vine.

She saw it droop and uncoil from the tree. It twisted at the ends, flopped around, turned like a worm… Linnasoeta could feel the other end of it give, loosen a bit. Her stomach fell to her feet.

To her horror, she saw the vine depress only a hair from the ledge until it fell into the ocean-sized cave.

And in less than a few seconds later, with a few victorious cackles from the Workclan below, Lin began to plummet.

She felt every ligament and organ in her body jump from her skin until all she saw was pure darkness.

CHAPTER 26

LIN'S CLOSE MEETING WITH DEATH

It was oil.

Lin froze at first. Then sheer terror waved over her. Drowning—Drowning! She panicked, thrashing in the burning currents of black thickness. She opened her mouth to spit out the oil, yet more poured into her throat. She saw nothing, not even the jostling of her own hand in front of her. Her eyes remained slits looking into the moving black around her. She coughed, more spilling into her lungs.

There was the sound of millions of gallons of black petroleum smashing against the side of a cave. Lin heard nothing, however, but her own terrified and screaming voice inside her head. She kept bobbing her head back under the poison: any minute, and she would die. The smell of the oil was nothing compared to the metallic taste of it.

Her heart was slowing. It was saying, "The time has come, Linnasoeta Choi, to join your mother."

But her lungs were screaming, "Swim! Find shore! Your body is half-filled with oil!"

And her mouth was screaming, "You cannot take much more of this. Listen to your lungs. Don't fill them with this slick, disgusting poison."

But it was too late.

The thickness of the oil coated her, sticking and freezing her into one position. She screamed and screeched for her life; her heart slowed down terribly. Her body depressed and buckled.

Mom... I'm sorry for every—

At that moment, her body straightened, her stomach elevating. Linnasoeta suddenly realized she still had a forgotten grip on the ropes. Her eyes felt heavy from the oil, but even her half-open eyelids spotted the brightening light.

As a hurricane formed in her stomach, she felt like stone. She ascended too rapidly, so rapidly that her stomach could not catch up with the blazing speed.

As Lin sensed the rope in her hand come back into her grasp, she saw the gray world come back into view.

CHAPTER 27
THE IMAGE...

Lin felt sick. She lingered over the trench and smiled.

The guards sucked in their breath as they saw the vine fastened around both trees, as if they had never cut it down. Silence fell after.

"CUT IT DOWN!" Yet there was no use.

Linnasoeta hollered as she flew down the vine. She felt sick all over; she vomited several times.

She was gaining on them, increasing with speed as she descended, the cold, freezing winds blowing against her cheeks and chest. She was closer, so much closer. The Workclan tried cutting it down, but then a horrified look was cast upon their faces.

"IT'S LINNASOETA CHOI!" They all were shrieking at the top of their lungs.

"WHAT?!"

Yes! It was Linnasoeta Choi, and she was, sick and tired and weak and cold, returning back to her village.

To save her father.

And to chuck Nyoka down the Thangos Trench.

Lin's feet touched the ground: she had made it. All the men and women gathered around her. "It is not safe here anymore, Linnasoeta Choi. You must not go to your father. He is ill."

Linnasoeta still felt a bit wobbly, and her legs felt numb. "Considering you almost killed me, I will do as I say and do as I want. Now move. I have to save my father."

"She will need help," a woman added in, "send three men down with her—!"

"—No! I can do this on my own. This is my fight. This is my father. STAY AND KEEP WATCH! We don't need any more *visitors*." She said the word while gritting her teeth.

Someone touched her shoulder, and she looked back to see a brawny man with wide-set eyes and an unkempt beard look down at her. "You are a traitor to these lands, Choi. Do not find comfort here. Remember that." And he walked away.

Lin heard his words ring in her ears as she dashed for the Wither House.

~

Lin felt her face burn. Her home was a ruin. The pillars that had held the building were crushed and crumbled and piled up into a great mass. The walls of the House were ragged and filled with holes—she could see the inside of the House, clear as daylight. The deck had been destroyed and the bushes ripped clean from their roots. The ceiling and chimney were torn off. Snow fell heavily from the sky and into her home.

It was a depressing sight, to see the House she had lived in her entire life in pieces.

But there was still a door, and the whole hallway was still there, so Linnasoeta halted her tears, mustering up any courage to destroy Nyoka and find her poor father.

She opened the door, the hinges squeaking, and put one foot inside. Then the other. She was inside her wretched, broken-down house, the nice sofa her mother had always kept clean...

Enough. It was always enough.

She shut the door behind her where it swayed in place for a while. There was no turning back. She was freezing in fear, and it was frighteningly quiet. The hallways were plastered with shadows and darkness, and the longer she looked, the darker it became. Her home was now something of a nightmare.

"Dad?" she whispered, almost too scared to talk. Nothing: the place was empty.

For minutes, there was only her own fearful footsteps tapping against the splintered wood, and her heart was ready to explode out of her chest if anything popped out at her. She kept her mind blank as she walked along. She was next to the kitchen.

Creak.

Lin dug her fingers into her neck. She looked behind herself to see nothing. Nothing but a shadow that lay unclaimed by no one, a shadow that was not her own. Her heart sped up.

Her mouth stretched in horror. It took everything for her not to turn back, her stomach sick with fear.

She tapped up the stairs to her bedroom, trying not to look past her shoulders.

Creak.

Lin held her breath. **Keep going. Find Dad.**

It brought tears to her eyes to know the father who may not have always been there for her was possibly dying somewhere in an old closet. The old man that had signed a deed long ago to keep her safe. Lin knew she would find him.

Linnasoeta's breath hitched to hear footsteps. She whipped her head around her shoulders to see nothing; nothing but the splintered door downstairs.

Her eyes watered: she didn't want to do it anymore. But she knew she could not leave, she was forced under her own will to not leave until every part of the house was searched. She had to do it, even though she knew something—or someone—was here.

The metal of her door felt wet against her hand, and when she looked down…

"Aagh!" Lin cried, noticing for the first time the red dripping down her spotted door onto the ground. The doorknob was soaked in glistening crimson; Lin was almost too terrified to enter. She sealed her eyes tight, and opened up the door. She stepped into her room, eyes still shut. Then she opened them. Her nose quivered at the smell before her eyes saw the image.

For a moment, she was numb, completely stunned and taken back. Then her mind had come into full understanding as she processed the image she saw.

She screamed. Loud and shrill. She lost her breath from the sight, she couldn't breathe. Her head tossed and she became dizzy. Mouthfuls of screaming obscenity exploded from her mouth.

She tumbled to the floor, shrieking. She could hear nothing escape from her mouth: just the static whirr of internal suffering. The image panged in her head. Her heart was knocking wildly against her chest. She was howling, crying, tears of terror. She was clawing her face with her nails. Her breath was lost. The image was glued to her head. Her vision pounced around from place to place, corner to corner, and over the image on the wall. She screamed, her lungs collapsing, but she could not stop screaming. Her father was—he was…Dead… Pinned…Bloodied…

The tears were exploding down her face, she was throwing herself against the floor, madly screaming, shrieking, crying for death. Crying out of complete and total terror. She was going to die, she was going to kill herself for this—

She heard laughter— and clapping—which made her fall dead silent.

Clap. Clap. Clap.

"Well done," a horrible, disgusting, evil voice sneered, "You found your father."

Lin stopped, her heart stopped, her breath stopped.

Nyoka.

CHAPTER 28
TOO LATE

I warned your poor, stupid, pathetic father that you were trouble. That he should have let you go and move on. Yet he did not listen. He ordered troops to find you, he so determined to find you, but you were long gone. Lost in the ice of Serabi. So, I asked myself, why the old man? What did he ever do for me?"

He walked over to the image on the wall and squeezed Shen's blood-stained cheeks.

"Why should I pledge my life to someone lesser than my own? He was weak. Weak and tired without his Kima. And his poor, stupid, pathetic daughter was possibly dying somewhere in the middle of Serabi... Linny, dear, he was practically *begging* for death. He could not stand this kind of pressure against his shoulders. The old man wanted it; so I gave it to him. In the prettiest fashion, so you could be amazed.

"Do you not like how the blood and spilling guts add some color to these old white walls, scuffed from failure? I especially like the little wording, the last message I wrote to you about him. These planks hold his little body up quite nicely. A bit of dark humor with his head being the 'O' in 'I *Love* You,' don't you think?" He turned toward Lin and gave her some sort of leer. Then he frowned when he saw no appreciation in her trembling face.

"But in any case, he's free of all his despair and worries.

"This brings me to my next point," he circled the room, "about this world. This so called 'Dark Earth.' We live on a rotating hunk of insufferable garbage. The world does not exist for us. We have no true purpose in even stepping on these lands, every single day, in the tired fashion that we do. The Sun knows nothing of us—not even our names—but we know *everything* of it. Wouldn't life be so much better if the Sun knew our name, Linny?

"And so I asked myself again, is there more? More of us out there, somewhere? I researched and studied and... well, there *are* more out there. Not only out there, but down *here*. There are creatures and beings so powerful they make our armies look like sharpened toys."

Lin coughed. Her throat was tight.

"You didn't free my father from anything. You're the monster." Her eyes welled with wrathful, infuriated tears, her blood boiling hot, the heat and anger from her blood burning her cheeks, teeth gritting, eyes flashing, wide, enraged, hair thrashing back and forth as she threw her head in madness.

"YOU SHOULD BE THE ONE TO DIE!" Linnasoeta screamed as loud as she could before Nyoka struck her in the back.

"Shut up and listen. Like I was saying—"

"GO TO HELL!" Lin threw herself at Nyoka's face, her hair surging like an opening fan and dug her fingers into his eyes. He yelped from the slice of her nails, and he unleashed a scream that shook the entire house. He threw her off and picked her up by the legs, punching her hard in the face as she dangled by his waist. She felt the crunch of his knuckles against her bones, a soaring pain in her nose. Blood dripped into Lin's eyes, stunned with darkness, nose spilling with red. Lin cried, but she swiveled up his back and sunk her teeth into his neck. Nyoka dropped her to the floor with a *CRASH*, falling to the floor himself, giving off several yelps in pain.

While he was screaming, Lin made a desperate run for the stairs. Her legs felt like someone was jabbing her with a knife— stabbing, sharp pains shooting from her knees—and her vision made the staircase split in seven. But she threw herself down the darkening stairs—actually falling—and scrambled to her feet and crashed downstairs.

"Linny," Nyoka was calling from upstairs in the bedroom. *"It's your daddy. I've got a surprise for you…"*

Lin felt a hand clench her shoulders, and she was flying across the room, smashing against the wall. She fell limp. She cried so angrily, so mad that she tried staggering up, and when she turned around to see Nyoka, she saw Shibun instead, his left eye swollen and puffy.

"Run!" he was whimpering as he clutched the leaking gash in his stomach. "Go!"

Nyoka, like a flash of black lightning, darted into the room, took Shibun by the head, and struck it down several times onto the kitchen counter. Lin could not hear the bone-crushing smack of his head, but she instead saw the blood dripping down Shibun's nose and onto the floor.

Shibun's eyes rolled into the back of his head, and he fell limp to the floor.

Lin was screaming *"NO! STOP! NO!"* at the top of her lungs, but could hear nothing come from her own mouth.

Not Shibun.

Before Lin could think, Nyoka was rushing full speed at her and grabbing for her heart. Stunned, she saw his eyes were a blaring yellow. They burned like acid into her own eyes, so bright, so vicious.

Without him raising a finger, Lin was soaring through the air once more, possessed and taken over. She tried to move her arms, legs, head, *something*, but Nyoka had her entire body under his command. He smacked her down to the ground.

Nyoka was controlling her.

"YOU SEE NOW WHAT I WAS SAYING, FOOL?" A deep, powerful thunder boomed through the house, shaking the walls.

"I WILL BE THE ONE! THE ONLY THING MORE

POWERFUL THAN HELL ITSELF!"

His voice was thunder, louder than a hundred screaming people, or a whole army of men stomping, and vibrating as if the world were experiencing a volcanic eruption, earthquake, and tsunami at the same exact time. Lin stayed there, unable to move. Her mind was ripping in half, her body was falling to pieces, her entire system was screaming in pain—

"NO GODS, NO CURSES, NO LIMITS!"

Nyoka's yellow eyes flashed into her own. Lin swirled, dazed. Everything was shaking, everything was fuzzy and white to her eyes, everything was split into ten. The house was ripping apart from the corners and tearing away like an unwanted page.

"THE WORLD WILL BE CONSUMED IN AN EVERLASTING DARK, AND I, THE MOST POWERFUL FINITE BEING IN THE WORLD, WILL GIVE THIS DARK EARTH A PURPOSE!"

The house was now only white. Whiter than snow, colder than night. Starch white, blank white, completely vacant—

Until...

There was nothing more than a dying girl in a forsaken house who wanted no more than her father.

CHAPTER 29

ACCURSED RED, NOW AND ALWAYS

Ismus sucked in her breath, listening to Lauren's steady heartbeat. "Breathe in, breathe out," she was saying to Ismus that night, her breath cool and fresh on her cheeks. "Breathe in, breathe out."

It felt a lot better sleeping with Lauren, but Ismus was still shaking.

She was to be attacked again.

The dream she had just finished contained an army of mutants, all in a wide-open field with a long, dark sky, in a time of night. The dead, yellow grass below them was swirling in a circle. The spirit things were huge, tall, and touching the skies. And they were hissing in some horrible language that Ismus could somehow make out.

"We can smell her. She lies accompanied, housed somewhere in the forests. Kill the witch, then take the soul of the girl. Amethyst is *ours*."

Ismus shivered. It was best to not think about that. She suffered through the night hearing Lauren snore, "Breathe'n, Breathe'o."

It was hard waking up the next morning due to the darkness. When they did wake the next day, they saw the sky was terrible.

The atmosphere was a slackening water of darkness. Purely and infinitively dark. It rippled like a swallowing ocean, deep in the trenches of dark waters. Wretched and cold, the clouds were black. They seemed to wrap the world in an endless embrace of shadows. They cast nothing but shaded evil across the lands… not a whisper to be heard, not a light to be seen.

It appeared to be nothing short of terrifying to be outside at that time, with the big, blocky clouds stacked upon one another, looming over like bandits with knives. It would have left a single child screaming, and a lone adult feeling lost and almost inconsolable. As Ismus gaped at the heavy sight of the atmosphere, she could not help but remember the sloshing of the waters in her own stomach when she had seen what had happened to Rodem.

The feeling was *much* more than fear. It was something far beyond that. Something *too* strong to describe.

"It's completely black," was all Ismus was able to say. But Lauren had already known, for she was lying on the bed, looking sick herself. Ismus felt a ping of fear in her stomach, and instantly she shut the curtains (which made the room no darker) and turned away, flustered.

Ismus's insides rattled and jittered. She glanced at Lauren who was now quite pale and decided to ask nothing of her. Ismus hung her head.

The answer must have been too obvious.

This all was because of Ismus. It was now or never to accept that. No matter how little sense it made to her.

"Do you want to eat?" Lauren blurted.

Ismus nodded, starting to all of a sudden feel a bit famished. Her mouth felt dry, and she removed a burning red hair from her bottom lip. "Yes."

Growl.

Breakfast was small. Plain toast with water. Lauren was making a fuss, saying that Ismus was not to eat too much or she might throw up.

"We don't want to have any accidents."

"I know, Lauren," Ismus swirled her water around. The toast was burnt around the edges.

"Um. I've been meaning to tell you, Lauren. I..."

Lauren waited. "Yes?"

"A few months ago—I was planning to tell you this—something happened."

"Tell me."

"When the beasts raided the camp that night, I had left without thinking about the others." Her voice stayed even, to her surprise.

"I had just run off, and since then I feel *terrible*. I didn't even think about anyone but myself." Ismus looked up to Lauren, to see what comfort she could insure.

Lauren sighed, putting down her dishrag. "You know, Ismus. People make mistakes. People are selfish. People can be greedy. People have sins they carry around for the rest of their lives." She walked closer to Ismus.

"This is only the beginning. It was not your fault to safeguard your—and your *alone*—well-being. This is only the beginning."

And that made Ismus quiet.

The day continued on, with the forest turning cold, so cold that ice was starting to form on the volcano itself, and the light that rested on the rim of the window glowed a dark steel. It made everything slow, slow and sluggish, and made time take an eternity to pass.

When the day turned into night, Ismus was trudging around and getting ready for bed. She dragged herself over to the closet, where her head was traveling faster than her feet, got out some clothes, and threw them onto the bed.

But all of a sudden she felt a huge *snap* in her spirit, and she threw herself onto the bed. She muffled her screams into the pillow. Her heart throbbed.

She sobbed into the pillow as it grew wet with tears. They were streaming down, Ismus not even bothering to wipe them. She just let them roll down her cheeks and drip off her chin as a new set came rushing down.

"Ismus, dear, I just came to… *Ismus?*" Lauren, with her pink silk nightgown and cap, came rushing to the bedpost.

Ismus spoke in a gravelly voice, "I don't want this to happen. W-why am I like this? All this pain… This disgusting world I've lived in… I have to say that it's *my* fault?"

She choked through her next words.

"I don't want to die." She gasped between breathless cries.

"But if I don't… Everyone else will… Even you."

"I am the last person you should be worried about," Lauren pulled Ismus in closer to her chest. The sobs that left her inhaling timed to the constant pulse of her heartbeat.

"W-would it be selfish," Ismus trembled. "I-if…I did stay?"

Ismus could feel Lauren go rigid.

"I am so sorry," she said in reply, eyes stinging. And then Lauren was crying, crying so lightly, so soundlessly.

"You cannot stay forever."

Ismus's heart broke at the sound of those four words.

Her mind could not form a cohesive reply.

Her throat hurt too much to say anything.

So she let the tears fall down her face.

"Dear—please Ismus, don't cry—I have always feared the arrival of this day, but I never thought that the curse would come seek my shelter. When you first entered the forest, passed out and burned, I knew you were special. Long, long, long red hair, skin paler than any cream I could ever make, and eyes more beautiful than a violet in any lush meadow. You were the body of Amethyst, and it struck fear into my heart to even let you into my forsaken cottage. I thought you would bring danger into my life.

"Foolish. You are funny and thoughtful, young, and smart. You are beautiful, and you have such a wonderful spirit, even though you are living in a suffering, bitter Hell. I would love with all my heart to let you stay—but fate will take your life somewhere beyond here, and there will be no force, not even me, to stop it."

Ismus, still hugging her close, had still not stopped crying and began wiping her wet cheeks. Lauren loosened from her grasp from this sudden hand movement, though Ismus was not ready to let go. Then the older woman sat upright.

"Think of the most beautiful thing in the world and tell me what you see." Lauren gazed at her, a small smile lifting the corners of her face. Ismus sniffed up the drips from her nose, trying to gaze behind the foggy dark haze, something full of *light* and *beauty*.

"Strain to see beyond this shadowing inferno."

But she could not. Ismus strained hard and harder, like on the day she left the castle for the first time and had to strain to see behind the endless fog. Completely cold and damp and dark, like a graveyard, like an infinite abyss.

"Black," Ismus choked, and tears rolled down her face. "That is all I see. The moon covered in total darkness. Blood below my feet—dripping. Pouring. Puddles and puddles of red.

"I can see nothing but black and blood. That is what I always

255

wanted to see."

There was a terrible fall of unwavering stillness as those words escaped from her mouth.

Horrified, terrified, petrified.

That was what Lauren was; her mouth and eyes were wide and quaking.

Her eyes poured into Ismus's, who only returned a blank, watery stare.

"I love this torture."

Lauren's eyes burned a dark red.

Ismus had never seen Lauren this way. With her eyes dark, with her cheeks glistening in tears, with nothing coming out from her mouth. Her stomach was sick at the thought of what she had said. Sick at the fact that she meant it, with all her beating, filthy heart.

Ismus opened her mouth but soon shut it from the croak in her voice. So she was just staring at Lauren, Lauren staring at her, and for minutes she felt an icy wave of heartbreak blanket over her.

This was not fair. Why should Ismus obliterate the lives of people around her with despair, worry, darkness, and sadness? She was a curse. She understood it now.

Ismus was formed from the Goddess of Death, Despair, and Loneliness; her hair burned an accursed red, and every time she walked, the people, the world below and above her, and everything else in her path would cower in fear and shrivel dead.

She *knew* that now, she knew she was nothing more than a spell, a spell of fear and isolation. Nothing more than horror and seclusion. Ismus was meant to be alone, to be away from human life.

For... she knew she was no longer human. Ismus was a *demon*.

She knew she would have to leave Irene Violet Sprout's cottage.

CHAPTER 30
A CHAOTIC INFINION

Aglittering stairway of ice and snow led up to the palace of Winterbreath. It was miles high, stretching up to the Highest Infinion, and once up the stairs, her palace of pure frost truly gleamed. It shone blue and white, glistening in the Light of Infinion, luminous like polished crystals. The castle's sapphire glow bounced off in all directions, touching all before it.

Inside of Winterbreath's demonstrative and vast palace of snowflakes was a meeting. A very important and fatal meeting that could determine the fate of Dark Earth forever. And invited were the Gods and Goddesses in the realm.

"Get to thy seats, are there manners whence thee came?" Winterbreath demanded, holding an ice-board with a piece of white chalk in hand. Her shimmery blue dress, catching the light from Infinion, flew about as she roared in her favorite form of early English. "Marry, a saucy soul such as thee—hark my words, Embore! Grammercy, Silvergrass, for shutting this lot up!"

"Please everyone, let us not make Winterbreath upset," Silvergrass, dressed in her dark green forest garb, spoke, "the meeting will be commencing in just a few short moments. Try and stay calm."

Waterleaf—with skin pale and hair silky black—sat in the background, the only one soundless.

Redtarnish, as tall and heavy as a tree, frowned with a shake of her root-colored hair. "There is no time to waste, the meeting must commence now." She smelled of tree bark and soil as she said it.

Embore flashed into a female, her slim, dark aura

shimmering as she moved.

"We can't start it now! We're missing the Novice Angel." She threw up a perfectly straight, beautifully white, wickedly evil smile and whispered, "Fun can only come of this."

"Won't this be a rare treat," Winterbreath grimaced as Silvergrass touched her shoulder.

"Do not talk like that. Kima Choi may be our last hope. Do not doubt her strength."

Winterbreath sighed and put down the chalk and ice board on a frosty table. "I know, Silver. But can we trust this not-even-Pre-Complete Angel? It has never been done, letting a Novice into the Council."

"I know, but as the higher Angel—Goddess—we are to be gentle and strong, not jealous and petty like mortals—"

"Yet this shows how hopeless and desperate we really are. It makes The Council look weak and fraught for answers. I am not bowing down to someone lesser than my own. I will not be the subject of hilarity."

"You *are* to stick to the plan. We cannot fight this battle on our own anymore, Winter. You know that. It has gone out of our control; there is nothing more we can do.

"We need Kima: without her all is lost. They have been training for this—"

"*I AM NOT BOWING DOWN TO SOMEONE LESSER THAN MY OWN! I WILL NOT BE THE SUBJECT OF HILARITY!*" Winterbreath screamed with anger and reached for Silver's neck.

The goddess faltered. Silvergrass's golden face wrinkled from the dying light of the world. "The darkness is taking you over, Winterbreath. You are becoming less and less God-like as the days go by. The Goddess in you is fading. Only death will come of us."

Winterbreath released her grip and looked down disgracefully at the floor.

Bwash. The solid ice doors smacked against the wall, a few stalactites falling from the snowflake ceiling, and in came an angel, hardly glowing at all. Kima Choi stepped into the room, the Gods and Goddesses staring down at her.

"Welcome," Silvergrass started, but then Winterbreath held up a finger.

"No point in welcomes. Sit down."

Kima dashed to the chair and closed her mouth, looking like a child compared to the tall angels around her.

The Goddess of Snow & Ice loosened the anger from her face and sighed, her breath as fresh as the air in winter, and said, "I am sorry, Kima Choi. May Infinion bless you for your arrival at this meeting, but we have something very urgent at the moment."

Kima closed her eyes. "Is this about my Linny? Or Shen?" Her hair swayed.

"No," Silvergrass interjected, before Winterbreath could say a word. "Not yet."

"As you know, Kima Choi, we Gods are the most powerful forces on this Earth, perhaps even the universe. We have been around since the very first stroke of light touched the earth, and have been keeping the world balanced ever since. However—"

"However, *you lost control.*" Kima smiled viciously. "While you sat upon your throne of power, and while angels like me slave away doing jobs for the Gods, you saw that darkness got too powerful for you... and now you come crawling for help."

Kima shut her mouth. "I am very sorry. I did not... Please— please continue."

"Well," Embore snickered and pulled up her striped thigh-high socks. "That's really what it is. We were blind. We *thought* we were safe, we *thought* we were the most powerful beings over this universe. But we definitely are not. Like... it's not even funny how wrong—"

"We have a task for you." Silvergrass stared at her soul harshly with her electric green eyes. "No, more than a task. It is a position. It is your choice if you want to accept it."

"I will do anything for you, Goddess of the Greenery," Kima said quietly.

"Embarion is dying. The very core of Their energy cannot survive the growing Shadow any longer. Light is dying, the very light of the Sun is vanishing from the skies. If there is no light, then all will die. Human, Angel, Animals, Plant Life... Gods. All will die. Even the Accursed One. All except for The Dark Goddess and her slaves will survive. The demons. It all will consume Dark Earth."

"What is in store for me?" Kima said in a curious and confused tone, one that made her feel more immature and imprudent.

Redtarnish spoke for the first time in minutes and replied in her masculine voice, "What's in store for you? A role. We need you to be the Goddess of Light."

Winterbreath rolled her eyes. "You can't just blurt it out, Redtarnish."

"No point in setting things up," Redtarnish bellowed with a shake of her moose-crown head. "Embarion is dying, am I wrong, Winter?"

"What?" Kima hesitated at the overwhelming possibility of her being something of a God.

"The Goddess of the Sun?" she repeated how a child would sound.

Silvergrass smiled. "You have full potential. The glow of scintillating joy and love comes from your heart. You are the light of Shen Lein and Linnasoeta Choi's life. You are a victim of the Accursed One. You are the only angel of both purity and untapped strength. Kima, you must be the Sun. Without you, all will die... in the most *torturous* of ways."

"What do you say, Saucy?" Embore smirked. "Are you going to take it?"

Kima stuttered, "I-I-I just don't... know. The fate of the world rests in my... Gods, I'm going to throw up..."

"NO! Not on the ice tiling!" Winterbreath clutched her pulsing forehead. "Our next proposal would be that we can send all angels and Gods to Infinity, but it would be very crowded—"

"We can't leave the Earthlings to die," Embore smirked again, "That would be cruel and unusual punishment."

"I'VE HEARD ENOUGH OUT OF YOU!" Redtarnish growled and stood up to her full, nine-foot height. The dirt from her hair fell to the floor. "NOW SHUT IT BEFORE I THROW YOU ACROSS INFINION LIKE THE CORPSE YOU ARE!" She shifted back into her chair with a loud PLOP and blew the scent of fertilizer around the castle.

Winterbreath coughed, pulling down her diamond-speckled, cerulean dress and ignored the two outbursts. "What say you, Kima Choi? Are you ready to become a Goddess? The last one to survive in all of Dark Earth?"

Kima stared down at the floor; she took a few deep breaths, thinking heavily. The room watched in silence.

"I have never been more gratified in my entire life," Kima answered firmly.

"I am ready to become the Last Goddess."

CHARACTER AND COUNTRY PRONUNCIATION GUIDE:

LINNASOETA: LIN-AH-SOH-EH-TA

ISMUS: ISS-MUHS

NYOKA: NIE-O-AH-KA

ALOES: AL-OHES

KIMA: KEE-MAH

AMETHYST: AM-A-THIST

SERABI: SIR-AH-BEE

RODEM: ROW-DEM

ACKNOWLEDGMENTS

Firstly, I need to thank my editor, Landa Torrence, for polishing my work and giving suggestions at my most stubborn of times. Without her, my novel would be an even more complicated and confused mess. There are two Carolines I also must credit: one for reading my manuscript and the other for FaceTiming me and acting certain parts out aloud. I must give my appreciations for my good friends Lauren, Violet, and Irene who let me use their names in my work. Their unique personas fused together into one of my favorite characters in the story. My younger siblings Elijah and Makenzie both gave me a fresh perspective and feedback whenever I needed it. Another important individual in this process was my father Elijah who acted as both an editor and first-drafter of my map. I also must give a gratuitous thank you to my book cover and map illustrator Joshua Chinsky; he captured everything I envisioned, and I could not be happier with how everything turned out.

However, it is my mother Kelli who started it all. The day I asked her to read my silly, two-page story about a girl with long red hair—crossing a vine-border with a bow—was the start of something I could not even fathom. All the hours of research, money, and scams are debts that I owe greatly to her. If it was not for her hope in me and her constant support of everything I do, Accursed Red, Ismus, and all of Dark Earth would have been tossed right into a trashcan.

ABOUT RAE S. VAUGHN

Vaughn is a high-school student with an avid love for writing, running, baking, ukuleles, YouTube, and anything to do with sugar and chocolate. She has two siblings, a pair of amazing parents, and a little Chihuahua named Larry. As of now, Accursed Red is the only title to her name.

www.ingramcontent.com/pod-product-compliance
Lightning Source LLC
Chambersburg PA
CBHW031711170626
46808CB00005B/1705